LAST SON of the WAR GOD

CLAY MARTIN

WILDBLUE
PRESS

WildBluePress.com

LAST SON OF THE WAR GOD published by:
WILDBLUE PRESS
P.O. Box 102440
Denver, Colorado 80250

Publisher Disclaimer: Any opinions, statements of fact or fiction, descriptions, dialogue, and citations found in this book were provided by the author, and are solely those of the author. The publisher makes no claim as to their veracity or accuracy, and assumes no liability for the content.

WILDBLUE PRESS is registered at the U.S. Patent and Trademark Offices.

ISBN 978-1-948239-82-0   Trade Paperback
ISBN 978-1-948239-83-7   eBook

Interior Formatting by Elijah Toten
www.totencreative.com

LAST SON of
the WAR GOD

For my son Ronin. Most days, I hope he never sees the world the way I do. But some days I hope he does, because anything else is a lie.

CHAPTER ONE

Bill's shoulders were starting to sting from the pole across his shoulder, a rough cut of pine with the bark still attached. As always, it was hewn from near where the hunt had ended, quickly. It was amazing how little you noticed the small inconveniences when work was a joy, your blood was up from a righteous chase, ended in a glorious finale. Maybe that was the problem. The hunts had been less and less of a challenge as of recent, which left them feeling hollow. It certainly wasn't the weight of the prize, that couldn't be more than 120 pounds, with Dean carrying the back half at that. And it sure as hell wasn't the distance. They were less than a mile from camp, which was also not unusual. Bill had been certain this one would be different, a hunt that would unleash the primal joy he so relished from his first outings. His first had been like becoming a man, all at once, all over again. Before the eyes of his group, he had proven himself an apt disciple, part of the family, one of them. The rapture he felt from proving himself a member of the tribe had almost been overwhelming. Nothing would ever be the same after that. Bill felt the change deep in his core, and thought at the time it would never pass. The look of approval on the face of the chief had been more important that the words he spoke, a ritual welcoming Bill couldn't remember a word of. That had been almost five years ago. For a time, he had ridden high. It was like being a different person all of a sudden. An event like this branded the soul.

Other men that knew could see it from a mile away. And the drones walking around living a "normal" life couldn't possibly understand. Bill felt like a titan among men. But like any drug, eventually the dose had less effect. At first he could quickly blink away any thought that the stalks were getting stale. What kind of a soulless creature could think that, high in the White Cloud Mountains? Running down game in the dark woods, only instinct and skill to guide him, choosing the path of a thousand generations of alpha males before him. To be a hunter was to be the chosen from among the race of men, a gift bestowed only on the strongest, fittest and most deserving. He could hear his ancestors crying out with approval as he neared the finish, telling him how the spoils proved he was truly of their line and blood. Still, he felt the pleasure slipping with time. He could see it in the faces of his tribe as well, though none ever spoke it aloud. Bill had tried to change things as well, to bring pride and satisfaction back to the game. As a member of the tribe, all men were expected to use their voice. To hold back one's tongue was a symbol of being a beta, and there were no beta's here. No sir. The Chief's word might be law, but only a coward would hold back his opinion. Bill had never been happier than to hear his latest suggestion receive the full blessing of the Chief, not to mention the raucous applause of his peers. It seemed the hooting and applause would go on forever. "Sheer genius, why had no one ever thought of that before?" they clamored. And for a time, it had brought the lust back to the field. It's why this little filly tied to the pine tree had a gag in her mouth, and it had worked. Bill reasoned that if you gagged them right after capture, they tended to save more fight for the spoils, and that always made things more fun. Like a kid with a new toy though, the shine had worn off quickly. It did help to make the spoils last longer, but it didn't do anything for the chase. And these stupid women were so predictable. Every time, they ran straight out of the clearing the camp sat in, left down the hill to the river bottom, refused to cross the stream, and holed up whimpering in the underbrush. The sign they left scurrying into a hidey-hole might as well be a neon sign to hunters like these, and it definitely wasn't much of a challenge. Bill often wondered if they were actually more scared of spending a night alone in the woods than they were of being caught. Not like the consequences of being caught hadn't been explained before they were released. Hell, they probably wouldn't even bother to run without that. It never took more than an hour or two to find them, thought to be honest, the few men they had hunted hadn't fared much better. Not that they took the spoils from the men. They weren't faggots. Chief said that men you hunted to prove your warrior prowess, that your skills were stronger. That you could dominate other men was supremely important if you thought yourself truly an Alpha. Women you hunted for the spoils, to share in with your tribal brothers. Always, by ritual, spoils until the sun crested the peak of the mountains, then the feast. Bill would always still enjoy that part, it was later that the empty feeling of the chase would haunt him. That was not okay. The chase was supposed to be the part that earned your reward. A weak chase always meant the reward wouldn't be as fulfilling. Ah well, he thought as they crossed into the clearing that served as the camp, another season is almost at a close. Dean had suggested that maybe a woman with a child in the equation would try harder, something they might have to explore next year.

CHAPTER TWO

50 miles away, Goose Neck, Idaho

Mike rolled off state road 56 onto Main Street of Goose Neck as the sun was setting. The Black Bronco's tires kicking up puddles as he pulled into the only bar in town. It had been a long drive from North Carolina, and starting with a hangover hadn't helped much. Long, but enjoyable, Mike felt free for the first time in his cloudy memory. Free to take in the scenery, free for the drive to take as long as he wanted, no worries about what he ate or how much he smoked. The reason he had come here meant none of that mattered for once. In some ways, Mike couldn't fathom the hand he had been dealt. Once a rising star, his career went up in puff of smoke seemingly overnight. Forced out in an early retirement, he had no chance of ever returning to that life. A bottle-a-day habit had played some part in that, but the writing had already been on the wall by then. And turns out, men like Mike should never have to spend so much time in their own heads. The demons of early success dashed on the rocks of injury hurt, more than most people would ever know. Not a lot of careers depended so much on physical capability, but he suspected pro athletes cut down by impairment in their prime would probably understand the most. It soon became apparent that Mike's marriage had largely been held together by his paycheck, with an entirely predictable but messy divorce soon ensuing. Two years down the line now, Mike was broke, broken, drunk, and out of shape. A long winding path of alcohol-fueled failures at new business and success with whores merged with a train wreck of self-loathing and lack of purpose. Credit cards were almost maxed, finances a state of chaos at best, and all of his relationships were an unmitigated disaster. Jesus Christ, he thought, the women that fell for the new Mike were all fucking insane. In his 35 years on planet Earth, he had never in his wildest dreams imagined such a bunch of lunatics could escape the asylum. It had been fun, but not worth the price against his decaying soul. As the months dragged by, Mike slowly felt himself sliding into the abyss. Some days he would turn his phone off, and distantly stare from the balcony of his filthy apartment for hours, chain smoking. It felt like his brain was turning inside out, like a stranger was in his body. No matter how long it took him to come to, he could count on dozens of missed calls and accusatory texts from across the country. At least one would undoubtedly be threatening to hold her breath until she passed out if he didn't respond RIGHT NOW.

One day, like the clouds parting, a moment of clarity. An epiphany burst through his addled mind. True enlightenment. Mike understood why so many men from his world ended up as suicides. Their numbers were high, but actually skewed to the positive if you knew the inside information. The official count didn't include heroin overdoses and drunk driving fatalities, or anything of the like. But the boys from the club all understood. None of that was by accident, at least not fully. Mike had come close himself, one of the only times he had felt truly alive since his fall from grace. Almost too drunk to walk, racing a borrowed mini cooper around the mountains of Kentucky, tires squealing without a care in the world. It had been exhilarating, pushing the little car well beyond its limits, zero thought for the potential consequences. And he had been truly afraid later when he woke up in a stranger's hotel room. His intellectual mind knew that was a sure way to get killed, even sober and in daylight. Just ask James Dean. But his spirit just didn't care. It felt like being locked in a cage with a sleeping tiger. You knew it was a matter of time, but there was nothing to be done to avoid it.

Mike stepped out of the Bronco on stiff legs and stretched for a moment in the parking lot. Today had been a long drive up through Montana and Wyoming. Twelve straight hours behind the wheel of a 90's model 4x4 was hard on the body, but this region of the country was what he had come out to see. Almost twenty years ago Mike had lived for a while in Wyoming, and the beauty of the West had left an impression. Many times over those two decades since he left, all he had wished for was to go back, live out his remaining days. Maybe part of his subconscious thought that being back here would jar him from his task, but his conscious brain just wanted to see it one more time. Without thinking he had driven all the way from Sheridan, up through Missoula, and all the way into Idaho. Why not Idaho? He'd never seen it, now was as good a time as any. Mike fully planned on spending a couple of relaxing days in the woods, finding a beautiful vista to watch the sun come up one morning, and then sticking his 10mm in his mouth. Maybe that would quiet the demons inside he couldn't drown with cheap whiskey.

The inside of the bar looked like every other run down shithole west of the Mississippi. Wire spools for tables, mismatched chairs that looked easy to break over some other drunk redneck's head, neon signs from ad campaigns for beer and liquor from decades in the past, sawdust on the floor to soak up the occasional blood from Friday nights when the farmers and ranch boys both got paid. A long bar on one wall with cheap stools and a cheaper gold flake mirror in the back. A light blue haze, and Mike was happy to see, glass ashtrays piled high near the bottles on display. The West, the last free place on Earth. The woman behind the bar was sizing him up with the look of small town bartenders the world over. Half disdain for strangers, half a look of welcome for anything remotely exotic. In a place where nothing changed for years on end, a stranger might as well be bringing news from Mars. With men, the disdain for strangers part was usually stronger, until you over tipped them once or twice. With women, the exotic stranger part tended to be stronger, but not by much. That could work out in his favor too. One nice thing about living a new life, his personal skills in deception and cunning were responsible for a lot of his problems. But they still had their uses. Lead me not into temptation, he thought, I can find the way myself.

"What'll it be Honey?" She asked in a gravely smokers voice. Samantha was well past her prime, in a job that tended to age one fast anyway. Crows feet were getting harder to cover with makeup, and she felt the sags in her equipment as much as she saw them these days. A girl doesn't stay 20 forever, and she was pushing twice that. Still, the lights in the bar threw her some favors, and her low cut blouse helped with tips, especially amongst strangers. Nothing was going to change the equation with the locals, not in the little fishpond Goose Neck had become. Too much time had passed, without nearly enough excitement. That was a nice way of saying everyone had already screwed everyone else in town by her age, it's just how things went. Outside of the occasional jealous husband or cat fight, things stayed largely tame, which also meant the hint of sexual favors wasn't going to garner any more coins. Strangers, on the other hand; well, a sucker was born every minute.

"Gin and Tonic, and one of those ash trays if you don't mind." Mike had been around enough to know how this game was played. The subtle lean over the counter to put her cleavage on display was as old as the day is long, and usually worked on younger men. A fool and his money were soon parted, and in your 20's that usually involved tits and no pay off at the end. Mike saw this play out in a thousand seedy little places just like this, and he was a fast learner. The bartender wasn't unattractive, in a country girl trailer park kind of way. Ten years ago she was probably rolling in enough extra at the end of every night to support a new Camaro and the occasional bump of coke. Time had been tough though. Still, he had nothing better to do tonight. He would drive up into the mountains tomorrow in the daylight, and didn't ever plan on driving back. Why not play one last hand? Win or lose didn't really matter, and it's not like he was concerned about the long-term consequences this time. The spider sat down and began to spin his web. The most dangerous men are always those with nothing to lose.

Samantha talked to the stranger for over an hour before she made an excuse to step back into the kitchen. He had just asked about a hotel in town, which was both a subtle come on and a key phrase for Samantha. The owner of the bar liked to be informed anytime someone stopped in town longer than it took to get gas. They weren't much of a tourist destination, and outside of elk season there was rarely a visitor for any length of time. Some Hells Angels had tried to use Goose Neck as a stop for poker runs a few years back, but the Sheriff put a stop to that right quick. Samantha didn't know why Tim always wanted to know about strangers, but she suspected it was trouble with the law somewhere far from here. Something was off with Tim. She didn't quite know what, but her female intuition told her something wasn't normal. He had never said a cross word to her, and had never shown a violent temper. But still, something in his aura flashed "warning, danger" like the markings on a black widow. Something deep in the primate brain told her not to ask too many questions, or try and get too close to him. Scary, but scary like a corpse that had been in the river all winter. Probably harmless, but the kind of thing you would still think about long after you should be asleep. The stranger in the barroom was a different story altogether. Something felt a little different about him too. Dangerous, but like getting your car too close to the crossing when a freight train went past. Inches away from more violence and fury than you could imagine, but totally safe as long as you didn't press any further. Tim had the week off, but rules were rules. As she dialed his number, her thoughts floated to what it might be like to ride that particular train.

CHAPTER THREE

The bartender came back out of the kitchen and continued to make small talk with him, edging on the mildly flirtatious. How much was an act to dig deeper into his pockets, how much was boredom, and how much was genuine interest was impossible to tell, and largely irrelevant. Mike didn't really care either way. He was bordering on tipsy, enjoying himself for once, and you play the hand you are dealt. The bar was deserted except for him and Samantha, one of those times of year a Tuesday wouldn't bring much business. Time passed, and eventually a scruffy looking man came in through the front door, stopping to size the place up before heading around behind the bar. Not a word was said, but the mood changed instantly. Samantha went from flirty to subdued, once in a while even looking at her shoes. The new man introduced himself as Tim, and asked Samantha to see to busing off the tables since they would be closing soon. It was spoken as a question, but there was no doubt it was a command. "Ah fuck, what kind of shit did I just step in?" Mike thought to himself. Boyfriend? Husband, was this a mom and pop shop? Tim was eyeing him from the moment he came in the door, and Mike knew what kind of evaluation it was. He hadn't been outright hostile, but it definitely felt like being sized up for a fight. Mike was in no mood for that, and felt his moment of action with the bartender slipping through his grasp. This Tim clown had cock blocked the magic, and a fist fight would put the nails in that particular coffin, no doubt. The guy hadn't made a further aggressive move or statement, but that probably owed more to Mike's size than anything. Quite a few men had thought they wanted to go down this road in his life, but most of them backed down once they really looked at him. 6'2 and 240 might not be a giant back in Texas, but most places it was enough to quell the storm. At least once it was apparent Mike wasn't the backing down type, and might even enjoy it if you didn't. Unless they were already drunk. For some reason, smaller men really liked to fight bigger men after the sauce took them, and it always ended badly. In the back of his mind, Mike actually hoped this clown had phoned some friends, so this would at least be entertaining if it was inevitable. If his night was going to be ruined, he at least wanted it to be worth it.

Tim asked a few questions of the stranger before he realized he was acting like a total weirdo. He had come back to town to grab some more beer and some steaks out of Bill's freezer, and hadn't planned on talking to anyone. It was so hard, barely twenty-four hours off the hunt, to contain his inner self. Christ, his cock was still sore from his turn at the spoils. He was third in line this time so there was still plenty of fight, and for the first time had stuck it in her ass. God that had been tight. Afterward he had momentary concerns that the other guys might think he was a secret homo, but nobody did. The tribe would never think that of one of their own. He was so turned on by it that he got hard again in time for seconds, before the sun came up. After the feast, the guys had sat around talking about how to improve the chase. Bill had suggested a woman with a child, but Dean thought maybe it was time to recruit another man as prey. Maybe if they put a man with a woman, which would make things more interesting. The talk had gone on long into the night, and by the next morning they were out of beer. Normally they didn't come back to town during the hunt week, but Chief had said it was okay this time. Maybe he was trying to salvage the experience, knowing that the chase had left the guys a little disappointed. When that stupid bitch Samantha called him, he answered mostly in case she had spotted his truck. Didn't want to seem like you're acting weird, answer the phone like a normal person Tim. What she told him was almost too good to be true. Large, fit man, passing through, alone, scouting elk locations for next year. Older truck, no wedding ring. That last bit was probably Samantha's answer to herself, not like it would have stopped the slut anyways. Sometimes he thought maybe she should come up to the camp. Not a fucking chance, Chief said. No one from around here. Not until we are stronger, not until the Return of Kings is upon them. Then it won't matter. You can do what you want in town, there will be no need for the camp. But not now, no exceptions. Now here Tim was, looking at this guy like he was fresh meat on the auction block. Get it together man!

"Sorry, I just came down from camp myself. You forget how to talk to people being out in the woods that long." Tim said, throwing back a shot of whiskey to calm his nerves.

"I get that, how long you been out?" Mike responded, still coiled inside waiting for an ambush.

"Bought a week. Needed a resupply." Tim smiled, holding up a case of beer cans from the bars cooler.

"I hear ya there buddy." Mike smiled back. It was fake as the day is long, but a poker face was one of his strengths. What kind of a twat needed a beer resupply after seven days at a hunt camp? This Tim dude was a strange one, no doubt about that.

Tim excused himself into the kitchen, and slipped out the back door. This was a golden opportunity he gleamed to himself. The stranger looked reasonably fit, Samantha told him he was in the area scouting elk locations, and wasn't due back East for weeks. The Bronco in the lot had North Carolina plates, which was a long way from home. Whole lot of miles between here and there for someone to check if he went missing. Decision made, Tim smiled. Alpha males took risks. It's what they did, how they survived, and only a beta needed a group consensus to act. The boys were in for a surprise tonight!

CHAPTER FOUR

When Tim came back in, he looked like a different man. Animated, friendly even, he started asking Mike all about himself. Mike stuck to a well-worn cover story about being a recently divorced, out of work construction worker. The conversation felt a little bit like a sloppy elicitation attempt, which made it easy to deflect. Still, Mike was a little on edge. Maybe this was the set up while the goon squad assembled out front. Well, if things got to out of hand, there was always the .45 ACP stuck in his waistband. An XD-S chucking ashtray sized bullets tended to even any odds.

Tim grew more and more sure of himself by the minute. The answers this stranger was feeding him were a gift from God himself. It seemed he was all alone, off the beaten path, and hadn't really told anyone where he was. Finding himself, something all these city boy fucks needed to do nowadays it seemed. Drones, all drones, slaving away for a system built on spend and earn, achieve status, be entertained. They weren't even really alive. It would be the greatest honor of this loser's life to get to die in a hunt. Hopefully this one at least had enough fire to die well. The few men that they had hunted before had finally whimpered and cowered when eventually cornered. So sad. They couldn't even really call themselves men. Why not at least die fighting? That would be a worthy death.

Tim walked to the back of the barroom where Samantha had busied herself cleaning tables, and told her to go ahead and take off. He would close up himself. That had never happened before, but Samantha didn't want to question it. Tim was acting strange, the new guy Mike was signaling tension in the air, albeit subtly, and she didn't want to be involved. Not her problem, once she got her purse and headed out the back door. Maybe Tim was about to ax murder this guy, and maybe this guy was about to stuff Tim under the counter. Either way, she wanted to be home and in bed by the time the Sheriff eventually asked what happened. This was definitely a weed kind of night. Smoke a bowl, turn the lights off, and forget this day ever happened.

Mike felt his heart sink when Samantha walked past and said goodbye, noticeable without leaving her number or a house key. If not his heart, certainly his libido. Well, that settled that. Tim was removing the only potential witness from the equation; violence was going to ensue. If this was some kind of unrequited crush, or just a your not local are ya boy kind of situation, the result was the same. He was going to try a be a grown up for once, walk away if this was a threaten "or else" party. Not like he was ever any good at taking a step back, but it beat having to shoot everyone if more than two other guys showed up. Or did it? He was here to probably end his life anyway, what difference did three yokels make? But he was also buzzed, which had a tendency to mellow him out. His end was supposed to be peaceful, not a last stand on the receiving end of a posse. Nothing else had been, the universe kind of owed him this one.

"No offense stranger, but I need to close up. You might drink like a fish, but one customer still isn't worth keeping the lights on for." Tim said with his best Baptist caught holding a beer smile.

"Not a problem, I had best be on my way to." Mike smiled back. Just a big dumb idiot with no idea what came next. No sir, officer, had no idea how fast I was going.

"One for the road? How about a shot of your choice" Tim considered just inviting him to the camp since it fit his interest. That would solve the Bronco problem, and the guys would subdue him the second he stepped out of it on principle anyway. But nope, not the way things are done. Tim was too smart for that. If something went wrong, he would be in deep shit. This required a bit more finesse. Besides, if they ended up hurting him bad in the take down, the bonus hunt would be shot. Like hitting a deer with your truck the second you get to your corn pile.

"How about Crown?" Mike shook the fuzz off. Probably shouldn't, but one more isn't going to make much difference for what happens next. He still had his wits about him, this was going to end fast regardless.

"To the line of Hunters" Tim raised his glass. Mike nodded and swallowed his drink.

"I'll walk you out so I can lock up." Tim said, sliding around the bar and coming even with Mike.

Fuck, here we go. So the it was the classic, ambush right outside the door. Well, Mike had seen this one before too. The door pushed in from the outside, hinges on the left side. Tim would open the door, ever the gracious host. Stutter step as they approach the threshold, duck the second his first foot crosses the opening, lunging to the right with a hook flying at ball level. A tiny minority of people were left handed, hence the ambush man would likely be on the right. With a little bit of luck, it would be a bat not a 2x4, and the shorter weapon would carry the hitter through the empty door, smashing Tim's teeth out for good measure.

Five steps from the door, Mike saw the world start to swim. Four steps and it all faded to black as he crashed to the floor.

CHAPTER FIVE

Mike felt himself floating to the surface of consciousness long before his body stirred. His brain was telling him to wake up, but it was hazy, like a whisper across a foggy marsh. The words weren't quite right, and the direction was far from certain, but the message was getting through. Why was it so hard to open his eyes? The last few years of hangover wake ups might hurt, but they at least snapped him to attention. He tried to move his arms to rub his eyes, but they wouldn't budge. Oh fuck, was he paralyzed? Did he drive off a cliff or fall down the stairs? His mind cut through the clouds like a suddenly too bright sun, and a refocused pull on his arms told him not only did they not move, but his shoulders were sore. Good sign! Pain beat feeling nothing at all. His thoughts went into overdrive.

Mike had been born with a super power, albeit one that wasn't normally very useful. He woke up faster from anesthesia than anyone he knew. Several of the surgeons that had worked on him in the past had commented on it, and it was mostly good for prank or two on the charge nurse, watching to see if you would return to the land of the living. No rhyme or reason, and certainly not due to clean living, but he woke up fast and clear. It was coupled with a larger than normal resistance to pain management drugs, which was less a super power and more a curse. When you have been hurt as bad as he had, and as often, the universe owed you some not feeling time. And like most things you are owed, good luck collecting.

Hands numb, shoulders sore, arms won't move. These are problems. Brain seems to be engaging, toes wiggle, and no source of blasting pain yet, that probably means not damaged. Or hurt extremely bad, the kind that is so deep it goes past pain, and straight to probably dying. He moved his head a little side to side and nothing shrieked at him. Good sign. Then he realized he could hear voices talking in relatively close proximity and went dead cold. His reassembling hard drive started putting together the last events he remembered.

"Sako? What is that? Sounds like a fancy European brand. I'm telling ya, this is some rich fuck, bought an old truck so he don't get robbed for being a city fella."

"With a plastic pistol shoved in his pants? Drinking? That ain't no city boy way to do shit, its illegal"

"Gym muscles. Some faggot assed office job, bought some toys to try and come out to the woods and recapture his man card. Done fucked up though."

"Them tattoos don't scream city life, and a couple big assed scars?"

"Tattoos are cool now. Probably got em off insta-book or some of that other computer shit. Hell, scars might be fake too. Perverts and weirdos from the city do all kinds of strange shit now days."

"300 Norma Magnum? Never heard of that shit. Its a big assed bullet though. Probably some pussy can't shoot, thought a big ole bullet would do the work for him. Bet the salesman laughed all night, thinking about some dip shit green horn cracking his skull with the scope when he drops the hammer on this."

"Wait till Chief gets back. He'll know what to do. Tim, you're either a dead man or a genius, and I can't wait to see which."

The last bit was punctuated by deep belly laughter from at least four men, on the way to intoxicated by the sound of it. Mike connected enough dots to remember he was in a bar, headed to the parking lot and likely a fight. Had he lost that fight and was laying half dead in a ditch now? Years of training kept him from opening his eyes or moving again. Keeping his chin slumped to his chest, he very slowly flexed his fingers. Or at least thought he did. All he was getting in response was pins and needles. Awakening his other senses, he noticed he could smell wood smoke. The dingy little hovel he had left only smelled of cigarette smoke. His mouth was dry and he was thirsty, but not ravenously parched. That said a short amount of time since he had gone under, three to four hours at worst. Could also be five minutes, but it hadn't been that long in relative terms. Finally his wrists solved why his shoulders were full of acid. As the feeling slowly came back in his arms, he felt the bite of a circle of metal on each forearm, which only could mean one thing. Handcuffs.

It takes an abnormally practiced man to stay still when he awakens from an uninvited slumber. Mike was that and then some. There are many situations where letting people assume you are dead has advantages. There almost no situations where upon waking up and discovering you are handcuffed, jumping up and screaming bloody murder has advantages. Opening his eyes would just tell a guard, if one was present, that he was ready to commence whatever came next. Being handcuffed and recently under his eyelids, that was probably not going to be any fun. Mike tried to breath normally and absorb any other detail he could.

Footsteps, and the movement of canvas. Footsteps moving closer. Mike dared not move from his fake sleep. He could feel a body close to his, like proximity siren going off in his head. A booted toe prodded against his calf. Stay limp, let it happen he willed himself.

"He's a big fucker. Think he'll be any good in the woods?"

"Hope he's better than most of these cunts have been. And the women too." A second voice chimed in, eliciting a chuckle from the first.

"Why's he got a bullet tied around his neck? Some new queer jewelry fetish?"

"I"M FUCKIN TALKING TO YOU BOY!" A mouth yelled inches from his face, spittle catching him above the eye. Mike didn't flinch in shock by sheer willpower. If they had taken his pulse, the jig would have been up, but these two didn't seem the thinking type.

"He'll be out for hours yet genius, this is my own brew. Years of perfection distilled drop by drop." Said the second voice, which Mike's recovering senses tagged as Tim.

"I still say he's just another pussy got lost in the wrong woods. Maybe Chief will give him a gun or something to keep this interesting. Otherwise we might as well just do him right here." Oh sweet baby Jesus, let that happen Mike yearned. A faint glimmer of hope sparked in his heart. Give him a Makarov and two rounds, and this equation would change real quick.

"I don't think Chief is in a giving mood. He was breathing fire and brimstone like a traveling preacher in a dry county when I told him the news. I'll be damn surprised if he even lets us hunt."

"Not your fault brother, you saw a chance and went for it. That's what alpha males do. Chief might be pissed at your judgement, but can't nobody fault you for making a decision. It's outside the way we do things normal like, but inside the code of how we live. Take what you want, it's the Return of Kings."

Shuffling away the same direction they had come, with the words fading," Yeah, but Chief is none too fucking happy. And that is not a man you want to piss off." Tim sounded a little dejected, liquid courage on board or not.

"Fuck it. Worst case scenario, we bury him with the rest, season is over, and we all laugh about this over beers for the next year. You took a risk, not just following like some drone. Chief will understand that, and the tribe does too."

No greeting to a third party, or words exchanged with one. Pretty good odds he was alone in a room. Rolling his head to the opposite side as the direction of the door, Mike risked partially opening his left eye. What he saw doused any hope of walking out of this one. Both men had masks on, the pull up kind with drawn on animal teeth. Under normal circumstances, laughable. But here, this had a very sinister connotation. This had nothing to do with concealing identities. Mike was under no illusion these men were concerned he knew who they were. For thousands of years, across every continent, a mask had been part of every warriors' attire. From the faceplates of the Romans, to the Samauria menpo, to tribal Africa, to arguably modern camouflage paint. Yes, it was partially designed to strike fear in your enemies, or make you appear other than human. But mostly it achieved a change in the human psyche. Put a dozen men in masks, and suddenly they were mentally capable of committing all kinds of barbarity. Take it back off, they returned to humanity, like peeling off a glove used for a dirty task.

Mike didn't know what was going on, or where he was, but he knew a couple of things about the human mind. So did whoever called the shots around here, and he knew enough to put his men in killer face as part of the ritual.

CHAPTER SIX

Chief, Bob to most people in the county, was not a man used to being second-guessed. A bear of a man with a hot temper, he dominated most interactions with people by sheer implied violence. God help you if you actually managed to piss him off. Some drunk had taken a swing at him a few years back, and Bob left that poor dumb bastard a vegetable, sucking down taxpayer dollars at a hospital over in Spokane on life support. Bob dropped him to the pavement with his first counterstrike, and just kept hitting him. Long after the man was down and out of the fight, Bob just kept pummeling him like a wet noodle. No one in town had wanted to testify to that, and with no witnesses any charge of assault evaporated. "Chief" had a reputation before that as someone not to be messed with. The incident with the drunk made mothers pull their children close when he walked down the street, and tempered the tongue of any man who even thought about challenging him around here. When he walked in the tent flap at the base camp, he was positively lit with rage.

"Tim, you dumb motherfucker, I should pull your lungs out through your asshole. What in the fucking hell made you decide to pull prey from our own goddamn town? Are you stupid, or do you just want me to kill you?"

"Now wait a second Chief, hear him out, Tim actually…."

"No one asked you to open your fucking cock holster Dean. Sit your ass back in that seat or I will sit you down." Chief snarled. Dean clamped his jaw shut and sat down in his chair like a scolded child. Chief kicked an empty chair across the tent, adding emphasis to his displeasure.

Chief was not the sharpest tool in the shed, he had solved a lot more problems with his fists than his head as long as he could remember. Still, even he could read the way the balance of power was shifting among the tribe. All of these dumbasses had been brewing this over as a good idea, waiting on him to show up and approve it. They were shocked he was not only rejecting it, but he was so angry he was on the verge of violence with his own kind. He needed to bring some finesse to bear. He had to regain control of the situation, but not in a way that permanently altered the dynamics of the group he had so lovingly built. "Goddamnit, we do things the way we do them for a reason. It's kept us safe and powerful for ten years. It's allowed us to build our tribe. It will keep us free and able to continue our ways until the Return of Kings. We fucking do it that way because its smart. Now you are all cunning and capable men, you wouldn't be here if you weren't. But you elected me your leader. You expect me to make the hard decisions for us, that is my burden. Someone want to explain to me exactly why we are in this situation?"

Tim was not a particularly strong man, in either body or character. He knew he had made a mistake, and was scared to his core that he was going to pay for it with his life. The cowards tongue took him, that silvery gift that has talked many a craven man out of the noose. He had one chance to fix this problem and walk out of here, with a little luck with his standing among the tribe still intact. Maybe even enhanced if he played it right. The words rolled off his tongue like water over a cliff, flowing to show Chief he had acted right. He recounted the story from the bar, how he had made sure there were no witnesses, how this was a loner from nowhere, how he had slipped the roofie into the strangers drink, then come back here to get help transporting the body and cleaning up any potential mess. Tim delivered a case worthy of a veteran prosecutor in a courtroom, watching Chief's face the whole time for signs he was going to be okay.

Chief sighed to himself. It was like dealing with children some days. In many ways, these were his children. Had he not created them after all? He felt his rage abating. He was still angry, but taking it out on the boys wasn't going to help anything. "Look, you took action Tim, and I can't fault that fully. But we do things careful for a reason. Yes, on the surface, this looks like a good catch. And I know the last stalk wasn't the greatest. That pussy was still good though, right Bill?" He said with a smirk. That got a little grin from everyone. Bill had lasted all of about ten seconds, which had earned him a lot of good natured ribbing over the last few days." You guys have grown as warriors, and you need a greater challenge. I get that. But the Return isn't fully here yet. There are too many things that could go wrong here. More people may know where he is than he let on, hell, he could have been running a Facebook live event when he pulled up. People do weird things. If nothing else, his phone has picked up signal in our town, which makes it a last known location."

Shifting to a sterner tone, with his hands on his hips, Chief continued. Looking down on his troops now. "The other thing is, we don't know shit about this guy. You don't just let a wild animal loose in your preserve, until you have some idea of what it will do. How would I feel if one of you got hurt? I don't doubt you guys could take on anybody, the tribe against one man, but you are all still growing. Hell, Jessup over there was Force Recon. But he was still squeamish the first time the ritual was completed. What if this guy spent his whole life trapping, and he catches one of you with a deadfall before we kill him? Is that really worth it right now, with so much hope for our future on the horizon?"

Chief's words had struck true. He could tell by the way no one wanted to meet his eyes anymore. When he had first entered the den, he had seen challenge and fury in several of these faces. Now all he could see was shame and doubt. Shame that they had disappointed the Chief by thinking they knew better than him. Doubt that they had dared to question his judgement. Check and Mate. The power was his again, and any threat to his leadership had evaporated like smoke.

"Now we can't just toss him in the bone pile. That won't work this time, we don't want him to just disappear. We are going to kill him right now though, because this is exactly how things get fucked up otherwise. Tim, this was your mistake, so you are going to take the lead in cleaning it up. First order of business, go in there and club this fuck to death. Head only. Then we will take him back to town, put him in his own truck, and roll it off the logging road southeast of town. People die in car accidents all the time. That is still inside our county, but as far from here as you can get. Then sit back and wait on someone to call it in. With a little bit of luck, nobody notices until spring. A long winter would play hell with forensics, if anyone even bothered."

Loyal soldier that he was, Tim stood and grabbed a fire log, following Chief to the tent flap. Glad he was out of trouble, he was experiencing massive relief and an adrenaline spike fueling what he needed to do. Tim wasn't the best in the tribe at killing, he usually thought about it long after when he was done. He couldn't sleep well for weeks, and when he closed his eyes he would see his victims looking at him, sporting impossible wounds. This was a secret he kept deep inside, no way he would let any of his brothers see his weakness. In time, he was certain it would pass, it was just another layer of forced civilization to shed. But right now? He would gladly cave this man's skull in as long as it meant returning to the fold after his mistake.

Chief was still relaying directions over his shoulder three steps into the room that held the prisoner when he stopped dead in his tracks. Tim bumped into him, a small accordion crash of all the tribe that had followed to see Tim earn his redemption. The room was empty. Time stood still as the gravity of the situation hit each man square in the disbelieving face.

"FUCKING FIND HIM!" Chief bellowed at the top of his lungs, cuffing Tim on the ear with a vicious blow.

CHAPTER SEVEN

As soon as the two clowns in Halloween masks left, Mike knew the clock was ticking. It might be amateur hour around here as far as warrior skills went, but there were no illusions he was a dead man if they found him awake and bound. Even if they were fool enough to let him out of cuffs, no way he was taking down six or more grown men with his bare hands. That was pure Hollywood fantasy. He was certainly going to try if it came to that, always better to die with your boots on than groveling for death in the face of unspeakable torture. He had no idea what they had in store for him, but he didn't want to stick around to find out.

Opening his eyes fully, Mike took stock of the situation as best he could. White canvas room, no doubt a straight wall tent. Bare electric bulb hanging in the corner, light hum of a generator close by. A bare dirt floor, with a small leak springing free under the uphill left corner from the drizzle outside he was just noticing. He was barefoot and his shirt was missing, though he still had pants on. Small comfort, maybe they didn't want to rape him first. His feet were unbound, which would afford some more maneuver room for however he was going to try and get out of this. His captors thought they had things locked down tight, no doubt, but he could see through the sloppiness of their methods. Unless you plan on walking a prisoner around, why not bind the feet as well? And what kind of a rookie left a prisoner unguarded in a prison with cloth walls? He was still going to need a bigger error in judgement than that though, if he planned on making it out of here. Moving slowly, still mindful of making a loud noise, Mike tried to sit up. His cuffs made contact with something and stopped his forward progress. Feeling around with his fingers, he determined it to be a steel pipe. Cautiously scooting to the right, while pulling tension on the cuffs, Mike felt the pipe slide down at a 90-degree angle. His mind's eye conjured a U-shaped pipe maybe a foot wide, and probably about the same off the ground. No doubt put here expressly for this purpose. Hoping for an easy win, Mike rolled onto his side, twisting the cuffs down the upward leg of his restraints, so that his fingers could scrape the ground. Fuck. Concrete less than a quarter inch down. They had at least done this part right. The size of the U shape also prevented him from maneuvering to get a foot in it, possibly allowing the much bigger muscle groups of his legs to press the apparatus apart. This was at least one-inch pipe, so that was unlikely to work anyway. Mike also seriously doubted they had been so lazy as to concrete one side of the U, but not the other. Nobody gets that lucky. Mike recovered to a sitting position anyway, and scooted his body to the left. At the intersection to the pipe and the other 90-degree bend, he found what he was looking for. The oversight that just might get him out of here in one piece. Whoever had constructed this restraint system had left four threads exposed from the pipe to the fittings, and now it was going to cost them dearly. Provided he had enough time.

There are many ways to defeat handcuffs if you have tools, and a few more still if you don't. Even if Mike had been able to break the U shape, he would still have the added problem that he couldn't get his hands in front of him without breaking the cuff. Some men he had known were that flexible, but he wasn't one of them. Not a lot of guys in the 240 weight class were. Without any specialized tools, like a professional would have tucked in his belt Mike thought morosely, the only option left was a brute force attack. He could beat himself up for getting soft later. Now it was time to do this the hard way. Pulling his hands as far apart as they would go, he inched his butt away from the U until he felt the chain of the cuffs bite into the threads. Leaning forward slightly to up the tension even more, he began rocking side to side. The trick here was to use the big muscles of your core, and not try to rely on arm strength. The cuffs dug into his wrists as the friction on the chain increased. As the pain ratcheted up, he felt the blood start to flow into his palms, and a wicked burn in the opening wounds as sweat poured into them. Between the exertion and the agony, he was sweating buckets. He bit down an urge to scream. His own rending flesh not only filled him with horror, but hurt like a hammer on toes. Focus on the prize, he willed himself. This is nothing compared to what will happen if you fail. He had an image of a coyote chewing its own limb off to escape a trap, which almost caused him to laugh out loud. Maniacal, crazed laughter, the calling card of the damned. Not the first time he had been here. His shoulders burned with the fires of Hell, but on he pushed. In training, they had always taped the wrists first. A little safety precaution, and we don't want our guys running around looking like emo teenage girls. They also checked the cuffs first for defects. These were mass produced, and if you tried this little trick on a set with a burr, you might not need to worry about escaping. You would bleed out and die before you got free. Ever onward, no way but forward, Mike pushed himself. If you can run until your heart explodes, you can take this. With redoubled fury, he leaned into the cuffs. And felt the chain pop and give as the threads of the pipe finally ground through the links to freedom. Leaning back, he let the chain go slack, and the broken link fell free, releasing him.

He jumped to his feet, listening for a sign they had heard him, praying the generator and rain had covered the noise of steel on steel. He hadn't heard a word for the last few minutes, both from the noise of the chain dragging across the pipe, and the necessary inward focus to complete the task. On a good day, it took less than three minutes to defeat handcuffs, but that felt like a lifetime if it was you in the hot seat. A new voice was mid-sentence with "go in there and kill him right now…", which Mike absolutely knew was for him. No sense sticking around then, and no time to listen to the outside wall in case there was a sentry. There is a time for caution, and a time for decisive action. This was no question the latter. Mike took three rapid steps in the direction he had seen water seeping under the tent, hit the floor at a dive, wormed under the canvas like a mad man, and rolled free in a dark rain. A lighting flash in the distance gave him all he needed to know, as he ran towards the tree line barefoot, like a rabbit from a pack of wolves.

CHAPTER EIGHT

Halfway out of the clearing, Mike was at a dead run. The muddy ground cushioned his bare feet from all but the occasional granite rock in the soil, but he was far from caring. Like it had all of his adult life, the tree line meant safety. In the open he felt naked, vulnerable, even in everyday life. Escaping from some backwoods nut jobs in the middle of who knows where, he wanted the concealment of the deep woods like a drowning man needs a straw. His legs pushed like pistons against the soft earth, running for cover a memory as old for him as time. It seemed like an unfairly large portion of his life was spent running toward the temporary security provided by a sea of green, it was home to men like him. Some people might call it the green hell, but not those who had been molded by it, forged into walking weapons by countless days playing cat and mouse in just such an environment. The truth was, nature was neutral. Those who learned to play by its rules, however, gained a huge advantage over those that resisted it, tried to shape it to their whims. Mother Nature would kill you in a heartbeat, but it would be impersonal. I told you not to touch the light socket, Johnnie boy, now you have to pay the consequences. Learn its heartbeats, its patterns, how to move in harmony with it though, and God help anyone arrayed against you. Because nobody else will. That is a lot easier to enforce with a rifle in your hands though, Mike thought grimly.

One hundred meters to go, a flashlight beam pierced the night, followed in rapid succession with a rifle shot. Mike redoubled his effort, shifting up to a sprint reserve fueled by even more adrenaline. A commotion to his rear, he was no doubt being pursued now. The only way his antagonists could have possibly missed was a choice of weapons. Mikes brain was calculating angles and odds even as he cleared the first of the giant pine trees. They had to be using deer rifles, which explained the one shot, with scopes, which explained the miss. Scopes are great for many things, but they don't gather artificial light worth a damn. Probably dialed up to max power too. The easiest way to make a standing off-hand snap shot with a scope is counter intuitively to drop the magnification down as low as it will go. The shooter either didn't know that, or he had caught them so flat footed they were reacting with panic. Hopefully a little bit of both.

Lungs burning with exertion, Mike kept up the pace as he ducked branches and scrub pines. The first rule of evasion, make enough space your pursuers don't accidentally land right on top of you. Fitness was a prized asset amongst all warriors, exactly for situations like this. As the lactic acid hit Mike's quads, he regretted every cigarette he had ever smoked, and every mile over the last two years he hadn't run. It had been so easy in the before. Fitness was part of the lifestyle, and the machine always had ways of checking. It might catch you slacking once, but the second would be the end of you. Out of the game, like many athletes, Mike's people had a tendency to backslide. They had been so superhumanly strong for so long, it felt like it would never go away. And regular people were so weak, it didn't really seem to matter. Like Clark Kent on a six-month bender, one day you woke up feeling like that last shot was liquid kryptonite. And of course, the universe throws you in a situation where you need it. His chest heaving and his legs turning to jelly, Mike tried to keep to a path across the jagged foothills that was basically level. Higher in elevation would require more stamina than his feeble body possessed at the moment. Not a chance he could disappear over a ridge in time to get out of rifle range. Down was worse, that is the default setting for almost every human lost or being pursued. The short-term gain in less exertion means being channeled by the terrain, a sure fire way to run into a trap. Ravines also usually have thicker vegetation, which makes you much easier to follow.

On and on he went. Speed was the only way to gain the gap he needed. The easiest way to never get caught is to be faster and deeper of lung than whatever is chasing you. Mike didn't know the terrain, however, and hadn't even the benefit of knowing where exactly he was. You don't go running blind in someone else's backyard unless you want to get headed off at the proverbial pass. Mike just needed a few minutes clearance to tilt the tables, and learn something about his adversary. With no attempt at counterattacking, he made a hard left turn. Dropping from a run to a fast walk, he mentally began counting his paces. Sixty-eight, left foot, sixty-nine, left foot, the same mental cadence he had been using for over a decade. His brain judged the distance for him on autopilot, allowing him to tune an ear to the noises that would mean the pursuit was close. At seventy-two steps, he turned hard left again, back the way he had come. As he walked, he stooped to pick up handfuls of cold mud, rubbing it on his exposed torso and face. Another seventy-two steps, which meant another 100 meters passed, and he turned left one last time, toward the original path he had taken through the woods. This time he slowed to a stealthy pace, taking care not to overshoot his original trail. That would spoil everything, depending on the tracking skills of whoever was behind him. A few paces from what would be a perfect square from the air, he halted and crawled low into a nearby bush. Dog leg complete. A recce trick learned from the older brothers in Vietnam, a lesson learned in blood and passed down through the generations since. Think you are being tracked? Circle back and rain fire on your enemies when they least expect it. Attack from nowhere, right in the soft underbelly while they think you are still moving. It tended to work a lot better with claymore mines and machine guns, a sobering thought at the moment. Still, it would teach him something about these other men. Could they track him at all? Could they do so in the dark no less? If they did pass by him, he would at least learn their numbers, and what weapons they carried. Would they walk in a formation? That would imply training, and that wasn't good. Would they be disciplined and silent, or a gaggle of yelling wild animals? As his hands found a fist sized rock with a nice jagged edge, he hoped maybe a straggler would be behind the pack. After all this time, to be left sitting in the dark, holding a fucking rock? Maybe this is how it all ended, clutching a Neanderthal level weapon and dying in a hail of gunfire.

Mike crouched in his bush for what felt like hours, the light rain cascading against his bare skin. He had been here before, and reminded himself over and over that your mind loses track of time in situations like this. He had spent many nights on the ambush line, waiting for a worthy target to cross into the kill zone, often going home empty handed. That is just how the game was played. At first there was always the excitement of setting up, followed by the adrenaline buzz of watching, waiting, alert at every little noise of the forest for signs of the approaching enemy. Then came the dreaded sleep monster. No matter how well rested you are, it is against the human psyche to lay in the dark for hours and not want to close your eyes. In training, that meant failure, and possibly expulsion. In the real world, it meant death. Not just for you, but possibly your entire team. Then came the aches and pains, usually with an accompanying itch somewhere inconvenient. Laying perfectly still behind a rifle disagrees with your body very quickly, regardless of how many times you have done it before. Movement at the wrong time will also cost you your life, so you bear down and take it. Eat your bitter. The price of doing business. Fat chance of the sleeps taking over here. The icy rain stung like pin pricks all over. The heat in his engine from the exertion of getting here had faded fast, and he was feeling the trembling in his muscles that preceded real shivering. He was freezing, sore, and vaguely becoming aware that he had damaged his feet. Hopefully not badly. Adrenaline can carry you through an amazing level of pain, but not forever. As the rain ran down his back and sought the last dry bit of his pants, Mike thought of how much easier this was in Gore-tex. Or in the desert for that matter. He thought of the Baghdad sun, his nemesis at the time, and how he would never curse its rays again. He flexed and released his muscles from feet to neck, trying to coax out enough warmth to go a little longer. The weak part of his brain, the little voice that always reminded him of the easy path, tried desperately to convince him no one was coming. Just take off, it screamed, they won't find you. You can find a road, or a Ranger Station, and be in a warm hotel by morning. Mike tamped that voice down. It was the same voice that wanted to quit when things got hard. The tiny little shard of cowardice that all warriors carry with them, the one that tells you to give up. It won't be that bad. You'll survive, everything will be fine. Courage was sticking that little voice back in its closet, and doing what needed to be done. Still, his practical mind was weighing the options. Maybe this crew had lost his trail, and they weren't coming. Hell, maybe they were scared to chase him in the dark. If that was the case, his best option was to make as many miles tonight as he could. See if these weak sisters could run twenty miles across the mountains to find him. That, he seriously doubted. No one could keep up with his kind in terrain like this. Half the job of a recce troop was to be able to out run an assault force. Even in his current less than ideal state, he didn't believe there were more than a handful of men on Earth that could keep pace with him across this terrain. Except for Afghans. They were definitely an exception to the rule.

Mike had very nearly convinced himself that he had lost his pursuers when he spotted the first rays of white light piercing the night. Coming from the direction he expected, a herd of elephants with flashlights bouncing willy nilly across the woods. He hadn't even attempted to conceal his sign, or counter-track, but he was still a little surprised they were able to follow him. Drizzle isn't the easiest thing to follow anyone in, regardless of how careless they are. Another forty inutes or so, and you would need a Malaysian on point to keep that trail. Lighting crashed again, offering him a snapshot look at the tribe. One man out front, flashlight down, slowly following his footprints. Not a professional by the look of it. His slow pace was due to his lack of skills, not the practiced caution a real tracker always exhibited. The trail does end somewhere, and it is best for you if that isn't in a well-planned kill zone. The rest of the group, seven or eight of them, was bunched up right behind him, flashlights out like scared school children. It was really too bad, Mike thought, that he didn't have a rifle. With his preferred weapon for this, a custom SAINT Edge AR-15 and its 2.5 pound trigger, coupled with an Aimpoint red dot on top, this would be over right now. Mike had been told, by the men who taught him and would know, that he had one of the fastest trigger fingers in the world. In under a second, he could unleash enough 77 grain killer bees to put every one of these men in the ground. The old Baghdad meat saw. A hurricane of lead and copper.

On they came. When they were within ten meters, Mike averted his gaze so that he could only see them out of his peripheral vision. The beam from multiple lights had fallen right on him, but he wasn't worried about that. You are either camouflaged enough, or you aren't. Low in a bush, he knew from experience that most people would walk right past. Without another clue, sitting still a man was almost impossible to detect in dense foliage. And human eyes don't reflect light the same way as animal eyes, which was very fortunate in his current situation. Something science still can't explain, humans often know when another human is looking at them. Mike looked away, just in case one of them was in tune enough with nature to feel it. At this range, his odds of survival if they detected him were zero.

The lead man came even with him, not three feet away. He had cut it a little close with his pace count apparently. He was so close, Mike could smell the beer on him. Mike started a cycle of short, slow, shallow breathes. He didn't want to hold it, in case they stopped for some unknown reason. He would eventually have to exhale, and that was likely to be loud. The leader hesitated a moment, found another foot print, and moved past him. God, he hoped someone from the gaggle didn't step away to take a leak. That had happened to him once in training. Some idiot bulk fueler, oblivious to his surroundings, pissed right on the leg of his ghillie suit. Mike stayed perfectly still, dumbfounded. It was harder for his spotter, three meters away. He later said it took every ounce of discipline beaten into him by their harsh school not to bust out laughing.

The gaggle of followers all looked roughly the same. Face masks of skull teeth pulled up, armed with a variety of hunting rifles, wearing a mix of earth tones and hunting gear. They were clearly pissed at being out in the rain, and at losing a prisoner. Whoever this Chief guy was, he was unhappy. Mike detected some fear, and that probably wasn't all from being out in the dark woods. There was some colorful talk about "skinning this motherfucker when we find him" and how "fucking stupid Tim was." Mike knew this kind of bluster from a lifetime of dealing with new guys and third world troops. Mostly it told him that this crew was undisciplined, weak, and had no idea who they were dealing with. Hell, a high capacity pistol would have been good enough to kill every one of them. He doubted they would even get a shot of return fire off they would be so surprised. Still, he wasn't out of the woods yet. He was holding a rock and mostly his bare ass, which wasn't near enough to flip the script. If they did find him, he had no illusions he wasn't in for a long painful time before an agonizing death. Their blood was up, they would follow through with a skinning. Men in groups are always more dangerous, the pack mentality can drive more cruelty and savagery than normal men are capable of alone. Not that Mike would be an easy capture again. He would make damn sure he died right here, preferably taking at least one of them with him. The first rule the Arabs had taught his generation of warriors, save the last grenade for yourself. The unspoken rule had always been, if capture is imminent and rescue impossible snipers kill your own. Better a .308 to the skull right now, than hours of a power drill on your joints. Not one captured soldier from the entire GWOT had been rescued alive. After seeing the corpses first hand, it was an obvious conclusion that being taken alive was a fate no one deserved.

After the group moved out of sight, Mike counted to sixty in his head. It would be dumb luck to have them quit the trail right as he popped out of his hiding place, but that was the kind of chance you didn't take when your life was on the line. He also prayed to the Old Gods for a straggler to come up that had fallen behind. Eight men, that is a fight you are going to lose every time. But one man, that you can blindside as an opening salvo? Good luck brother, the ravens will be picking your eyes out come sun up.

After a full minute had passed, Mike bolted out of his hiding spot and back down the trail he had made on the way in. It was difficult and slow in the dark, but he needed to follow his exact path. The plethora of footprints made by his pursuers would mask his own, hopefully sowing enough doubt about his direction that they called it off completely. The rain started to pick up, thankfully, which should do the rest. At some point down the track he would just turn left, wipe his footsteps away for a few feet, and bolt into the night. Not good enough against world class, but these guys were far from world class. He was reasonably sure it would be good enough. Suddenly, a smile creased his face. Out of nowhere, all of his Christmas's came at once. A lone flashlight beam shone through the trees, coming from the direction of the camp. And from the sounds of the heavy breathing behind it, the tribes least in shape man was trying to catch up to the big boys.

Mike spotted a large pine tree slightly off trail and quickly ducked behind it. This new comer wasn't exactly following the tracks, but was coming close enough it should work. He crouched down with one eye peeking around the trunk. If it looked like the loner was coming straight at him, all he had to do was slide around until his body was out of view. And if he passed from too far out to grab, well, this worked equally well from behind. Gambling on percentages, he lined up with what he hoped was the stragglers right side. Only 10% of the world is left handed, which meant that a man carrying a rifle tends to point the muzzle left. Right hand on the trigger, it is the most natural way to do it. And if it was only carried in one hand, that also tended to be the dominate hand. Getting control of the gun was step number one. All the hand-to-hand skill in the world falls apart with a 7mm magnum in your chest. There are a number of ways to take out a sentry in the real world, none of which are likely to ever make it into a Hollywood movie. The preferred technique was ten rounds of suppressed rifle fire from extremely close range, followed by a coffin kill in the head to be sure. A 175 grain Sierra Match King from down the street was a close second, but neither was really an option right now.

His heart quickened as the light grew closer. He thought again of how much time he had to get this done. He was at least 500 meters from the main pack, unless they had doubled back. Possible if either they knew his trick, or just grew weary of following. He hoped he had a least a minute of separation, or this was likely to go bad. There absolutely wasn't a better option though, he needed a weapon badly.

And even without a weapon, he was likely to freeze to death tonight without clothing or a fire. He had checked his pockets on the ambush line, empty as the day they left the factory. It was now or never. The man was almost on him. He closed his left eye, so that at least one of them wouldn't lose the adaptation to darkness. It took thirty minutes to fully adjust to the dark, one of the quirks of human vision. Painful after all the time in the gloom, he kept his right eye on the light so as not to lose track of its holder. He inched around the tree to fully conceal his body as the man came closer still. He felt naked with just the tree bark between him and an armed assailant, as the beam cut both sides of the big pine. This man was lost, which was making him move slower. Not what Mike needed at the moment, time was not on his side. This was not the kind of ambush you could spring from any distance but touching, and he needed this chump to hurry it up already. Incredulously, he stopped five feet from Mike's tree, panning left to right trying to find the trail. Mikes heart was beating like a race horse, he didn't have time for this.

The moment was on him. Sometimes fortune favors the bold, and he was running really low on alternatives. He sprang like jungle cat from his hiding place, moving in fast from the hunters left side, right arm raised for a downward plunge of the rock. The man turned his head, and froze like a deer in headlights. Two steps away, Mike realized with the perfect clarity of a mind honed in combat that his gamble was wrong. Left hander, muzzle pointed right at him. House always wins. Mike shoved the muzzle away with his left hand, right coming down with a chunk of granite he prayed would be a killing blow, but tangled in his own parry of the rifle barrel. The gun discharged, powder burning his tricep. A quarter second slower, and the trees would be wearing his brains as a decoration. The flash temporarily blinded his right eye as he processed that he had delivered a glancing blow with the stone. No time to worry about that now. Years of dealing with a world where everyone carried automatic weapons instinctively drove him to jerk the rifle free and toss it away. No one, in a life or death struggle with a lunatic on top of them, would have the presence of mind to cycle the bolt of a hunting rifle. But habits die hard. Even with a knife stuck through their skull, hadji was likely to lay on that trigger until he hit the ground. With an automatic weapon, that could be deadly. Mike had lost an XO that way one time, shot by a dead man in the streets of Karbala. Mike brought the rock around in a circular blow, but the man had covered his face with both forearms. The impact stopped with the crunch of bone, but not the ones he needed. His plan was turning to shit quickly. Mike slipped his right arm underneath the man's forearm guard and grabbed the back of his head, at the same time raining left elbows as fast as he could muster. As the straggler tried to turn and fend those off, Mike slipped his heel up under his forward knee, dropping them both in a tumble to the forest floor. As they hit the ground, Mike drove his knees up under the man's armpits, dropping his weight onto his chest. His left arm swept away the guard and pinned it to his own chest, as a howl escaped the lungs of the hunter pinned beneath him. Broken bones hurt like nothing else to move, and Mike used that to his advantage, holding them out of the way of the work he needed to do. He raised his stone over his head and delivered a savage strike to the orbital socket. It was a solid hit, but still the man struggled on. Short, sharp blows, Mike hammered the rock down as hard as he could. He felt bone break, the sickening crunch as the orbital socket gave way, and the mushy strikes that meant he had broken the skull. Mike was exhausted, and wanted to collapse on the man he had just fought. But the first rule of fights where he came from, make damn sure the other guy never gets up. Mike grabbed a fistful of hair on a limp neck, rolled the chin back, and smashed the stone one final time into the stragglers windpipe. If it wasn't over before, it was absolutely over now.

Mike saw half a dozen flashlights bounding through the woods. The fight had taken much longer than he intended, and the rifle firing hadn't help him any. He took a quick look around for the rifle, but knew there was no way he would get that lucky. To search for it in earnest was no doubt a death sentence. He could hear the pack yelling someone's name, and they were almost on him. Reaching to the dead man's belt, Mike located a hunting knife and pulled it free. Better than nothing. No time to be subtle, he cut the man's boot laces and yanked his boots free. His prizes in hand, he took off into the night like a wraith.

CHAPTER NINE

The rain arrived in earnest as Mike slipped into the woods. He was moving as fast as he could, but that little tussle had taken a lot out of him. " Jesus," he thought to himself," I'm in worse shape than I thought. Forty-five seconds of fighting and I'm wheezing like an old man." He pressed on, though within a few minutes he was fairly certain he was no longer being pursued. Better safe than sorry. The knife in his hand at least felt like a weapon, though it was no match for a 30.06. Still, it gave him comfort to have something cold and steel, and it beat the hell out of a rock or a stick. As he was making his way deeper into the woods, he saw the flashlights searching frantically for a few minutes, and then stop at what he assumed was the corpse of the man he had just killed. There was some gnashing of teeth and wailing, followed by some sporadic gunfire. Not even close on that one, he didn't even hear the bullets hit trees. Some of that would be anger, but he hoped a touch of fear too. He was guessing the local militia might be a tad more hesitant to follow him into the darkness with one of their own rapidly assuming room temperature. That is how it usually worked. Everyone wants to play warrior until people start dying. And right now, he also knew he must look like a demon incarnate. Blood dripping off his knuckles from hitting his opponent, blood washing down his face from the spray of the rock meeting flesh at high impact velocity, and a chunk of razor sharp steel in his hand now.

Odds were good they were going to call it a night. Tracking him now would require some very real skills, and it was getting more difficult every second. It was also a fact that most cultures won't leave their dead if they have a choice, and that generally also trumped pursuit. Outside of Africa at least. In the darkest Congo, best to just keep running, especially if the blood was up or the khat was flowing. He had never been to a place with less respect for human life, and suspected that if we found hostile life on Mars, it would retain its crown. He had been there as an "observer", providing eyes and ears to another of the infamous African tribal genocides.

At what he felt was a long movement, Mike stopped to listen and put his newly acquired boots on. He gave himself a few minutes to acclimate and watch for light behind him. Maybe the Timmy squad had switched off the torches in a moment of tactical brilliance, but he doubted it. Mike often wondered how more cops didn't get killed, looking around with a giant target indicator piercing the night. Habits die hard. He couldn't hear anything but the falling deluge, which was more than enough at present to mask an entire battalion on his trail. Fuck it, time to slap on his spoils of war. He had a funny thought, of many years ago when he was a cherry new guy in the infantry. His new roommate, Garbage Man Raubeson, had passed on a piece of absolute grunt wisdom. "If things go bad at some chicks house, always remember. You can get further with shoes and no pants, than with pants and no shoes." He smiled, hell of a time to be remembering that.

He forced his right foot in, and silently cursed the son of a bitch he had taken them from. Wishing he could kill him all over again, he forced his left foot in. He must've killed the only midget in three counties, the boots were at least four sizes too small. It was better than nothing, but not much. As he moved once again into the darkness, he hoped the previous owners dick had been as small as his feet. He deserved it.

Mike moved now with energy conservation in mind, it was going to be a long night. Long, angled approaches when he needed to cross the small ridges that littered the landscape, and avoiding directly uphill. Not only was he running low on gas, every foot of elevation gain would make it that much colder. When a bolt would light up the sky, he would pause and try to assess the terrain. A flash picture wasn't much, but it also kept him from stepping off a cliff in the seconds he was blind after. He was near the bottom of a ravine when a lighting flash stopped him dead in his tracks. Was his mind playing tricks on him? He wasn't exhausted enough to be hallucinating yet, that usually didn't happen until the third day without sleep. Another lesson he had learned more than his share of times. He felt his way to a tall pine, big enough to keep most of the rain off him for a moment, and waited for another flash of light.

It came, and what it revealed sent a jolt of fear up his spine. Not the new fear. An old, primitive fear, built in at the reptilian level. Even to someone of his mental fortitude, it took a moment to shake off. The floor of the ravine was littered with skeletons. At least a dozen, and probably more. What he had seen was unmistakable. No way to fool himself these was animal bones. What would it be anyway, a great deer graveyard? When the Gods lit up the sky, he found himself staring into the eyeless abyss of a human skull.

He willed himself forward. The dead can't hurt you, only the living he told himself over and over. Mike was not a superstitious man, but no soldier is totally immune to the ancient notions once in a while. It had been an extremely weird night. Touching the skull, he gently felt around for a long bone, finding a femur. He held it close to his face and hoped the tiny detail his subconscious had collected was just an overlay of a different time and place. As the heavens split again, any doubt vanished. The bone was human, and it had been split longwise. There was only one reason for that. Cannibals.

However bad this had been before, it had just gotten a lot worse. This was a level of savagery not often seen by Western eyes. There was the occasional fruit loop serial killer, but nothing on this scale. He had a better chance of winning the lottery twice in the next fifteen minutes than this being unrelated to his kidnapping. If there was an entire group of men willing to engage in cannibalism, they had gone well and truly off the rails. This supreme taboo act was more than enough to bind them together, and they would hunt him to the last man to keep this kind of secret safe. Whoever the leader was must have some kind of spellbinding control of them, to take them down this path. It was a far bridge, something like this. Amongst civilians, even murder is pretty abnormal. With group murders, most often one of those involved can't live with it, and comes forward to cleanse their soul. This was something else completely. And given the amount of victims, they had been at it for some time. Anyone capable of keeping a lid on this had absolute god like power over his followers. Eating of human flesh is far enough outside the bounds of normal to get you stoned or hung instantly in most cultures on Earth. To create a group of men ritually bound by a secret so dark as this was incredible. Apologizing to the dead, Mike walked away with the femur still in hand. If he did make it out of here, he needed something to convince the authorities he wasn't crazy.

With his adrenaline wearing off, Mike knew he was in trouble. He was soaked, and the air temperature was at best in the forties. Even with the cloud cover, these mountains got cold at night. The best way not to freeze to death was to never stop moving, an old recon trick. Like most old recon tricks, that was easier said than done. As a young man, moving all night under a ruck had kept the fires burning hot enough to stay alive. The closest he had come to hypothermia had been in of all places Georgia, during a thirty-five-degree monsoon. He had been fine during the all-night movement. Not happy, but he didn't get paid to frolic through the daisies. The bad part came in the subsurface hide they built to observe through the day. That had been a long, miserable experience. Wrapped in GORE-TEX laying in three inches of water, trying to hold still while looking out a dug in viewport. Writing report after report as the 82nd Airborne's satellite communications array took shape, hands cramping with the cold. Finally, the team leader had the sense to scrub the mission. To stay underground was suicide in those conditions. They crept out of the hide and deep into the woods, and ended the day huddled under poncho liners in a kitten ball. That had been one of his first experiences with speaking truth to power too. Command was furious, but his enlisted team leader held his ground. The mission had been scrubbed because to continue it would have meant certain death. Something the officers would never understand, sitting in a warm Operations Center drinking coffee.

Mike stumbled on. His only hope was to keep moving, but that was getting harder by the step. He was exhausted, still half naked, and the temperature was plunging. There is a limit to how much heat your body can make, and if that threshold passes, you die. All the tough in the world won't save you from that. He was still shivering, which meant he wasn't quite dead yet. His legs felt like wet concrete. It was becoming an effort just to put one foot in front of the other. Several times he caught himself from falling over, and he knew it wasn't just the ill-fitting boots. He had to keep his mind focused on the task. Just one more rise, he would tell himself. Every piece of micro terrain became a mission. Just get up there, and then we can rest. He would struggle and fight to complete that short little fifty-meter mission, rewarded with a tiny sliver of accomplishment, and start another. During training, his friend Franco had been fond of saying "I quit everyday, I just don't ring out." That was how you finished an impossible task. One brutal step at a time. Just make it to that tree. Just do one more lap. Quit tomorrow if you want, but just survive to the end of today. Many times in school Mike wished he would just die. It was insane that death was preferable to the shame of quitting, but that is how they got you. Running through the mountains of Greece, following a gazelle of an instructor who had recently tagged in, Mike saw the tunnel closing in around his eyes. Not a physical tunnel, the black at the edges of your vision that means you are about to pass out. Desperately he hoped he would fall off a cliff when it happened, so that the pain could be over. For miles he looked at ravines in the rock, willing it to happen and be quick. Like all forms of torture, eventually it ended. He made it. No quit in this boy. That had been a recurring problem in his life, and part of his strength. He was apparently just too stupid to know when to give up. It was the same trait amongst his people that put amputees back on the battlefield in this war, entirely by choice. Goddamn, how that had changed the game. If the guy missing a leg can come back and fight, how the hell are any of you other pussies going to quit? Those were some seriously hard Mother Fuckers, and the M-F was always a capital. Mike had seen a bomb maker take a beating from a prosthetic leg on target one time, a Wahabi they intentionally left alive. Not many bomb makers or beheaders made it to detention, no quarter for those fucks. This was an experiment in psychology though, and it had worked. Several weeks later, the chatter picked up across the sector, tainted with a supernatural panic. Not even bombs killed these men, and they came back with metal limbs to exact a terrible vengeance. Enemy morale crumbled, and IED incidents fell dramatically. The original bomb maker died in a Predator strike a few days after his release from Camp Cropper. It seemed none of his proteges wanted to pick up the job.

Mike's mind was fighting confusion. He kept forgetting where he was, or what he was doing. His body demanded rest, and that call was harder to fend off. Arms wrapped around his core, the goosebumps on his flesh felt like sandpaper. Intellectually, he knew he was done. It was just too cold, he wasn't going to make it. On TV, the survivor always makes a fire at times like this. Mike had never been good with a bow drill, and there was a snowballs chance in hell of one working in conditions like this. The first rule of survival fires had always been, carry a firestarter and collect tinder in a waterproof bag long before you need it. He had neither. He was going to die. Not a real problem with that, he had come to these mountains with just that intent. Maybe not this way, but the end result was the same. He was proud he hadn't let the amateur hour cannibals kill him, and had taken one of them to Hell for good measure. His only regret was losing. He cursed himself for not following them back to camp, at least he would have a chance to finish them in the night. Go out in a blaze of glory at the very least. He stumbled and fell. This was it. After all the bad shit and terrible places he had survived, he was going to die like some lost hiker in bum fuck Idaho. When the forest service found his body in months or years, they would probably assume he threw his clothes away in a hypothermic craze. Happened all the time. Mike closed his eyes, too beat to get up, and curled into a ball. The warm mud caressed his face like a lover's touch.

Warm mud? Was this the last stage of freezing they always talked about? The moment your body releases all the blood it has shunted to your core back to the limbs in a desperate last move to survive? He forced his numb fingers up to his face and dug them into the ground. He felt very real heat. Sweet mother of God, he had fallen near a hot spring. Rolling onto his stomach, he used his fingers as guides to locate the source. Volcanic hot springs are sometimes boiling, enough to cook a man or a dog in an instant. Right now, he didn't care. Salvation was at hand, and he would gladly scorch his bones, if only to die warm. He traced the path of the warmth and crawled into it, inch by inch. Laughing out loud, he burrowed into the silty mineral dirt that showed the source. He was saved. And that meant some people he'd recently met were going to get a lot more than they had bargained for.

CHAPTER TEN

It was Tim's flashlight beam that first found the body, and a smile flickered across his face before the realization of who it actually was face up in the grass. Somebody must have gotten the stranger, it would explain the rifle shot, and the head on the body certainly looked like a high velocity rifle round could have done it. Not that Tim would know, he'd never seen anyone shot before. As the rest of the tribe bunched up around him and the pool of light grew bigger, his spine ran cold with the dawning awareness that Dean was at his feet. He was hardly recognizable, only his paunching belly and red hair gave it away. The red hair that wasn't stained with fresh blood at least. The left half of Dean's face was completely caved in, a pile of mush that distorted the shape of his undamaged right. Tim was stammering something about an ambulance when Chief slapped him across the face. " This is your fucking doing Tim. One great fucking idea you had dipshit." Chief's mouth was so close his teeth looked like ivory tusks, and Tim was vaguely aware of spittle landing on him despite the rain. Someone in the group was whimpering, a strange sound against the angry yelling for retribution coming from two others. Chaos ensued for a few minutes as flashlights bounced across the trees. Somebody announced they found Dean's rifle, and a gaggle of feet went that way. Jessup was screaming to set up a perimeter, and finally started grabbing people and setting them in position in a rough circle around Dean's body, kneeling facing out. Thunder crashed, and Lee fired off a round into the night. The unexpected shot triggered a sympathetic panic, and every man on the perimeter opened fire, rapidly emptying deer rifles in a one sided firefight with the trees. Tim almost jumped out of his skin, and was raising his rifle to fire at the phantom in the trees when Chief ripped it out of his hands.

"Stop goddamn shooting you fucking morons." Chief yelled, voice just enough to get through the ringing from a volley of rifle fire. The world went eerily quiet. Chief was dangerously close to losing his temper, he never talked to his boys like this. And the last thing any of them wanted to see was the Big Man actually enraged. God in Heaven himself would be afraid to see that. Tim was shaking, and it had nothing to do with being cold. For the second time in as many hours, he wondered if Chief would kill him as an example of screwing up.

"Jessup, Bo, get the fuck over here." He bellowed. The pair snapped out of the circle and ran over. Chief motioned them into a huddle, Tim unwillingly joining as well. He doubted he was still supposed to be here, and after his mistakes knew he had no business in the decision making process. But he was too afraid of Chief's wrath to excuse himself and slink into the autonomy of a rifle on the line like everyone else. Jessup had the most military experience of the tribe, and Bo was the lead tracker.

"Bo, how's the trail look? And how far are we from camp?" Chief asked.

" Rain has done a pretty good number on the trail, and us coming in here like a herd of elephants didn't help Boss. I might be able to find it, but it's getting worse by the second. Clock is ticking for sure. Less than a mile back to camp"

Chief paused a moment to take this in. "Jessup, what's your take? Keep chasing this guy into the night, or regroup and run him down in the morning?" This was very rare. Tim couldn't remember a time Chief had asked anyone's advice.

It was like he always just knew what to do. When the Return of Kings was complete, Chief would be one of its legends.

Jessup already stank of whiskey, which seemed to be his default setting. "It's like this. We got the wrong guns for night work, and most of our guys are more used to daylight hunting anyway. Maximum advantage with us and scopes in the day. Easy to get ambushed in the dark. Gotta figure, this guy is looking to hole up tonight anyway. He isn't dressed for this shit, and probably scared as fuck too. One more thing to think about, lost people tend to walk in circles, and this bitch is assuredly lost. But some bad luck might be circling his happy ass back to our camp right now, and that wouldn't be good. Guns, not to mention trucks. He could actually drive out of here, and then we would have a shit show on our hands."

Chief went white in the face. That was something he hadn't considered until right now. Addressing Bo and Jessup, Chief's words were sharp and to the point. "You two, take two others, and high tail it back to camp. Bo, you're going because you can get back here. Once you get there, Jessup, secure the camp. Shoot this motherfucker if he shows up, but I want him alive. After what he did to Dean, he doesn't get to die easy. Bo, keep a man with you, and bring a truck back for Dean."

"And you Tim. You sit your fucking ass right here next to Dean, and think about how you are going to make this better."

Jessup, Bo, and two shadows bounded off into the night, leaving Tim next to his dead friend, ringed in a circle of LED white and uncertainty.

CHAPTER ELEVEN

An hour later, headlights appeared, ending the apprehension Tim couldn't shake. Impossible, but he had an ominous thought that maybe the stranger had ambushed and killed the four that had left. No fear at all that he had escaped, that he could deal with. Best case, he just kept on running. Worst case, they all ended up in jail. Tim had been to jail before, and it wasn't pleasant. But at least you knew what to expect, and the guards kept order most of the time. The sight of Dean with his skull bashed in had done a number on Tim's psyche. He didn't want to end up like this, and it could easily have been him. Or anyone else. Dark thoughts swirled his mind, and right now he just wanted to be home in bed, maybe a nice whiskey drunk to drift him off to sleep. He kept seeing the shadows move, each time fighting down panic that the stranger had returned for him. The sight of the truck brought him back to his senses. Civilization, or at least a product of civilization, a grab at normalcy. Even the grisly task of loading Dean's stiffening body seemed easier, with the high beams keeping any boogie men at bay. At Chief's direction, the rest of the tribesmen loaded up after, and Bo slowly drove them back to camp. The distance had seemed immense running around in the dark, but incredibly short in a drive.

Back at camp, Chief seemed to have regained his composure. Leadership means knowing when your troops need an ass chewing, and when they need a pep talk. The tribe was cold, tired, wet, and the reality of taking their first loss was sinking in. Chief needed to shore up morale, before the dam burst.

"Men, I hope you all took a good hard look at Dean. That is part of the life we have all chosen to live. We took a risk every single time we hunted other men, because only when death is a possibility are we truly living as Alphas. We knew that eventually one of us would fall. But he would fall surrounded by his brothers. It's what makes our hunts the apex of our rituals. What will give us the strength to forge a new world. The fucking, sating the hunger, taking what we want as men- that is the reward only given by the crucible of hunting. It's not tragic about Dean. He died with his boots on, locked in the trial of combat with another man. And hell, we don't know, he could have already inflicted a lethal blow that this ambushing coward slunk off to die of in the brush. Dean lived as a true man, and he died as one. He finally got to chase the ultimate prey, and there is no tragedy in that. Mark my words men. The bitch hunts we do, those are for fun, and because we deserve it. I was angry at Tim for grabbing prey without consulting us, but I'm not anymore. Men we hunt to prove we are better. We are the Alpha Males, and we prove it to them over and over. We have not had a worthy adversary yet, and Tim just may have given us one."

The sulking men started to perk up. With fawning eyes, they looked to their leader. The fire in his words was infectious.

"Now this cocksucker is running around OUR woods. Cheap shooting, ambushing little prick. He had better hope Dean succeeded in killing him too, because if not, vengeance will be ours. At first light, we are going to go find this motherfucker, and make him pay. I am personally going to cut his balls off, and then shove them up his own ass." The crowd smiled. Tim couldn't believe he was worried a short time ago.

"Now not all good news. We still have a big problem, because we still live in a society none of us chose. Dean will be missed, and the sheep back in town knew he was with some of you. Day or two of the hardware store not opening, and people are going to start asking questions." Chief was leaning hard on his authority, and his skills as an investigator. He needed his guys pumped up enough to go take care of the stranger, and they were going to have to do it without him. No other way. He wasn't scared, though he seen the fear in some of his men's eyes. He needed them to know he wasn't afraid. They had to know that. If they doubted for a second, the whole group would break. Maybe even run. And they couldn't afford that. It was time to see just how strong the bonds he had created were.

"The only way I see to handle this, given Dean's injuries, is to fake a car crash. Which I will then be called to investigate. We can't dump him like he looks in town, or the mayor will be up my ass to find his killer. People will get suspicious, start phoning in anything out of the ordinary, it will be a circus. One of the reasons I keep such a tight leash on crime in this county. We don't need people looking. Now I am open to suggestions, if anyone has a better one. I know some of you are a little scared, and that is okay. For most of you…" He said winking at Jessup,"…This is the first time you've had a loss of a comrade. It can be a little unnerving. My partner got shot my third day on the job back in Salt Lake, and I still remember how it felt. Me not being here, and asking you to go into harms way, is asking a lot. Not something I take lightly. So does anyone have a better idea?"

Chief looked around the room, making eye contact with each man in the tribe. He didn't see a winkling of doubt, or a fracture of his hold on them. Good. With a bit of luck, they would come out of this a stronger unit. And he was going to torture this son of a bitch that had killed Dean so hard, his not being present for the capture would be forgotten.

"We need to put Dean in his jeep. Tim will drive it. Tim, I'm not mad anymore, but you did get us into this. I need your help getting us out. Stuff Dean down in the passenger seat footwell, we don't need anyone seeing him. Tim, wear a hat in case we meet any other traffic. You are going to follow me over to the old sawmill, I know just the spot. I can fake a car crash with the best of them. It's how I got rid of my second partner back in Salt Lake, after he caught on to my after-hours activities." Grins from the peanut gallery. "A drop down the Arrowrock Ravine would produce injuries consistent with his head trauma, especially if he gets thrown free of the jeep. So we will take the doors off first. Splash some booze on him too, makes it more plausible. We want to do this in daylight, so hopefully he gets found early. The sooner I can go investigate the crash, the sooner we can get back here. Tim, you were seen in town with the stranger. So after we drop Dean, you need to be seen in town, doing normal shit. Go buy gas, eat at Margie's, whatever you do on the regular. We leave at sun up, should get us to the spot before any traffic out that way. Jessup, you are in charge of finding Dean's killer. Go get em."

Jessup took to his newfound authority with a seriousness in his voice. "Starting now, we are running this like a military operation. Tonight, there will be a sentry up at all times, one-hour shifts. Rifle in your hands, just in case. I am making a list of who has what hours, I'll pass it on to the man I wake up. I'll take first shift." Which looked a lot like an excuse to keep drinking. The tribe settled into bags for a fitful sleep. Five miles away, a demon was awakening.

CHAPTER TWELVE

Mike slept the slumber of the dead, if only for a few hours. He was partially panicked when he awoke, a nightmare of being buried alive. He had a dream about that once in a while, since a job at seventeen laying water lines in Wyoming, deep trenches to avoid the freezing air. No cave ins on his watch, but the fear rooted deep. The coffin like bunks on the USS Nassau all those months had made it worse. Stupid choice in dreams to haunt him after all he had been through, but those are the breaks. Mike sat up, uncomfortably warm after his nap. He was still amazed at his fortune, he should be dead right now. He took a moment to assess his situation. He still had the knife he had taken from the dead man, and his femur. No idea how he kept a hold of that in his hypothermic stupor, but he had. He was clutching it so tight he had to pry his fingers loose, aching from being contracted so long. Checking damage to his body, he found it wasn't as bad as it could have been. Feet were a little chewed up from running barefoot, followed by the too small boots, but he had taken worse. His fingers hurt and one was numb, but it didn't look like frostbite. Right hand had some abrasions from swinging the rock, and feeling them brought back the memories of the fight. He felt no sympathy for the man, in fact he kind of relished the moment the bones in his head finally shattered. The moment the battle was won. There was always a moment, right when a victory was yours, elements set in motion that could not be stopped, that was magic. The action had been done, but it wasn't complete. The bullet was in the air, the bomb was falling, or your weight was dropping with an off-balance opponent if you preferred judo analogies. Nothing but the intervention of a supernatural force could change the outcome. You had already won, but the moment of success hung in the space of no time. Those were the moments a warrior takes to his grave. You only get milliseconds to recognize them, but you savor them forever. An imposter had tried to play Spartan with a real one. That outcome was decided years in the past.

Mike cut the toe boxes off of the boots, improvising half sandals. Not ideal, but it would work for now. Laying back in his nest of sulphur, he thought about how he had arrived here. No doubt he had been drugged back at the bar. No point in kicking himself over that one. Not exactly a common occurrence, and he didn't have an enemy within a thousand miles twenty-four hours ago. He had been brought here for some kind of twisted hunting fantasy, by a crew that had done this before. Mike wondered if they knew who and what he was, if that was the reason they chose him? Doubtful. So far, this crew didn't seem like it could pour piss out of a boot with directions printed on the heel. A ten-minute head start, and they would never have a prayer of catching him.

Finally, his thoughts turned to his miraculous survival. Training and experience counted for a lot in staying alive, but pure, dumb, luck was the only reason he was still breathing. That was a common enough life experience for him. He had buried a lot of friends and teammates that were stronger, equally or better skilled, and more experienced. Skills matter, but the longer he was in it, the more combat seemed an awfully lot like a dice roll. A 39-cent bullet from an AK will kill the hardest bastard in SOCOM just as dead as a new private. You stack the odds as much in your favor as you can, but you only have to get unlucky once. Mike had a pistol holster with a bullet hole in it once, a fact he didn't notice until his tour was over. Two inches had been life and death at some point in the last six months, and he didn't even know it.

Like most soldiers of this era, the professional ones at least, the lifers; belief had turned into a mixed bag of mythology. Everyone he knew thought they were going to Valhalla, himself included. Ben Bitner's final wish had been to be cremated, his ashes stored in a can of blasting caps, which his wife had honored. Mike had only known one God in the last twenty years, the God of War. He was an unforgiving, cruel bastard, but Mike and his kind followed him anyway. Even with friends dying face down in the sand on a regular basis, and the really unlucky ones returning maimed and burned, they kept going back. Mike couldn't imagine a world where that wasn't his task. And one day, they came in and took it all away. He didn't bleed out in some far away hellhole, or turn into pink mist in an IED. The powers that be just decided he was unfit, handed him a pink slip and a retirement check, and turned back to the job. Enjoy being a civilian, don't bother to write or call. We have things to do.

An epiphany exploded into Mike's brain. He knew why he was here. The War God had kept him alive, all that time, and brought him here to use him one last time. It wasn't to punish the cruelty of these men, or right the wrongs they had done. Policemen are for that, and the War God doesn't care. They needed to be destroyed because they were false warriors. Sniveling, worthless, wannabe soldiers. And in this soft land, they were getting away with it. They were stronger than the simpering weaklings around them, no doubt. That wasn't a high bar. Their failure had been to pretend to be disciples of the God of War, when they were not. And so he had put one of his favorite sons among them, to punish them for their sins.

This was a heady revelation to Mike. It took him some time to grasp the gravity of his task. Finally, a mission. A reason to exercise his skills and talents. He was giddy like closing the hotel door with the prom queen in tow. It was time to make the imposters pay, and pay dearly.

Quickly drafting a plan in his head, he set off the way he had come, backtracking. Along the way he kept an eye out for a straight six-foot limb.

As the sun was breaking the horizon, he located the camp where he had been captive. Selecting the side where he could see a sentry standing inside a tent flap, he curled up in a bush to wait.

Like astronauts and fighter pilots, people from his line of work tended to have physical abilities bordering on mutants. "Panda", a killer of the first order, had once described his old squadron as a cast of comic book characters. Quite fitting in most cases. Mike had vision so clear, they stopped testing him at 20/5. Hundreds of yards away, he might as well be having coffee with his captors.

The light of dawn revealed some interesting developments. The tent he had been tied up in was actually one of two, identical white canvas models with a breezeway between them. Both had smokestacks indicating the presence of wood stoves. These guys set up for a while apparently. That was a lot of logistics to handle on the fly. From the worn paths around the tents, Mike guessed that this must be private property. Logic dictated that you wouldn't set up such an elaborate dwelling in a place it would draw attention from the Park Service. Probably an island of private land in a vast sea of national forest. Such things did exist, and would be priceless for the enterprise these men were in. In front of the tents was a large fire pit made of stone, though not shored up by masonry. At either end was a steel, forked post, a ready receptacle for spit roasting game. That brought a grimace to his face. Sick bastards. There were six vehicles parked to one side of the tents, all in a row. Five models of trucks or 4x4 SUV's, and most interestingly, a Crown Victoria painted County Sheriff. Not Sheriff's deputy, the man himself. Mike wondered if these nitwits had tried to pass off the corpse from last night as a hunting accident. Or told the local Sheriff they had been jumped by a drifter gone homicidal. That might make things interesting. One hint of a siren or helicopter rotor, and he was going into full blown Escape and Evasion mode. This was not the time to go peacefully with some Good Ole Boy Sheriff, who believed Mike was murdering townsfolk at random. He knew exactly how that story played out. Same here as any Louisiana Bayou, Mexican Border town, or Eastern European checkpoint. Shot while trying to escape, saves the county a trial. He would have to hoof it to a place big enough for an FBI office, and hope the Feds gave a shit enough to spot the holes in the local investigation.

Mike mentally laced up his running shoes as a man in a police uniform walked out of the tent. He was talking with a large bearded man, like they were old friends. Two men behind them carried a body by its limbs, which had obviously started to stiffen. More men shuffled out behind them, but stayed a few feet back from the dead. Like it was contagious. Moral support, but from over here. The mass bunched together, a normal human reaction to fear. Like cattle. Another clue about lack of experience in a hard world. A single machine gun burst would have killed all of them, and touching distance of your bed doesn't mean safe. Rookies. Moment of truth. Where was the corpse going? Despite the morning chill, Mike's palms were sweating. His body found a reserve of adrenaline and dumped it into his system. Dying in battle was one thing, but living in an iron and concrete cage was a special kind of hell. He didn't want the Sheriff to be part of this; it complicated things. But he also didn't want to outrun and potentially outfight the resources of a State sanctioned manhunt. He had fought a long time to protect this nation, he had no desire to engage its Police forces in mortal combat. He willed the body to go anywhere but the Sheriffs car. Moving it was already highly unusual, he thought a coroner would not like that. But maybe this far out in the boonies, it was normal for "accident" victims. The grisly procession stopped next to the passenger side of a green jeep, and someone came forward to open the door. Game on then. The deal was sealed. Nobody, anywhere, transports a body in the front seat of a jeep. Apparently a friend was too good for the bone pile, but not too good for a convenient disposal.

Mike watched as the man he recognized as the bar owner got in behind the wheel and fired the jeep up. The Sheriff got in his own car and headed down the mountain, jeep right behind. The man with the beard yelled indiscernible commands, and his troops fell in around him. After a few minutes of drawing in the dirt and talking animatedly, the group formed into a rough line, one man ten meters in front. Beard man walked up and down the line, forcing the spacing between men further apart. The herd instinct was still going strong, it took him longer than he wanted to achieve his desired interval. He spoke again, and the lead troop slowly started forward. The squad followed at the same pace, like a horse dragging a plow. Beard yelled stop, and the entire formation stopped. Go, and off they went again.

"Not bad", Mike thought," not bad at all." This was a decent counter to his dog leg from the night before. Spread out in a picket line, they stood a much better chance of sweeping him up if he tried the same trick again. It had its own weaknesses, which he was going to be more than happy to point out soon. But they could at least adapt. This might be interesting after all. And thank you for showing me your cards early, it's been very helpful. Mike ran off to make some tracks. It was the courteous thing to do.

CHAPTER THIRTEEN

Jessup was eager to show Chief that he could handle the task, that he was the right choice to leave in charge. Jessup had no doubt that he would one day be the heir apparent anyway, and this was as good an opportunity as any to prove it. The first thing he had to do was whip the tribe into shape for a new kind of pursuit. They had been caught with their pants down last night, he wasn't going to let that happen again. The other guys looked up to him, he had been a Marine after all. Big, tough, scary ass kicking motherfucker. He commanded almost as much respect as Chief already. If anyone noticed that his stories tended to change the more he had been drinking, they never said anything. He had been to combat, and a stern glare was more than enough for cowing any thought of challenging him. Time to get the troops in order.

"Bring it in here close men. Listen up. We got our noses bloodied a little last night, no doubt about that. But we are still going after an unarmed man, scared to death and mostly naked in the woods. He got Dean's knife, but let me tell you something. Knife ain't much good in a gun fight, seen that happen once in Fallujah." He hefted his rifle to emphasize his words. Jessup was the only one carrying an AR-15, a semi-automatic, magazine fed, open sighted adaptation of the famous military M-16. Some of the boys had openly jested him about that in the past, but not today. Jessup said he liked to keep a real killing tool at hand, not some fuckin hick deer rifle. One fool had questioned his rifles diminutive "poodle shooting" round a long time ago. Jessup got right up in his face, barking that it had killed over 100 terrorists in his skilled hands, would you like to go for 101?

"Now this motherfucker done killed Dean, and we are going to get some payback. Chief wants him alive, but you get an opening, you shoot. We will deal with the fallout later. I see him first, I'm going to cut him off at the knees with this here meat saw." He continued, patting the thirty-round magazine sticking out of his AR." Yesterday, we ran after him like a gaggle fuck, and it cost us. Not today. Today we are going to move in a formation especially good at finding little rat fucks hiding in the bushes. Bo, you will be on point, tracking." Blank stares greeted him. "That means Bo will be in front, since he needs to follow tracks. So you all don't herd of elephants over all the sign." Light bulbs went off among the brighter of the crew.

" Donny, you will be right behind him. And I mean right behind. Bo is watching for tracks, you are watching his back. So Bo don't get blindsided. Everybody else, spread out in a line, ten meters apart, or just far enough you can see the man to your left and right. Zeke, left flank. Bill, right flank. That means the ends. Solid anchors on either side. Terrain changes the distance. If it gets real thick, move closer to the center. When its thin, spread out more. That way, we cover more ground, and we don't miss this fuck crawled up in the undergrowth. Make sense?"

"Bo, take us back to where Dean got bushwhacked. We will start there, see if we find a trail. Lot easier to track in daylight than with a flashlight. Form up!"

Bo moved to the clearly visible truck tracks that led off into the treeline, and halted for orders to move. He knew how to take direction, and Jessup was in no mood to be trifled with. Chief had interrupted his morning beer. The rest of the tribe was bullied and cajoled into a line, until they looked like Pickett's Charge. Jessup gave the order to move out, and off they went.

Arriving at the scene of Dean's death brought a somber silence. The main body of troops held back without a word from the circle of trampled grass where he had given up the ghost. A gash in the mud showed where his body had been driven hard to the earth, never to rise again.

Jessup moved from the rear to hear Bo's assessment.

"Just like I thought, he came back here. Probably looking for something else he could use. Gait looks like a panicked walk. Skittish, desperate even. I am kind of surprised he found it again, but maybe he never left. Could've been fifty feet away, hunkered down behind a tree. Most likely made this morning by daylight. He circled here three or four times, made a few passes up that way. Hoping to find Dean's gun no doubt, but we beat him to that. Heads off to the north east, tracks are deep. Should be easy to follow in this mud."

Two hundred yards later, the tracks changed. Bo had to slow to a crawl, deliberately looking for the tiniest disturbance in the earth. Thirty or forty yards later, an obvious print would appear again. After a few cycles of impossible, obvious, impossible, obvious again, Bo held up his hand to stop movement. Jessup came forward again.

"What's up? Problem?"

"No, it's just weird. One minute these tracks are like a freeway, the next it's like nothing at all. Almost like it's on purpose."

"Broken clock theory dude. Broken clock is right twice a day right? Scared little rabbit, bound to get lucky some of the time. You're also tired, we been doing this all day and night. Keep it up, we are keeping the pressure on. He is going to run out of gas sooner or later. He's a smoker, and we live in these woods. Easy day."

Jessup clapped him on the shoulder, and moved back behind the picket line. Command and control spot he said.

Easier to maneuver the boys when the time came. Left unsaid, it was also arguably the safest.

The pep talk did nothing to ease Bo's nerves. Something was wrong. But it also wasn't worth an argument. On he went, at whatever pace the tracks dictated.

The sun neared its peak, and still on they trudged. Miles into the vast wilderness, and not so much as a glimpse of the quarry. The tribesmen might be from here, but they were not endurance athletes. As the day grew longer, their feet grew uncomfortable. Unlike soldiers, they weren't accustomed to humping a rifle across vast distances. Heads slumped, looking at the ground instead of the foliage. Jessup finally had to resort to calling breaks every hour for ten minutes. He was starting to wonder if the stranger was heading to Canada, high tailing it for the border. What the fuck had Tim found, the only marathon runner sponsored by Camel?

At noon, the tracks disappeared completely at a dry streambed. Bo searched both banks, and found nothing. Less than nothing. He wondered if man had ever stepped foot on the other side of it. Returning to the near side, he prepared to give Jessup bad news. Left or right was the gamble, and they might have to split forces to be sure. As he opened his mouth to give his analysis, he heard a scream from the right, followed by a rifle shot. It was answered by two more in quick succession, and he and Jessup both hit the dirt when a 30.06 round cracked overhead.

CHAPTER FOURTEEN

Without a starting point, Mike assumed they would come back to the place of last night's action. In lieu of other options, it's what he would do to. The rain might well have washed away all the tracks leading out of here, but some chance was better than none. It beat walking around in the woods, hoping to cross his path by chance. So Mike gave them what they wanted. He wanted a tracker to read him as scared and lost, so that was the story he crafted. Four rapid trips from the imprint of his victim uphill. Mike didn't even bother looking for the gun, he was sure it was long gone. Only a complete fucking idiot wouldn't have made certain they found it last night. And if they even thought for a second it was in his hands, this morning's behavior would have been a lot different. No one would be that stupid, no one. And anyone with any sense would have at least driven the trucks into a circle to form a barricade. A truck won't stop a bullet, but it stands a pretty good chance of deflecting one. And it beats nothing. A smart man would be sleeping in the woods.

With the story complete near the body, he headed off towards the northeast. As he went, he switched back and forth from sloppy movement to counter tracking. Mike wasn't the best counter tracker in the world, but he certainly wasn't the worst. The easiest method is not to make sign in the first place. Deliberate steps, hard spots underfoot, green vegetation that won't snap and preferably recovers quickly.

With a lifetime of practice, you can still move relatively quickly this way. And for an amateur tracker behind you, the time is magnified ten fold. Mike needed a perfect set of conditions for a killing ground, and at mid-morning he found it. Taking someone out of a picket line with a rifle is easy, but requires a bit of finesse and planning with a close range tool. Now he needed to make his escape. A half a mile later, he found what he was looking for. A dry streambed would offer the pause he needed. Deliberately walking right across the soft ground to the edge, he stopped and removed his boots. No dirt on the rocks for his next move. Gingerly, moving stone to stone on the balls of his feet, he walked downstream. In a matter of minutes, his sweaty footprints would disappear, dried by the sun. A very experienced tracker would notice the slight indentation and loose dirt around the rocks he stepped on, but he doubted this crew was up to that challenge. And he only needed a minute of pause anyway.

Five hundred meters downstream, Mike made for the bank and pulled his boots back on. Silently slipping back into the forest, he found the rock face he had spotted jutting out of the mountainside from his initial track. It was inaccessible from the forest floor, at least without some serious effort. He judged it to be 150 meters from his track anyway, which put it out of the line of march for the flanks of his pursuers. Shaded by a large pine, it would be hard to see into from below, and offered a great vantage point for observation. Mike settled in to wait.

Eventually, Mike was rewarded with the sound of a twig snapping. He had almost dozed off, his night catching up with him. Minutes past, as he heard rather than saw the movement below him. The tracker soon appeared, hunched over, desperately trying to stay on the trail. Mike noted a lack of a sign cutting stick, a tool that would have made this immensely easier on the poor bastard. Behind him, shapes slowly turned into men as the pickett line tried to keep pace.

Far right flank was falling behind a little, and the occupant of that position looked winded. Left would have been easier, but like lions on the savannah, weakest prey dies first in times like these. Mike ducked below the crest of the granite, eliminating any chance he could be seen, and waited on the passing noises of pursuit to subside. Two minutes counted off in his head, and he chanced a look. He was just in time to see the bearded man pass out of sight. He counted two minutes more. He couldn't afford a straggler like last night, catching him in the open during his descent. That would be the end of the line. Sure everyone was accounted for, Mike slipped down the rock face. Quiet as a ghost, he maneuvered to the far right end of the line and fell in with the tracks.

Just before the dry streambed, the vegetation grew noticeably thicker. This is true the world over. Smaller plants have a chance here, vines and brush not seen in the shadowy forest where trunks rule the sky. A running creek not only supplies water and nutrients, but the flood of spring storms washes away the saplings that try and take root. Thick undergrowth binds and holds together, tree roots wash out and topple from the weight. The tribesmen, new to this game and worn out from a long pursuit, had stopped the accordion effect of shrinking their lines when visibility was restricted. Now it was time to pay.

Mike spotted his intended target twenty meters away, leaning against a tree to catch his breath. Silently advancing, keeping to the shadows, wraith like he closed the distance. At ten meters, his victim's ears perked up, and he moved his head in a wide circle, sensing danger. Mike froze, slowly kneeling from his hunched over walk after the man's gaze passed over him. Movement is what gets you seen. The moment passed, and the right flanker resumed looking to the center for direction. Inch by inch, Mike crept forward. A branch breaking right now would mean getting shot, and that wasn't on his agenda. He felt every step before he committed his weight, sliding his toes left or right of anything that felt thicker than pine straw. At seven meters he committed. In one fluid motion he swept his freshly minted spear over his right shoulder, cocking his arm for a throw. The femur attached as a spearhead was carved to a pinpoint, secured with repurposed boot laces. The need for stealth gone, Mike planted his left foot hard on the ground. Right flank idly turn his head to the noise, and his eyes turned to dinner plates at the horror. Too late to react, the six-foot oak shaft released from Mikes hand, moving forward at the speed of death. 240 pounds of weight whipped into the throw, hurling it forward, a javelin of retribution. The spear penetrated the man's front and rear ribs like paper mache, shoving him backwards as it embedded in the pine behind him with a solid thunk. His victim felt the wind go out of him, both from the impact and his newly perforated lung. Blood bubbled around the wound, a sickening pinkish froth known battlefields the world over. The agony of his lung collapsing forced a weak gurgle from his lips. Mike never stopped moving, arriving a half second behind his deadly missile, scooping the unfired rifle out of the still shocked hands holding it. Kicking off the body pinned to the tree, Mike immediately sprinted for the safety of a shallow ravine he had picked on the way in. As he rolled over the crest, he heard a bullet hit near him and ricochet off a rock. Jerking onto his chest, he fired two shots in return, expert hands running the bolt like a sewing machine. He didn't even try for a hit, just enough lead back to let them know he had a gun now too. Running in a crouch to keep his head from getting blown off, he hit the end of the ravine and disappeared into the foliage. Time for phase two.

CHAPTER FIFTEEN

There is an advantage in knowing where all of your opponents are, one never seen on a battlefield. Mike shook off the recce instinct to go to ground, to hide until the next time to strike. He needed to do some real damage to his enemy's ability to make war on him, something with some teeth in it. He might have delivered a couple of jabs by killing two of them, but human beings are adaptable. Even the dumbest rock farmer in a third world militia is capable of learning, and if they live long enough, they get dangerous. He needed an uppercut that came all the way from the floor, something to knock them completely off balance. And he knew just what to do. Running flat out, no concern for noise, Mike booked it back toward the base camp. He needed all the head start he could get.

Half a mile away from his destination, he stopped to listen. Hard lessons learned, Mike knew it was imperative to keep an ear open. You could often hear foe long before you saw them. With no way of knowing if the camp had been reinforced, or if someone was there conducting roving sentry duty, he had to approach carefully. Silently he moved five steps, crouched, and listen again. Shadow to shadow, planning multiple moves at a time, his pace slowed to a crawl. Three rounds left in a rifle of questionable zero was no way to get in a surprise firefight. He needed to get the job done, but years of reinforced training kept him cautious on approach. "You're in too big of a hurry to die" one of the old hands had told him the first time he ran point on a training mission. Non Commissioned Officers, NCO's, handled the hands on assessment and training of new recruits. Officers might be overall in charge of the school, but that mostly meant sitting in an office doing paperwork, and occasionally leading morning PT. The NCO's were the gatekeepers, and at any moment they might decide you weren't good enough. Failure to heed advice such as this, or a recurring inability to adapt, would have you doing the walk of shame with your seabag right back to the unit you came from. And with good reason. Those same NCO's would rotate out in a year or two, and anyone they let pass the gate might be their teammate then. The lessons learned were written in blood, first from the Gods who stalked the jungles of Vietnam. No fighters had ever existed like those, nor might ever again. The best a man could hope for was to carry their torch forward, and never bring shame on the units they built.

Finally, Mike reached the edge of the clearing. He set his internal clock to ten minutes, and observed the camp. Longer would have been better, but that was a luxury he couldn't afford. The camp had been built on a relatively flat meadow, with the tents set right in the center. 200 meters of open ground on any side was a lot to cover, if he wanted to get this done quietly. There was a lone man, sitting on a log turned up right, poking at the coals of a dying fire. His rifle was leaned up against the guyline three feet away, which showed a decisive lack of concern. The bane of sentries the world over, the man had given in to boredom. He was failing at his most basic of tasks, to keep alert to any changes. Still, three feet was too close to cover the distance presented. Mike considered just shooting the bastard, but that wouldn't really solve his problems. Right now, Mike needed information. He was still operating in a complete fog. He needed troop strength, assets available, known enemy strengths. The obvious play was to shoot him, steal a truck, and high tail it out of dodge. That, however, presented other potential problems. A stolen car report, a little extremely real evidence of the two murders he had committed in the last twenty-four hours, and some fabricated evidence could make him an enemy of the state very quickly. Given some creativity and thought, he could face a slew of charges that would keep him from seeing the light of day as a free man forever. And just running around killing his captors seemed very shortsighted. It was a simple mission, to be certain, but it left a host of problems as well.

Mike looked the camp over again, calculating the odds. Worst scenario possible, he was caught halfway to the tents by the man to his front, and all his friends from behind. He was unlikely to survive that if he had a real gun. With three bullets at his disposal, the odds were zero. Reading the micro terrain with a practiced eye, he caught a shallow wadi that flowed down the mountain, behind the canvas bunkhouses, and off to one side of the vehicles. Two feet at best, with maybe a foot of grass on top of that. Known in the business as a pool table stalk, because from above it resembled crawling across a sea of felt. Absolutely the most time consuming way of moving, it would work. It wasn't going to be pretty, but it was the only option available. Without a ghillie suit, front covered in slick canvas, it was also going to be painful. But sometimes that is the cost of doing business. Mike started pulling small patches of grass and bushes to hold in front of him like a fan of correct colored vegetation. As he prepared to step off, movement to his front froze him. Incredulously, the sentry went to one of the trucks, rummaged around in the backseat, and headed for the tent flap. Mike stood frozen in slack jawed amazement, but his eagle-eyed vision wasn't lying to him. There was a girlie mag of some flavor in the man's hand. He was going to get a combat jack in. "Oh, you dumb son of a bitch", Mike voiced to himself, "I hope your family puts tits on your tombstone because you just signed your own death warrant." With glee, he set off at a high crawl, moving much faster than he otherwise would have dared.

CHAPTER SIXTEEN

Robbie was bored to tears of sitting on his ass on a goddamn stump, waiting on something to happen. He had started this morning with righteous indignation at being told to stay behind as camp guard. He tried to argue with Jessup, then pleaded, then all but begged. Jessup had finally told him "Shut the fuck up, we don't have time for your bullshit, you're doing it. End of story." That had put a nail in his dissent. It was unfair, and they both knew it. But Jessup wasn't the kind of man to argue with once he was red in the face. Robbie backed down, even though he knew it was a stupid choice. He was younger and stronger than half the tribe, and a better shot than the other half. He had grown up in these woods, before his daddy got shipped off down state. He and his mother had done the obligatory visits every month at first. Then the time started growing. Pretty soon the weather was too bad one month, and we ain't got the gas money the next. Not a year later, his mom had a new beau living at the house, then another in a never ending string. A decade past, and when his pop's got released, he never even bothered coming to look for his boy. Last Robbie heard, he was in California, shacked up with some biker skank. Lesson learned early, all women are whores. Robbie was never going to let one get the best of him, no sir. All through his young life, Robbie had kept his deer rifle stashed deep in the mower shed, a place his mom would never think to look. Or her worthless scum fuck toys, they might slip and fall into some hard work. He would retrieve it at the start of deer season, heading straight to the woods. All that time, he never failed to fill the freezer, not that he cared about providing. He knew he had the respect of the men in town. Young man, no mentor, doing what men are put on this Earth to do. Old Roscoe, who ran the processing shop, let him work the first few slaughters off, sweeping up the place and other menial tasks. After a few seasons, he finally sat him down and showed him how to do it himself. Said he admired the young man's tenacity. And that had eventually brought him to the attention of Chief. His mother had been initially concerned that he was friends with the Law, that sort of thing didn't sit well with his family's habits. And she had been right to be worried, but for the wrong reasons. When he was twenty, Chief had showed him how to suicide someone off a bridge. He inherited the house, and had been part of the tribe since shortly after.

Thinking of Chief, Robbie set to his task of guarding the camp. Chief had put Jessup in charge, so it must've been the right thing to do. And he bet Chief would have a quiet word with Jessup about this particular decision. Robbie was one of his favorite proteges, and he didn't deserve to be treated like this. Robbie knew that if they bagged the stranger, while he was sitting here in camp like moss on a rock, he'd never hear the end of it. They wouldn't rib him out loud, at least not at first. It would be "You shoulda been there man, it happened like this" and "We nailed his sorry ass, it was so great." Then, after the drinking started, it would be a new totem pole. Who was there and who wasn't. Whoever got to shoot the sorry motherfucker would be at the top of that, followed by Bo for tracking him down, and finally ending with Robbie, bravely guarding camp like a housewife. "You get the dishes done while we were out avenging Dean?" They would all laugh at that one.

Then Robbie secretly hoped the stranger was doubling back, hoping the camp was empty. Scurrying to find a cell phone, some car keys, some way to get help. And here Robbie would be. In his first draft, Robbie just shot him, dragged him over by the fire, and waited. Late in the day, his brothers slunk out of the woods, tired and defeated, not a glimpse all day. Robbie would be sitting on his log, nonchalant, sipping a cup of coffee, foot on the bandit like a prize trophy. He could just see the face that smug bastard Bo would make, some goddamn tracker. Couldn't find his ass with both hands, while Robbie got the job done. Then he thought maybe he would drag the body into the bunk house, chain it back to the prisoner rack, like nothing even happened. Wait on someone to find it, that would get some laughs for certain! The final version of the fantasy was the best, after countless re-writes. In that one, the stranger came bounding out of the treeline, pursued by the tribe in full flight. He was too far ahead though, he was going to make the safety of the trucks. In this one, Robbie threw down his gun, and slowly pulled out his hunting knife, steel gleaming in the sun. In full view of his "betters" Robbie guts the stranger like a pig. The man falls to his knees, begging for mercy. But Robbie has no mercy in him. He plunges the knife into the stranger's chest, just as Chief drives up. Wild cheers erupt, and Jessup has to explain to Chief why he left Robbie behind, but Robbie ended up saving the day. That was the one he liked best.

Catching himself falling asleep, Robbie tried to patrol the area around camp. He was half scared to miss the stranger slipping into camp, so he kept to the grassy meadow. He tried to listen for approaching footsteps, or maybe gunfire deep in the woods, something to break the monotony. Give him a clue as to what was happening. By mid-morning, he grew weary of walking around in the grass. If the stranger wasn't some kind of fucking idiot, he was hauling ass towards a highway, as fast as his feet would carry him. At least if he got away, it couldn't be Robbie's fault. He was guarding camp, like he was told. He bet that was it. Bo would lose the trail eventually, if he had even found it yet. The guys would be back, empty handed, by sunset.

Robbie sat, bored again, stirring the embers of the fire he had made to ward of the chill of dawn. No way the tribe would be back before late afternoon. Jessup would be loath to give up the chase, Chief would have his ass if they came back early. That meant Robbie had hours to go.

Chief was adamant that no pictures ever got taken in camp. He said it was a capital offense, and he wasn't messing around. Not just of the rituals, but no pictures that could ever place any of his men in this area. It was too bad, Robbie thought, some of these whores we fuck are downright stunning. Some pictures would be nice to relive that. Recently, Robbie had taken to collecting titty mags of girls that looked like the prey from the hunts. Close counts in horseshoes and hand grenades, he mused. Chief also said no titty mags in camp, and that the tribe should stop abusing themselves to porn anyway. It made you weak, spilling your seed to fiction, less hungry for the hunt. Keeping it bottled up made you more ferocious, both for the hunt, and for the Return of Kings. After the Return, you could sate any desire you had. But you had to earn it first. Blood and sacrifice. Robbie always mentally rolled his eyes at the porn part. He wasn't giving up digital pleasures, and he doubted anyone else was in the privacy of home either. He had just bought a new Hustler Beaver Hunts, and the cunt on page ten looked exactly like the little hooker they brought up here last season. Dirty little whore, she actually came while Robbie was giving her a pounding. Fucking slut secretly loved it. Chief was right about them. They wanted to be put back in their place. It was too bad that for now, they had to kill them right after. In the Time of Kings, he could keep a stable of his favorites. Until they displeased him at least. He hadn't even jacked it to his new mag, and the thought stirred his loins. He would have to be quick, just in case the tribe came back early. It wouldn't do to get caught jerking it when he was supposed to be on high alert. It would be even worse if they came back with a body, they would mock him endlessly, and no doubt tell Chief. "Hey, we bagged this asshole early, and came back to Robbie playing with his pud looking at fuck books." The illicitness of the need made him tremble with excitement. He would just knock one out real quick, put the magazine back under his jumper cables, and no one would ever know.

CHAPTER SEVENTEEN

Before moving out, Mike took a second to remove the round from the gun, stick it back in the internal magazine, and closed the bolt on an empty chamber. The safety on a deer rifle was mostly a decoration, and only a fool would try and crawl with one in the pipe. It was the same way he had done it with his M40A1 when he was learning. A bolt action isn't much use in a surprise, close range encounter anyway, so why risk sparking it off and telling the world you are here? Looping the sling in his left hand to secure it, butt stock dragging, he took off at a fast high crawl. Keeping the stock elevated just a few inches with his forearm kept the scope from taking a lot of abuse, dirt from clogging the muzzle, and the ground from derailing the bolt. He thought of just making a run for it, but with his luck the sentry forgot his hand lotion. He needed to make the most of his time, and a high crawl seemed the best option. If someone appeared, he could instantly drop down in the grass, most likely avoiding detection. If he laid still, odds were in his favor the whole pack of idiots could come strolling in here and never notice him. He would just have to wait for dark, slip away, and come up with a plan B. If he was so close the sentry finished early and spotted him, it was a simple motion to sling the rifle forward, rack the bolt with his right hand, and blast him. The devil is in the details. The sun warmed his skin, and he was sweating profusely as he closed the distance. He had to be down to his last reserves of water, his tongue was on fire for a drink. Still, he stopped every few seconds to listen for sounds of the main group. He didn't have the ability to watch his front and his back, so this was the next best thing. Damn it would be handy to have a spotter at a time like this, watching his back with a semi auto from the safety of the pines. On he went, moving as fast as he could manage. Ten steps out, he jumped up and ran for it. Too close to miss careful inspection anyway, and that much closer to fresh weapons. Carefully, he crept around the corner of the canvas walls, hand on a bolt already drawn back. A loaded weapon would have been faster, but half charged gave him options. Pausing at the closed tent flap, Mike put his ear to the canvas. He was treated to the sound familiar to a hundred thin walled porta shitters in a dozen third world war zones. Boys will be boys. Mike smiled. Time to pay for your sins. Ripping the tent flap open, spilling sunlight across the dark interior, Mike covered the distance to Robbie in two rapid steps. Robbie flailed, trying to cover himself, knowing he was busted, face a mask of confusion at what he was seeing. At the last second, Mike remembered he wanted to talk, and drove the butt stock low from its arc at Robbie's head. It hit him in the chest at half the speed intended, but was still enough to collapse him in a heap. In a move practiced thousands of times during close quarters combat training, Mike caught the bounce of the weapon off his chest, changed the angle up on the rebound, and smashed it butt first into the man's kidneys. Robbie spasmed with the pain, and as his head snapped up, Mike looped it with the rifle sling. Crossing his hands and planting his feet into Robbie's freshly abused lower back, Mike rotated his wrists over in a savage modified Gi choke, cutting off the blood supply to Robbie's brain. In ten seconds, he was out like a light. Mike secured his hands with his own bootlaces and went back to the door. Twenty seconds had passed, max, less time that it took most men to cover 200 meters. And it had been relatively quiet. But still, its easy to get caught with your pants down once the action starts. Nothing quite so unforgiving as getting so caught up in the axis of advance, and forgetting your flanks. Lots of dead men learned that the hard way. Glassing the trees from deep in the shadows of the room, Mike saw nothing out of place. Robbie started to say something, so Mike walked over and calmly kicked him in the stomach. While he was trying to catch his breath, Mike pulled a water bottle out of a nearby cooler. Twisting the cap off, he raised it to his lips, and quickly dropped it. Fool me once echoed in his head. Reaching back in the cooler, he pulled out a handful of ice and filled his parched mouth. Drugged water bottles, entirely possible. Drugged ice, highly unlikely. The melt off and volume of water would make it less effective, and you would need a huge batch to start with. No one would go to that trouble for a random chance encounter. Remembering the bar lit an ember of rage, so he rabbit punched Robbie, knocking him out cold.

As his eyes adjusted to the dim interior, Mike set about looking for the tools he would need. Shoved in a corner, he found his own gear, or at least most of it. Giddy like a kid on Christmas morning, he picked up his battle belt. The pistol was still in the holster, a monster of a weapon. He had been very flush with cash when he splurged on a Dan Wesson Fury. Chambered in 10mm, a handgun round powerful enough to handle a grizzly, it had a huge capacity at 14+1. He checked the chamber, and found it still loaded. With its integral red dot sight and 1.5-pound trigger, this was enough to change his fortunes all by itself. His Randall #16 knife was still in it sheath, so he set about cutting fist sized holes in the tent, one each cardinal direction. The canvas wouldn't even slow a bullet down, but at least he could see now. The small size made it easy to see out, but still hard to see in, and the added light helped him in his search for the useful. Stripping off his sandal boots, Mike put on his own footwear with a rising spirit. He had never been so happy to see his friends Zamberlan left and Zamberlan right. He didn't even bother looking for socks, priorities of work needed to be done. His .45 caliber plastic carry gun was with his jacket, right on top like it was waiting for him. Finally, he checked the load on his Sako TRG M10 rifle. One bullet missing, but no time to bother looking for it now. The other seven in the magazine would make these hillbilly fucks regret it dearly if a firefight started now. Basic survival tools acquired, Mike sat down to ask some questions.

Robbie came to slowly. Mike was afraid for a moment he had hit him too hard, killing him ahead of schedule. You do have to break a few eggs to make an omelet. Cold water on the face finally did the trick. Robbie awoke to find himself sitting in a camp chair, arms and legs tied down, pants still around his ankles. Mike knew there were better, more reliable ways of interrogating. The best in the business never even laid a hand on their detainee, and wrung every last drop of information from them. But those methods all took time, a luxury he didn't have at the moment. He needed answers fast, and there are more direct, if less moral, methods in the book too.

"You are probably wondering why you are tied to a chair, and more importantly why your dick has its own special binding. That knowledge leads to the further realization that said tiny dick is actually tied in four directions over a log. Now believe me, I didn't enjoy touching your tiny pecker, especially after I caught you in here stroking it to gay porn. Nasty little fucker. And also believe me, you don't want to find out why I bothered. I am going to ask you a series of questions, and you are going to answer me. Got it?"

A seemingly cobbled together statement full of lies and half-truths actually had psychology behind it. First, naked means off balance to most people, unless they are in a very intimate setting. Even then, a level of comfort first generally has to be achieved. Being of the same sex made it worse. Most men haven't been around other naked men since they were in a high school locker room, and the awkwardness of it broke down barriers otherwise in place. Humiliation at acknowledging his actions, combined with the lie of homosexuality, leveled up the shame. Introducing the idea he was caught with gay porn, combined with his penis's new wrappings, led him to subconsciously question not only his own sexuality, but also his interrogators. And a tiny penis insult for good measure, to further illustrate the balance of power. If he had a female interrogator to run this gambit, it would work as a standalone. But he didn't. Steeling himself, he knew what came next.

"Fuck you motherfucker, you don't know who you are fucking with. Chief is going to skin you, you're a fucking dead man. You fucked up big time. The tribe will be back any second, and they will eat you alive cocksucker. Best thing you could do right now is stick a gun in your mouth, save yourself some pain. I ain't telling you shit!"

Dammit, why did it always have to be this way? Mike kept his poker face, and never moved from his own chair, inches away from Robbie. In a fluid motion, he brought up the thick, wooden tent peg he had secured for this purpose, and brought it down in a hammer fist on the head of Robbie's cock. Smashed between two unrelenting piece of oak, the transfer of force was devastating. Robbie's eyes bugged out of his head in agony, and his screams filled the air. Mike shoved a dirty sock in his mouth he had found in the tent, jerked his head back by the hair with one hand, and poured a water bottle down his throat with the other. It was a poor version of water boarding, but it had the desired effect of shutting him up. Mike waited on the wailing to subside, and sat back down, never removing the sock. Robbie's chest was heaving, and he contorted against his bonds. Mike calmly folded his hands until Robbie wore himself out of spasming. Making eye contact, he gestured with his left hand in a V. Point back and forth from his eyes to Robbie's, he pantomimed "Look at me." Robbie looked at him like a whipped dog, but some defiance was still in there. Never breaking eye contact,

Mike brought the tent peg slamming down again. Then he got up to observe the wilderness until Robbie composed himself. He was in a hurry, but he needed to appear that he had all the time in the world. He had to break his spirit, and that was going to take some punishment. It was the same problem with the ragbags overseas. The hardest part of the interrogation was making them understand they hadn't been captured by the regular Army this time. The regular Army was awesome at tank battles and artillery barrages, but they were woefully out of their depth at counter insurgency. The poor bastards actually seemed to believe what the generals and politicians said, at the least the officers did, and that was enough. They would follow the rules, no matter what idiotic order came down the pipe. First it was no bags on heads, you have to use goggles. Bags are inhumane. And don't write on them with a sharpie. And chain of evidence. And we can only hold them for three weeks unless the local government wants to put them on trial. One of the most embarrassing things Mike had ever seen actually made the cover of the Stars and Stripes. Some fucking idiot general had decided to empty the prison at Camp Cropper, and had the 4th Infantry Division Band outside the gates playing for them. American soldiers, playing Danny Boy or whatever a band does, while hundreds of terrorists walked to freedom. Mike had flown over Cropper almost every morning that deployment, returning home from missions a lot of his teammates never would. He had often thought of expending his last grenades in the prison yard, wondering how many at prayer in their yellow scrubs one would take down. And some spineless fucking idiot that wouldn't know what cordite smelled like let them all go. Mike's troop rarely brought in prisoners after that. What was the point?

Returning to his seat, Mike saw that Robbie had mostly gotten over his last dose. He plucked the sock from his mouth, dropped it on the ground, and twirled the tent peg into a two handed grip at chest level.

"I think we have had a failure to communicate here. Or at least, you have failed to recognize who you are dealing with. Let me put this in some perspective for you. I killed the fat one last night. Not because I had to. I beat him down because I had to. And then I killed him. Because I am good at it. You clowns might not have recognized it, but I crushed his throat when I was finished to make sure. Whatever you think you and your "tribe" are, you're strictly amateurs. And I have played a very long time in the big league. I've killed more people than you've fucked, and probably done so in a single day. You are already going to walk out of here hurting. If you have any shot at still breathing when I'm done, you had better start answering. Now I am going to ask you a series of questions........"

Robbie eventually broke. Everyone does, it's inevitable. And once he started talking there was no shutting him up. He told Mike all about how Chief had recruited them, how they came here once a year to hunt men, how Chief selected and acquired prey in faraway locales, what Mike's fate would have been if he hadn't escaped. But like a career criminal, he stuck close to the parts Mike already knew. Mike prodded him with questions to steer the interview, but held some of his cards back. When he started talking in circles, Mike assumed he had exhausted the current line of stories.

"Now tell me about the bone pile." Mike stated flatly. No hint of emotion, no accusation, like a mother asking a child where the candy in his pocket came from.

No response. Mike brought the tent peg down next to Robbie's still captive penis, now purple and mangled. The noise shocked him, and brought pre-emptive tears to his eyes.

" I already know about the bone pile Robbie. I just want to hear it from you. Earlier today, I turned a femur into a spear and ran one of your boys through with it. That's why they haven't come back yet. They are carrying another of your dead or dying. So answer the question Robbie. There is no need for more pain."

Mike stared him in the eyes, willing him to break. Time was running short, and he needed the threat of violence to be enough. Pain has a threshold, and if he reached it, Robbie would either pass out, or shock would make further damage irrelevant. Mike's face was a stone mask. Gently, he put the tent peg down. And slowly, he pulled the Randall fighting knife from its sheath. Turning it in the air, he let the light glint off the stainless steel, seven-inch blade. The threat was as real as it was going to get.

"Last chance Robbie. I want to hear it. Tell me the truth, and we can be done here. But if you don't tell me, this can still get a whole lot worse."

The moment held. Robbie's face was pure terror. Mike braced himself for the next move. Robbie took a deep breath, exhaled, and rolled the dice.

"Fuck man, I'll tell you. The Return of Kings is…….."

On he rambled, spilling the entire mythology of the tribe. How the Time of Kings would come again, how they took the spoils to prepare for that day, why they ate the bodies of the women, but only the hearts of men. Mike was sickened, but he prodded him on. Now that the story was flowing, they were the best of friends. Tell me how long you guys been at this. You must all be very crafty not to get caught. Wow, that is amazing.

"Your a hardcore dude. Chief would let you join us, I'm sure of it. You killed two of ours, but that just strengthens the tribe. Tribute paid on the field of battle. He will be back here soon, I'll talk him into it." Robbie finished, rambling on into drivel.

" So let me get this straight. You guys kidnap women, bring them up here, turn them loose, hunt them, rape them, and then cannibalize them in a ritual sacrifice? Because you think this is how mankind functioned up to a few hundred years ago? And you think you are bringing about a time, the Return of Kings, when this is socially acceptable to do again? Any piece of ass you see, you just go take it because it is your right as the Alpha Males of this soft society?" Mike asked mystified. He had been around the world and seen some savage shit, but this was taking belief to a different place. At least in Africa they didn't write mythology about it. It was just the way of tribal warfare, from a society that didn't have the wheel yet. These were US Citizens, in the age of the internet and air conditioning. Whatever had popped the screws loose in this group of misfits, there was no redemption for.

"Yeah, pretty much." Robbie cowered. He had put it all out there. It was a dangerous gamble, but what kind of warrior could resist a sales pitch like that? Whatever this Mike guy was, he was definitely a warrior.

Mike considered his options. There was an appropriate response forming in his head, and sometimes it paid to let these things form fully before acting.

Reaching down with the Randall, Mike cut Robbies leg bonds. Keeping his left arm up to guard in case of a ruse, he then severed the bonds holding his arms. Dropping his knife hand back, he pulled Robbie to his feet, and stepped back a pace.

"Imagine that, finding an entire tribe of warriors in the ancient tradition, all the way out here in God's country."

Robbie couldn't believe his luck. He chanced half a smile, which Mike returned fully. He was going for it. Chief really might invite him into the fold, and it would be Robbie's brilliance that had done it. Or Chief might kill him on sight. Either way, Robbie was going to be just fine. He struggled to hold himself upright after the beating he had taken, and winced as he reached down to pull up his pants. As he did, Mike very gently pushed him back upright.

Voice even, still smiling, Mike peered into his soul. " One problem though. The God of War doesn't like you. You prey on the grazers because you are the weak. You play like you are hard, but you don't know what that means. You are soft, so very delicate, and yet you think you are men. The God of War grows angry when soft things pretend to be his disciples. It is why he has sent me. To punish you."

Recognition slowly dawned in Robbie's eyes as he absorbed the words. A question rose to his lips. He didn't understand, he needed clarification. Mike rotated the Randall, held reverse grip, so the point was horizontal. In a savage blur of motion, he ripped the blade across Robbies lower belly, turned into an upward arc to his sternum, and sinking the blade deep, dropped his weight behind it as he plunged it all the way to his hip. Robbie still stood with an idiotic look on his face as his guts fell out of a foot wide triangle shaped carved out of his torso. In Sayoc they would call that a blue worm strike, and his instructors would be proud if they could see this one. Mike stood as the realization of damage finally made it to Robbie's brain. He tried to stuff what was falling back in the hole, and fell to his knees as shock set in. Grabbing Robbie by the hair, Mike pulled the seven inches of razor-sharp steel into the sky. His eyes lit with fury, Mike administered the only last rites he knew. "See you in hell. Your friends will be joining you soon." And with that, he proceeded to hack Robbie's head off, a necessary part of phase three.

CHAPTER EIGHTEEN

Jessup's command was slowly falling apart. The guys had been pushed too hard, and taken too many licks without giving any back. They were fraying at the edges, snaps of anger at each other, and a wild eyed fear at what was lurking behind every bush among some of them.

Bill was in bad shape, and if they didn't get him to a doctor soon, he wasn't going to make it. Jessup was feeling a little overwhelmed himself. Back at the river, things had turned to chaos as soon as the shooting started. Half the crew just opened fire in a random direction, while some ran toward the action. These guys had never trained for fire and maneuver, and had no idea what they were doing. Bo and Jessup almost got shot by their own guys, fucking Wade mistaking them for phantoms sprawled out on the rocks. Thank god the dumb shit was so excited he jerked the trigger half way to China, sending his bullet careening off a rock behind them. Zeke ran in front of someone taking a shot, and got half his ear blown off. Dumb son of a bitch was lucky it didn't canoe his head. It took almost two minutes of Jessup waiving and screaming to restore order, and he was kind of surprised he didn't get blasted in the process. He was an inviting enough target. His troops back under control, he had half of them lay still, while the other half tromped down the streambed in a flanking move. Then they were too scared to beat the brush towards the sound of the contact, lest the jumpy men on the firing line open up on them by mistake.

Finally Jessup said fuck it, ordered everyone to hold their fire, and took Bo to investigate. They found Bill pinned to a tree with a spear, gasping for breath and desperately trying to pull it out of his chest. Jessup tried to pull his hands away from the shaft, prevent him from doing more damage, as he screamed for Wade. Wade had paramedic training, the closest to an expert they had. All the guys came tumbling in, and froze with horror as they saw what had happened. "Perimeter you fucking jack wagons" Jessup screamed, snapping them out of bystander mode. " His fucking rifle is missing."

Wade was out of his depth, but he knew enough not to remove the projectile. It was the only thing keeping Bill from bleeding out. He opted to try and cut the spear on both sides, keep a section in place to control bleeding, so they could transport him out. As he looked to see how the spearhead was attached to free it from the shaft, he noticed a detail that had so far been missed. Dropping his knife, he motioned Jessup over.

"This is a bone."

"No shit it's a bone. Can you fucking get him down or not?"

"Specifically, its a femur."

Jessup looked at him and made a "so what" gesture with his hands.

"A femur is a leg bone. It's not his."

Jessup's eyes grew wide at the implication. "You sure?"

"Absolutely positive. This isn't no fucking animal bone. It's a human leg bone. He found the spot, and he's letting us know he knows. This is bad. We gotta tell Chief."

Fuck. News was getting worse by the second. Well, if they were going to get shot, it would have happened by now. And no point in hiding what everyone was going to find out pretty soon anyway. Jessup passed the news to his guys on security. Keeping two of them close to guard Bill, he sent the rest out in pairs to find some appropriately thick branches to make a stretcher. At least someone had the sense to pack a poncho today. And fuck the trail. They had to get Bill to a hospital, and they had to let Chief know that their darkest secret was in danger of being dragged into the light. He would have to pull out all the stops now. Everything they had built depended on it.

That had been hours ago. They had been tromping through the woods ever since, doing their best not to drop Bill's dead weight. They had started off noble enough. But as the miles dragged on, the aggravation grew. The rough bark dug into palms, pressed by 200 pounds of flesh atop it. Forearms burned and grips gave out. Four men walking, holding a fifth, trying to find a rhythm over the uneven terrain. Stumbling, jarring the package, which always brought inhuman, gurgling screams from Bill. Resentment grew, cursing Bill out loud for being dumb enough to get stuck by a goddamn spear. On they went, fighting against the coming darkness. They were exhausted, even with rotations on the stretcher. A mile from camp in an opening, Jessup called a halt. Bill was lowered to the ground unceremoniously, and the stretcher bearers collapsed in heaps.

"Rest ten minutes, then one last push back to camp. Bill is counting on us, and we don't leave our own behind." Jessup announced, trying to sound more in control than he was. Calling Bo over, the two huddled to confer.

"'Bout a mile left, right?"

"Give or take. We are damn close."

"We better be. These fucking dudes are beat. Chief needs some answers, and I need a drink. We gotta get this fucker, but the boys ain't up to it tonight. You gonna be able to find that track tomorrow?"

"Sure as eggs is eggs. Not a cloud in the sky tonight, they gonna still be there. And I could track a dollar bill through a Miami titty bar with the fleet in town."

"Not a cloud in the sky, but what about that?" Jessup was pointing to a new column of smoke rising above the trees.

"What the fuck? Robbie must've started a goddamn bonfire, in case we didn't beat the sun. Bet that stupid little shit used every scrap of firewood we got by the look of it."

With an uneasy feeling growing, Jessup and Bo turned back to face each other. What if it wasn't Robbie?

"Everyone up! Move your fucking asses! We gotta go!" Jessup screamed, pulling men to their feet. A few resisted at first, until they saw Bo moving out at a rapid pace. Stirred by an unexplained excitement, the tribe moved to follow. Rapidly they bounded down the hill, breaking brush and half running to keep up. Bill was bouncing on his stretcher like a rag doll, but no one seemed to notice.

Breaking into the clearing, a scene of utter devastation greeted them. Instinctively, they huddled together behind Jessup as he cautiously stepped forward. Never in their wildest dreams had they imagined such a thing could take place. The stretcher bearers dropped Bill without a word, falling in behind their leaders as something drew them like moths to a flame. In the center of the ritual fire pit was a newly erected tent pole, with Robbie's head staked on its peak.

CHAPTER NINETEEN

There are many ways to strike fear into the heart of your enemies, and picking the correct one is vital to success. Choose wrong, and you only harden your enemies resolve. In Baghdad, Mike's Task Force had opted for a long strategy. They would simply appear out of the darkness, green eyes guiding them through the night like monsters from a science fiction novel, exterminate whatever cockroaches needed killing, and leave before the local jihadis could mount a counter. It took a long time, but eventually the terrorists panicked about the unseen, silent death that stalked them. Executions and torture of suspected collaborators did nothing to stem the tide, and only served to help dismantle the organizations from the inside. They self-destructed on a national level, leaving only small warring factions that killed more of each other than the Americans did.

Africa was different. Over there, the name of the game was to match them brutality for brutality. The local allies Mike's team was sent to help laughed out loud when he gave the US mandatory briefing on the Law of Land Warfare. What silly white faces these were, telling them they could not eat prisoners. A few weeks of witness to the atrocities of the Dark Continent shaped a new understanding. The UN peacekeepers sent before would break and run before they would gun down child soldiers. The Americans, hardened by years in the GWOT, had no such compunction. Military age male might mean grown man at a DC cocktail party, but out in the real world it meant anyone big enough to hold an AK-47. In the jungles of the Congo, you hit harder, pursued faster, and massacred without mercy the moment you had a chance. And always let one witness go, to tell the story.

In both conflicts, Mike was always struck by how easy it was to defeat any culture steeped in superstition. All the way back to fighting the Indians, the smart man looked for cracks in the armor. Comanches thought that if you died at night, your spirit wouldn't be able to find the after world. Night attacks broke their will to fight. Arabs had the issues with pork and graven images, and the Africans had enough voodoo logic to fill an encyclopedia. Using the belief of whatever faction you face won't break the leaders. High enough up the food chain, there is no such thing as a true believer. The people actually in charge only want money, power, expensive hookers, and top shelf booze. But the poor sap in the trenches, that is a different story. Take away his magic, and the ranks will shatter.

He didn't see an easily exploitable Achilles heel in his present opponents, except maybe that they believed they were strong. Leaving a head on a pike should help correct that, and all he needed was to knock them off balance for a few precious minutes. Combined with the carnage he had wrought, he hoped it grab their collective attention long enough to finish them.

Immediately after hacking off Robbie's head, he had set about gathering his own supplies. Enough to keep him combat effective for a few days, in case his plan didn't work. No more freezing to death at night, or spending precious time trying to purify water, or catch squirrels for food. He could function a few days without food before incurring serious deficiency, but it wouldn't be fun.

Next, he dragged enough assorted stuff out in the open to outfit several men comfortably. This was his honey pot, in case the tribesmen were smart enough to stay back in the woods. They might last a while, but eventually the lure of food and shelter from the elements was bound to drag them in to try for it. Known as a baited ambush, this was frowned upon by the Geneva Convention, but Mike wasn't playing by anybody's fucking rules anymore.

Turning his attention to the assorted vehicles, he located one with a spare key stashed under the fender. The rest of the keys might be in the bunkrooms, or some spare pants, or out with the goons pursuing him. It would be a waste of time to find out. Every car besides the one designated his escape hatch, he smashed a hole in the tank with a hatchet and slashed the tires. Can't have someone getting lucky and driving off into the night. On a whim, he also snatched the registration from each one, in case he had to go find these bastards in the real world. A response by State Police or some other neutral party could still drive him off, but he wasn't the forgive and forget type. Hell or high water, everyone here was going to pay. Robbie's registration, he stuck in his dead mouth.

Last, after staking out his talisman on a requisitioned tent pole, he set the rest on fire. Collapsing the tents first kept the blaze contained. He wanted enough smoke to attract the attention of his quarry, but not enough to get noticed by the Forest Service. Wouldn't they be surprised, driving up in a wild land fire truck? He didn't want anyone spoiling the party early, there was still a finale to come.

Work complete, Mike found a vantage point with a field of fire covering the entire meadow. Deep enough in the trees to make this a very unfair fight, he surveyed his masterpiece. It looked sufficiently like hell on Earth. Robbie's head was visible in the waves of smoke, illuminated by the embers of what had been a base camp. Breaking the windshields of the trucks left little doubt they had been disabled, but just enough hope some might run for them anyway. Everywhere you turned was ruin and devastation. Most importantly, there was nothing left to hide behind. Working the bolt on his Sako rifle had been like the caress of a lover after a lingering absence. It was over caliber for killing men at 400 meters, but it would do. Even with the bucking jolt of recoil associated with the magnum cartridge pushing a 230-grain bullet at 3,000 feet per second, he could manage three shots per second. This was a custom built extreme long-range gun, wholly unsuited for a relatively close range, multi target engagement. But the terminal effect would be like a hammer blow from an angry God. A hit anywhere would put a man out of the fight, and he could always mop up after. To further reduce the chance of organized resistance, he decided to ensure his first shot killed two men. If they bunched up, that was an easy enough task, and three wasn't even out of the question with a bullet like this. He turned his scope down to the minimum magnification to expand his field of view. Happy with his position and set up, Mike prepared for the wait. Most of the men he was about to kill would never even know they were in a fight, and this would all be over inside of ten seconds once his first shot pierced the sky.

Mike's wait proved long, his freshly recovered watch told him in excruciating detail. He had worked fast earlier, a by-product of an unknown enemy. After the spear attack, his worst-case scenario gave him an hour-long head start. If these men were real savages, they might have just left their dead pinned to a tree and come right after him. He banked on the threat of a rifle in his hands to slow them down some, they didn't appear fanatical enough to just charge him with superior numbers. One of two things was happening now. They were bringing back a body, or they saw through his ruse. If the later was the case, they might well be glassing the tree line right now, looking for him. He had by necessity picked a position with an open field of view, but had camouflaged his spot with carefully placed vegetation. He doubted all but the best of counter snipers could find him as it was. If they did, they better get him with the first shot. Counter battery fire would be coming like Thor's hammer itself.

Finally, after hours of waiting, he heard the sounds of movement coming from his 12 o'clock. Much too large to be an animal, unless an entire herd of elk had taken flight. Mike pulled the butt stock into his shoulder, his right hand loose on the pistol grip. Double checking that the safety was off with his thumb, he mentally rehearsed his movements. He had done this pre fight ritual a thousand times, but habits die hard among professionals. "Shot placement doesn't matter, just get some hits" he drilled over and over. The Berger hybrid match bullets he was using were enough to take a T-Rex off its feet. Against men, all he needed to do was get some lead in them fast. He could be having steak and eggs in Spokane by morning.

The bearded man from earlier was the first to come into sight. Keeping both eyes open, Mike tracked him to his center cross hair. At 450 meters, his bullet only dropped five inches, and there wasn't enough wind to even begin to matter. He stood frozen for a moment, and Mike had to actively resist the temptation to drop the hammer. "Stick to the plan" he murmured to himself. Beard moved forward at a glacial pace, and behind him came a tangle of limbs as the rest of his posse reached the clearing. There was a stretcher with his earlier victim on board, which explained why it took them so long to get here. Mike counted, making sure everyone was present. It wouldn't do to get wrapped up a killing spree, only to get hit from the flank. Doctrine said to never take more than two shots from one position. One shot is almost impossible to identify the source of, but two narrows it down nicely. Three almost always gives away your exact location. Mike needed to take at least six.

Staggering into the open, on the tribesmen came. Mike gave it enough time to get them all well into the open. They had no idea what was coming. Two men matched paces, and his finger tightened on the trigger. Tiny bit of take up, a custom feature of all his personal rifles. He liked the mechanical movement to give him a tactile assurance he was set when fingers where numb. Long years of practice let him add half the pressure required to fire as the scope tracked the man in the rear. As soon as he came abreast of his buddy, they were going to die as one. Half a step to go, Mike released the breath from his lungs. Natural respiratory pause, the ideal time to shoot. Inches until they met square, and a bullet tore through both of their torsos long ways. With this much kinetic energy in the projectile, he was likely to get all four lungs and both hearts. His left hand fed micro adjustments to the stock of the rifle, balanced on its bipods. He started his gentle squeeze of the trigger.

And stopped abruptly. This wasn't the way. The War God hadn't kept him alive for it to be this easy. He had all of his tools now, he could end this at any minute. He thought back to what he had told Robbie before he gutted him. It was true. Those might not even have been his words, the War God was speaking through him. Channeling him back to a purpose. These men deserved to be punished. Not the easy death of shot in the head so fast you don't know it happened. There might or might not be a hell in the afterlife, but he could certainly create one here. And maybe this was Mike's redemption. He had felt useless, lost, and he had come up here to kill himself. But the last two days, hunting and killing men that deserved it, with just the tools of the Stone Age? On reflection, he had never felt so alive. This is what he was born for.

He was suddenly glad he had left them with supplies. He wanted them fresh enough to play. They didn't have enough to be happy, which was also good. They needed to eat some bitter before he ended them. In these last moments, let them gain an understanding of what a real soldier went through. Then they would be allowed to die. Cold, hungry, and afraid, just like they deserved.

Decision made, Mike turned his rifle to the surviving functional truck. The one he had planned to escape in. No one would be escaping now, he knew, as he sent a copper shanked meteor crashing into the engine block. One shot, and off he went into the safety of the forest. It was time to plot and scheme. He thanked the War God for the chance as he melted into the wilderness.

CHAPTER TWENTY

Every step drew Jessup nearer. He already knew what it was, but he needed to be closer to make it real. Like his eyes were lying to him. If he could just get right up to it, he would see it was something else. Or a fake. Robbie playing some extremely elaborate practical joke on them. Burning the camp was going pretty far for a joke, but that was Robbie. Immature fucking kids.

No amount of self-delusion could make the image change though. It was like watching a train wreck in slow motion. He wanted to, but he couldn't look away. Fifty feet from being able to touch it, he felt tears running down his cheeks. No way Robbie could be dead. Not like this. His hands were extended in a futile gesture of touch as he numbly closed the distance to the devastation. A rifle shot like the earth cracking split the air, and Jessup shit his pants.

The rest of the troops hit the ground, an animal instinct ingrained from the first clap of thunder ever heard by an ape. Jessup stood, paralyzed by shock, the mess of his evacuated bowels leaking down his leg. Wade, playing the hero he had seen on TV, bolted and tackled him to the ground. Impacting his former mentor, he felt a soft squish were none should have been as their combined weight collided with the soil. No one moved.

Minutes dragged by, stunned silence holding in the air like time had stopped. Gone was the grabastic return fire from previous encounters. No one had a clue which direction the shot had come from. His senses returning, Bo called for a status report. Universally scared that a voice could draw the next round, he received no answer. For a brief moment, Bo wondered if he was the only one alive. Maybe one shot had actually been many. Maybe everyone else was already in the Elysian Fields, and he was soon to join them. Cautiously, he lifted his head, and took a look around. It remained attached to him. He stood up and surveyed the rest of the tribe, many of whom were now looking at him like he might spontaneously explode. Some looked as though they might be trying to burrow into the earth like badgers. Anything to escape the killing ground they were so obviously laying in.

"Get the fuck up you fucking pussies. I need to know who is hit!" He thundered.

Gradually, one by one, the rest of the tribe shakily got to their feet. Wade gave Jessup a dirty look and conspicuously moved a few feet away from him.

Bo took charge in the way that a shipwrecked crew elects a new captain. That is to say, by default. Jessup was still catatonic, walking around Robbie's staked head in circles. Bo sent four men to retrieve Bill, and set the rest to surveying the damage. The record was not good. Bill had died of his wounds sometime during the melee, his face was turning purple with pooling blood. All of the vehicles were badly damaged, and would require parts to ever move again. Robbie had not only been killed and hung like a trophy, his truck registration was in his mouth. A chill fell over them as Bo announced what the paper stuck in his teeth was. It didn't take a degree in cryptology to get the message. The stranger was telling them all "I know who you are, and where you live, and we will settle accounts one way or another." Zeke was secretly very pleased he had carpooled this time. The supplies set out in the open felt like a taunt. It was a sleeping bag per man left, with a meager supply of food and water. Right on top were several boxes full of bullets. Like having them wasn't going to make any difference in what was to come. The only hope left was that Chief had an answer. He had been attending to other business, but he would know what to do. No one got the best of Chief. Not ever, bet your life on that.

As twilight approached, the tribe was quietly separated into two groups. One group was gathering wood and building a new fire pit. No one was willing to deal with Robbie's decapitated brain bucket, like it was a curse. And the other was Jessup, silently sitting on a log, staring off into the distance. A flicker of hope sprang as Chief's car came tearing up the dirt road to camp.

Chief parked his car in the usual spot, a force of habit from being at this place so many years. He was to all appearances unfazed, but his mind was processing detail at an alarming rate from the moment he noticed the lodge was no longer standing. He had been a busy boy today, and already had bad news to give. What in the holy fuck had happened while he was gone?

Bo met him a few steps from his car door, alone. Some reports are best done without an audience. After a few minutes of muffled conversation, Chief strode over to where Jessup was seated. He stood without speaking, Bo a pace behind and to his right. The rest of the tribe unconsciously formed up around Jessup, looking to Chief like lost puppies. Broken, spirits drained, ever hopeful that their prophet knew the way. The look on Chief's face was pure rage, and cowering, they braced for the onslaught.

"Jessup, what exactly does a 175 grain Sierra Match King, tied to a green piece of 550 cord around a man's neck mean?" Chief might have been a criminal, but he was also a very competent investigator. One did not prohibit the other. And he knew the power of an ancient ritual. Some trials must be conducted in public.

Jessup looked at Chief dumbfounded. He had no idea what this line of questioning meant. Finally, he shrugged his shoulders.

"You were in Force Recon, yes?"

"I told you that before. All you guys. I didn't shit my pants either, it's just that…."

Chief cut him off with a raised voice. "I don't care about your fucking pampers. I want to know why the fuck you can't answer my question."

Jessup's eye's widened. He knew. Jessup didn't know exactly how or why, but Chief knew his darkest secret. Slack jawed, his brain scrambled for a solution.

"A 175 Sierra Match King, or a 168 grain in older specimens, configured like that means a very specific thing. Something you should fucking spot in an instant if you are from Force Recon. So what is it? Answer the goddamn question." Chief unholstered his sidearm and pointed it at Jessup's forehead, eliciting gasps from the spellbound audience.

Jessup looked at the gun, and past it to Chief's eyes. There was no mistaking the homicidal intent. Chief was going to kill him, right now, if he didn't have an answer. For the first time in many years, he went with the truth. Lip quivering, and fresh tears trickling down his face, he couldn't look him in the eyes as he said it. "I was a cook. I was in Force Recon, but I was a fucking cook. Not an operator. I made omelets. They have all kinds of support jobs in a place like that, and technically we are in the unit. But I wasn't on a Team. I got busted out my second year for stealing morphine from the aid station. I never even left the country." He put his head in his hands, as audible sobs escaped him.

Chief held the pressure on the trigger. He was so goddamn mad he wanted to beat Jessup to death instead of shooting him, but the gun was already in his hand. Between Tim's fucking bright idea, and this fake commando motherfucker, everything he had built was going up in smoke. Bashing his skull to shards in front of the rest might also restore their fear in him, which he was going to need if they were going to have any hope of winning this. But he hadn't survived this long by making rash choices. He was also going to need every swinging dick that could lift a gun. Slowly, he put his gun away.

"A 175 grain Sierra Match King, on a green piece of 550 cord, is what they give you the day you graduate from Marine Scout Sniper School." Chief let that sink in, noting the fresh shock in the faces of his men. He continued before hysteria took hold. " I found that out on the internet today. Thank you Google. Green 550 cord, I am sure you astute specimens have noted, is basically thick green string. Remarkably like the kind around the stranger's neck yesterday, as described to me by Tim. With a bullet hanging off it. I didn't get a chance to pull out my reloading scale, but it is a pretty good guess that was a 175 Sierra Match. Anyone disagree with that cognitive leap?"

Heads shook left and right. Chief pressed on with his lecture." The story they tell is, each person is destined to die from one bullet. That is the one with your name on it. You might get shot by others, but the one with your name on it is the one that kills you. The one that is gifted to you, the day you graduate by your instructor, is yours. As long as you wear it around your neck, so you always know where it is, you can never be killed."

"So basically, Tim released a Marine Sniper into the woods for us to hunt. A combat proven, trained, professional Sniper. That also believes he is invincible. And our own hero class warrior spent his career asking if you wanted ham and cheese or Denver. Un-motherfucking believable. Jessup, you're a pants shitting coward and a phony. You got Bill killed with your bullshit, acting like you have any idea what the fuck you are doing. These men trusted you today, and you failed them miserably."

Chief walked away to gather his thoughts. The tribesmen murmured to one another, but made no move to disperse. A few minutes later, Chief came back from his car carrying a duffle bag, heavy from the thud it made hitting the ground.

Showing a disconnect none the others could muster, he also removed Robbie's head from the pike, and placed it on Bill's corpse, now located by the ruined trucks. He ordered a fire started in the pit to restore some sense of normalcy and control. For what he needed to tell them next, he had to be able to read their faces. Cracks in the dam were showing badly, and he needed to shore up what was left. In the dark or under the lights of his car was no way to do that. He had to remind them of their place as hunters, strength gathered by the light that had served their kind since time immortal. His council once again seated, he began.

" No man is bullet proof. Not a fucking one. You put some lead in King Kong, he will fall over dead too. Mike. His name is Mike. Just a man, just like any of us. We underestimated him, that is why we have three gone. We didn't know we were dealing with a professional, but now we do. Guess what though? We are all professionals too. We have been stalking these woods for years, and our skills are as good as anyone. At risk, gentlemen, is everything we have built. Our entire way of life. We have to put this fucker down, or we will be looking over our shoulders from now on. Not just for a coward's bullet from the dark, but for the State Police. The FBI. Any agency he could contact that might believe what he told them."

"Snipers are good at shooting people that don't know they are coming. We know he is coming. Fucking pussies like that aren't real warriors, they just sneak up and hit people that aren't ready. So we are going to be ready. I don't want any of you thinking we are going to get in a sniper dual with him. That is foolish. We don't play to his strength." Reaching into the duffle bag, Chief pulled out an M-4 carbine. "As soon as I found out what he was, I stopped by the Sherriff's dept armory. We gotta get these back before anyone notices, but I brought each of you an assault rifle. No more deer rifles and scopes. These are purchased from the military by DHS for us, made for killing men. Full auto switch and everything. Next time we see him, pin him down and kill his ass with superior firepower. No more problem."

Jessup lied to us, deceived us, but he is still one of us. He has partaken of our rituals, he is still part of the tribe. We will hold a council of judgment when this is over, but not until. We need all hands on deck." Jessup breathed a sigh of relief at his reprieve. He was still in trouble, still going to hear about this. But for the moment, he was okay. The guys would never let him lead again, but he still had a chance. Maybe he would be the one to get to shoot this Mike fuck, then all would be forgiven. They would see then. His alcohol addled brain commenced to telling itself he was a Force Recon veteran again. He had been living the story so long, most of him couldn't be convinced it wasn't true.

Chief continued "We have one last card to play. Old man Johnson runs the dogs for this county, as you all know. He's not on the department, we just pay him when we need him. Never enough need for our own dogs here. Johnson runs a moonshine still off in the woods too, which we all know I overlook. Something you don't know, word is he sent out a bad run last month to his distributors. Already spent all the money they fronted him on crank and whores. He is in a bit of a bind. We would never bring an outsider here under normal conditions, but these aren't normal conditions. He's an old mountain man, they understand feuds. I think we go get him, tell him this is personal, and offer him all the coins we can muster. If he sees anything he shouldn't we just add him to the bone yard when it's over."

The gathered men murmured assent.

"I am going to have to go get Johnson myself. Anyone else drives up they're likely to get shot. He's on a bender, and probably jumpy as hell. I'll be back as soon as I can. Bo, you are in charge until then. Don't go off and chase this fucker through the woods just yet. That's what he wants. And if he wanted to shoot us right here, he would've earlier today. He's playing with us. He wants you to follow him into another death trap. If I'm not here by morning, just go beat the brush a little. Keep him on his toes. Don't go following his trail, whatever you do. Let me get the dogs here, and we will let em loose before he has a chance to react. Can't nobody beat a pack of dogs alone, I don't give a fuck what kinda soldier you are."

Goodbyes said, Chief had done all he could do. He slipped into his car, quickly shutting the door to keep the dome light off. Careful not to touch the brakes the whole way down the hill, he drove into the night.

CHAPTER TWENTY-ONE

Mike could tell from the lack of reaction that his enemies were on the ropes. The complete absence of return fire wasn't newly gained discipline or tactical skill, it was defeat. The battle had just started to get fun, and already their will was collapsing beneath the weight of surgically applied attrition. It was pathetic. The Arabs, backwards though they may be, had lasted for years under the constant attack of both commandos and an unchecked Air Force. A subject of frequent discussion amongst his peers, Mike often wondered if he would have the balls to fight on against a Spectre gunship he had no chance of shooting down. Or what it would be like if his enemy could drop bombs from the sky, in the same hole if needed, with no concern of retaliation. Put mildly, we would have to fight bullet proof space monsters that could beam into our living rooms at will to face a comparable technology gap. This bunch of pussies was folding like a cheap suitcase over a couple of hard hours. What these men really needed was sleep, a few hours of safety, and a strong leader to guide them. Mike was going to make damn sure they got none of those.

Extremely confident that pursuit was absolutely out of the question, Mike spent some time learning his surroundings. Moving to a nearby peak cost some energy and time, but it afforded him an understanding of the terrain he never would have gotten otherwise. Time spent in reconnaissance is rarely wasted. He found a shallow lake that could serve as a resting place for his rifle. Too impersonal for now. He hated to submerge his beloved Sako for what might be days on end, but he couldn't risk it being found. Rust is slow to set in, but the glass concerned him. A scope with moisture inside is useless. He had purchased the toughest glass on the planet, a Night Force ATACR 7-35, routinely used in the military to two fathoms deep. It should be fine, but it was a risk. And it felt somehow wrong to intentionally cram his best tool beneath the water, water being the enemy of steel. He had felt the same way the first time he learned to cache a zodiac beneath the ocean, engine and all. It worked, but it took some getting use to. In regular units, it would be your ass if any of your equipment ended up on the ocean floor. Here, it was mandatory to pass training. At least he wouldn't have to worry about tidal shift making his rifle harder to retrieve this time.

Mike was so happy having boots and warm clothes, he felt like the king of the world. It was the same way in training. Come back from some ten day patrol, socks constantly wet, minimal food, covered in chiggers and ant bites, with an E&E exercise at the end for good measure. Exhausted to the last drop. Just a warm shower without a ruck on your back feels like Heaven after that. And a cold beer tastes good enough to bring tears to your eyes.

Happy with his newfound knowledge, and comfortable he wasn't running blind anymore, Mike returned to a vantage point outside the camp he had recently left in desolation. Not the same spot he had taken his shot from, on the off chance they found it. Extremely unlikely, they would have to first be out, and then have crossed his trail. Or gotten unfathomably lucky. Still, habits die hard, and he wouldn't go to the same spot twice in a situation like this. No longer needing to shoot, he deliberately stayed further into the safety of the trees. The smallest branch can deflect a bullet, but not a concern with observation. The technique was called burning through vegetation. With bino's or a scope, vegetation very close to you meant almost nothing. The power of the glass would see right past it. But looking in, you were near impossible to detect. Mike was very glad for his Ziess pocket binoculars, secured to his war belt. Small enough to fit in one hand, extremely light, and only 8 power. But they were well built, and punched far above their weight.

The bearded man was off by himself, looking for all the world like he was suffering from shell shock. "Wow, that was fast" Mike thought, " Weak sister indeed." The rest of the tribesmen were huddled together, with the tracker seeming to take the lead. He was a wiry looking man, all forearms and shoulders, longer hair that the rest pulled into a greasy ponytail. Some kind of neck tattoo on the right side, file that for later. The best way to end a rally was a decapitation strike. Mike chuckled at his own joke, thinking of the one they called Robbie.

As the sun was starting to set, the County Sheriff's car appeared again. This was intriguing. Mike still hadn't worked out exactly how to solve that problem. Citizens disappear all the time, but elected officials tend to be missed. And other law enforcement tends to take it very personally when you kill one of theirs, no matter the reason. It was going to take some thought. A Sheriff with a hole in his head was a good way to find yourself pursued to the ends of the earth. And making an entire car disappear was a trick in itself.

Mike was losing the light, and even his binoculars couldn't help him anymore. He had to get closer, without exposing himself to a potential compromise from headlights. All it would take is one idiot flipping a switch at the wrong time, and this could go pear shaped. And no telling if the Sheriff might try and just extract everyone crammed in his car. Mike couldn't let that happen. He was days away by foot from safety, and they might have a plan put together to blame this all on him by then. Sometimes you are left with only bad options. Hell or high water, these boys weren't leaving this mountain in anything but a body bag. A pistol wasn't his optimal choice to enforce that, but in the dark it beat a scoped rifle anyway. Before he left, he pulled his pistol and ensured it was loaded, and the tritium sights were glowing. Be a fine time to realize he didn't have a front sight post. Not like it would have fallen off in the last six hours, but pre combat checks were part how you stayed alive.

In order to cover his approach from potential headlights, and cut off escape if absolutely necessary, Mike circled toward the parking area. The mostly useless trucks further provided a screen to his approach from the woods. Coming from the rear of them, he angled toward the end furthest from the Sheriffs car. He aimed to finish twenty meters to the right of the furthest truck, perpendicular to the functioning Crown Vic. He would stay low in the grass, banking that no one would see him at the far edge of the periphery if the lights did come on. He would have preferred the left side or rear, but they offered potential dangers. If the Sheriff left alone, or with a few others, that would mean he was coming back. Better to let them go, deal with the ones he had here, and then clean up when they returned. Mike wasn't ready for the party to be over, but if he had to end it tonight, much better to do so against split forces. They only had to get lucky once, and working on smaller groups upped his chances tremendously. If the Crown Vic did leave, it had equal odds of reversing or turning left in a wide circle to find the road out. Just his luck to spend all day avoiding bullets, and get run over by a damn car. Best not to chance that. Right in the middle of the 4x4 graveyard would get him close enough to listen, and reduce his chances of being run over to zero. But you never knew when some unfortunate dumbass was going to remember a stashed pint of whiskey from his back seat, or need his teddy bear to go to sleep. Discovered laying under an F-250 would make fighting his way out complicated to say the least. So he settled for the grass, good enough concealment, no cover, and a fifty-yard shot if things went loud. Risky, but the best he could do under the circumstances.

Mike was losing his capacity for tactical outrage slowly, but he couldn't believe his eyes. Not long after he settled into his firing position, a fire roared to life not thirty feet from the charred remains of the tents. Mike absolutely could not believe it. He had guessed that possibly the Sheriff character would have more sense than the others, but he had guessed wrong. Mostly he had moved closer, so that when they tried to move under the cover of darkness, he could easily follow. Only a complete fucking idiot would stay put in the one spot he absolutely knew where to find them. And a fire? Really? Was it fear of the dark, a habitual need for the comfort it provided, or the primal safety of the circle of embers? Fire light might have kept wolves and saber tooth tigers at bay, but it had been a bad idea against men since at least the Civil War. You wouldn't see that bullshit at Passchendaele or anywhere on the Eastern Front, you could bet on that. Animals might be afraid of fire, but ghosts certainly weren't. And Mike was as ghost as they come.

Still, the rising fire had one negative effect. Mike was pinned in his hiding spot, the circle of light just on the edge of overtaking him. He was comforted by the fact his pistol was in his hand, no need for unnecessary movement to secure it. He was confident the grass would keep him hidden, but it never hurt to be extra cautious.

Mike settled in for a long wait, there was no telling how long this might take. Fortunately long waits were part of the DNA of snipers. Sometimes, you might wait three days for something that never happened. Long, lonely hours on the glass, waiting on your subject to appear. Cat naps of rest while you rotated duties with your spotter. The thousand jolts of adrenaline when something might happen, but then didn't. The satisfaction was only heightened the longer you waited, for that one beautiful moment of payoff. That made it all worth the chase.

The crackling of the fire and the distance made the conversation unintelligible. The Sheriff seemed to be giving the troops a pep talk, Queen and Country, or whatever passed for that with these psychos. At least with Al Qaeda and the Jayesh Al Mahdi, Mike could understand the seventy-two virgins bit. His version would have replaced those with the dirtiest girls around, but the motivation was at least conceivable. The weird, cousin fucking, cannibal hillbillies around the fire? Mike was actually kind of glad he was missing the hooah speech. It might give him bad dreams later.

To kill the time, he considered his options. The leader was a good choice for who died next, but the tracker was an obvious problem too. Earlier today he had won the contest, walking him right into a trap of Mike's choosing. You don't win against a skilled tracker forever, no matter how good you are. They might get lucky and see through his next one, or they might manage to move so fast after him they caught him off guard. He also had no idea how well anyone else could fill that role. For all he knew, everyone out there had an equal skill set. Unlikely, but possible. Either one was a good option, but he might have to settle for a target of opportunity. You play the hand you are dealt.

The Sheriff stood. It was time to find out how the chips fell. In thirty seconds, it could be time for a hellacious firefight, time to slink off into the woods, or time to endure the gaze of high beam halogens. Cutting off his peripheral vision, Mike closed his left eye. He would hate to be using it for a pitch-dark fight alone, but he had to preserve some night vision. His hands started sweating as pre-combat chemicals flooded his system. Even after a lifetime of experience, you have to lock side effects down. He forced his breathing to stay regular, and reminded himself of the possible scenarios. He didn't want to jump the gun needlessly. If shooting became necessary, the Sheriff was going first. He was the freshest of the pack, and not a far stretch to assume the most experienced in a gunfight. Besides, the car keys were in his pocket, and no one was leaving without those.

The Sheriff paused at his car door, looking into the night. Mike swore he made eye contact, and felt the second wave of fight drugs come on board. His right hand tightened ever so slightly on the grip of his pistol. A huge part of staying alive in bad places is knowing when to start shooting, and when not to. The second you know you are compromised, the only sane response is to lash out as violently as possible, as quickly as possible. Letting someone else start the fight is a good way to end up dead. He held the Sheriffs eyes, hoping not to see recognition. "Don't do it fucker, don't do it" Mike willed him. Look away, you see nothing. The Sheriff's left hand was fingering his flashlight, right still on the door handle. If the flashlight came up, a 10mm was headed that way before it switched on. The Sheriff turned his head slightly left, and then right. Whether he knew it or not, that would help. Human night vision was better at angles, due to the placement of rods rather than cones. All part of the fun biology of not getting eaten thousands of years ago. Mike lay stone-like, mentally projecting himself as part of the grass.

The moment broke. The Sheriff opened his car door at a shallow angle, dove inside, and shut it again. He fiddled with a switch, followed by the ignition, and drove off slowly in a wide circle, no lights. Mike noted that he was at least thinking, between what was undoubtedly an auto switch for headlights and decisive lack of brake lights. He also wondered what could possibly be dragging the leader away again so quickly. He hadn't taken either of the new bodies, a development without an answer. Mike could see no tactical advantage either way. He let out a sigh of relief, and returned to focus on the remaining opposition. The Sheriff leaving was a big question mark, but it did sort out his target deck by default. Take what you are given, the rest will fall in place.

For hours, Mike watched with fascination as the men around the fire acted like they were on a camp out. Like the danger had passed. Canned soup was heated and eaten, the smells stretching far into the night, even over the fire smoke. At one point, a pair did bumble around in one of the trucks, returning to the group with a flashlight. It was nowhere near Mike, and hence no danger, but they had no way of knowing that. Incredible. The fire burned lower, reducing the depth of light, but would still be visible for miles. Up here, in the starry vast wilderness, a match was detectable to the human eye for two miles. Around midnight, sleeping bags were laid out haphazardly, with a single sentry pacing the opposite side of the fire.

At least he was walking, that should prevent him from falling asleep. " See, they can learn!" Mike smiled to himself. But another serious tactical blunder was taking shape. The sentry had put the fire between those in his charge and himself, effectively making him blind on that side. Most probably remembered habit from the years living with the lodge in place. A tired brain associates things that once existed with standing barriers. Mike had seen that first hand with the advent of the wall charge. A wall charge was useful for blasting assault sized holes in the compounds favored by the Iraqi's and Afghani's. Many times, if you sparked one off in the dark, the return fire would concentrate on the unoccupied gate anyway. Force of habit, it was the only entry point the occupants remembered. Not all, but often. Nothing like killing some dirt worshipper pouring AK fire the wrong direction, back turned to a newly established threat. The sentry was creating another problem by constantly walking about. His angle was better to see an approaching threat, but his own steps created noise. Subtle, but a rhythm you could follow. Human beings are creatures of habit, and repetitive cycles take root quickly. Ten steps stop, look around, ten steps back, stop, look around. A dark plan unfolded in Mikes mind. He wasn't the most creative man alive at most things, but killing was his canvas. "You boys like fire do you? Keeps you safe from the monsters? Special treat, coming right up."

Mike quietly reholstered his pistol, holding down the retention in the Safariland ALS device, releasing the button slowly when the sentry was farthest away from him. He needed both hands for this. Ideally, he would have waited until the witching hour of 3-4 a.m. More time for a sentry to get sloppy, miss a change over, sit down and go to sleep. As it was, he had no idea when the shift change would be. Timing it for a few cycles also put him closer to sun up, and potentially closer to the Sheriff returning. Besides, he didn't want his friends getting any rest. They had awakened a walking nightmare. They bought the ticket, that meant the whole ride. The tracker had taken a spot right on the edge of the glow. Matching pace with the sentry, Mike crawled forward. Left arm, right arm, left leg, right leg, pause, left arm, right arm, left leg, right leg pause. He was a few movements short of the sentry cycle by design, giving himself time to rest, avoiding the breathing of heavy exertion that could give him away. A few feet from the trackers bag, Mike stopped and reached into his jackets chest pocket. No soldier in his right mind ever slept inside a sleeping bag. The zippering of cocoons had dumbfounded him earlier. Sealed up tight, there was no way you could react to danger in time. It might as well be a body bag if Apaches were afoot. A soldier might drape one over him, or wrap up in one unzipped if it was dangerously cold, but never closed up tight. Mike looked at the head to be sure he was still on target. Fogging breath escaped a stubble-covered mouth, head turning from the fires heat. A neck tattoo showed like a beacon. Mike pulled the yellow bottle of lighter fluid from his pocket, and opened the cap. Originally Mike had taken it as a survival item, in case he ended up walking out of here and met another storm. Bow drills and flints worked great on TV, but they sucked in real life. They would work, but it required a lot of prep and effort. Zippo fluid was the great emergency option, known as "white man's fire starter" in his youth. His present opportunity was too good to pass up though. He was confident the memory of what was about to happen would keep him warm enough if he had to hoof it.

Synthetic sleeping bags are better than goose down when wet, and tend to be cheaper to boot. But they have a very real downside in combat. His people had learned quickly that nylon is a bad idea around hot explosions. A pile of horrific burns from melting jackets and gear prompted the arrival of new, fire retardant clothing. It was expensive, but the burn ward at Walter Reed wasn't exactly cheap. Those materials were a long way off from becoming standardized in civilian camping equipment.

Mike held still a few moments, to ensure that the new smell of naphtha didn't wake anyone or draw attention. It was an unmistakable odor, and he was counting on the fragrance of smoke to cover it. Starting at the bottom of the trackers bag, Mike carefully dribbled a trail up a little above the zipper. This would hopefully melt the opening together, preventing any escape. He stopped well before the shoulders, daring not go further. Not everyone will wake up to a foul stench, but some will. The nose is a powerful weapon in the arsenal, if often under-utilized. Besides, trapping him in the bag without killing him quickly would provide a much better object lesson, upping the horror, and hopefully helping to cover his escape. Next, he traced large loops over the width of the bag, just shy of saturation. The foot of the bag being thickest, he soaked a trail down to the ground, tracing it back towards his face. To ensure his fuse was continuous, egress was going to be difficult. He had half the bottle left, and he hoped it was enough to get him to cover. Planting his right thumb on the ground, and feeling the oily texture of the fluid, he wormed his legs backward. Then his left hand drew a line of lighter fluid back to just under his nose. Right thumb retracted and planted again. Pushing off his left hand, he inched his legs back again. Progress was slow, but necessary. He was only going to get one shot at this.

The cover of the trucks beckoned to him like a siren. The further he got from the firelight, the faster he moved. He wasn't sure how long it took lighter fluid to evaporate in these conditions, so he was laying it on thick. It was a race against the clock of the initial drops though, far away on a bedroll, occupant dreaming of a victory he would never see. Mike felt the urgency, and shifted his angle to intercept the third truck in the line. He had worked too hard to let this fail. Better to up the risk than to miss. His feet touched the driver's side front tire, and Mike looked back toward the bivouac. Oh shit, the sentry was changing his pattern. Had he been spotted? The sentry walked directly over to the bag holding the tracker. Was he going to smell the combustible fluid! Fuck! Mike felt a small panic as he desperately fumbled for the lighter. Shift change, the sentry was shaking the tracker awake! FUCK FUCK FUCK! Mike wasn't in the position he wanted, but it had to go now! And if the firing chain was broken, he was about to have incoming.

Ripping the lighter from his pocket, he sparked it against his right thumb. He would pay with a small burn, but no time to bungle the start point of combustible fluid. The fuel took, racing a line back to the bag. The sentry's eyes opened wide, not comprehending what was happening. Why a glowworm was screaming through the darkness right toward him. His rifle came to his shoulder just as the flames reached the tracker, erupting in a fireball of fumes and nylon. He cranked off one shot in Mikes direction before he fell backwards from the surprise combustion inches from his face, tripping over another man in the process. Finger still on the trigger, another shot went straight up in the air. The Tracker woke up screaming, nylon sticking to his skin, tearing both loose as he struggled to escape the inferno. He managed to get to his feet, stumbled a few steps, and crashed to the ground. The blaze consumed him.

As soon as the trail took, Mike was on his feet running, desperately waving his hand to put out the flame. His burn was a small concern, but it was bound to draw fire as he sprinted to the safety of the trees. He clamped his left hand over the flames as bullets poured into the vehicles behind him. Universal truth, cars are bullet magnets to the untrained. No doubt the trail was still burning, and they may have caught his shadow moving into the trucks. Convinced he was using them for cover, they were now chewing them apart with rifle fire. Mike registered full auto bursts, and understood why the Sheriff had come back earlier. Better hunting tools for the prey at hand. Not a development he had expected.

Bursting into the cover of timber, Mike threw himself to the ground and turned to watch the show. Minuscule chance of getting hit in the prone, and less likely to draw more accurate rounds than moving. Panting, he took in the chaos. Everyone was on their feet, some dashing here and there, others trying frantically to douse the tracker with water bottles. Two of them were shouting conflicting orders, while some fired rifles at shadows. Finally, someone bounded to a truck, flipped the lights on and returned with a fire extinguisher. The Tracker was finally put out. Dead or not though, he was out of the fight. Just the legs would cost him two years of recovery in a burn center, and Mike was certain it was worse than just the legs. Satisfied with his nights work, he ambled off to catch some sleep himself.

CHAPTER TWENTY-TWO

Chief had been a busy man since he left the boys back on the mountain. He felt genuinely guilty about leaving them out there by themselves, but he didn't see any other way. He made some appearances around town, checked his inbox at the office, and talked for a brief while with the deputy on night shift. Business as usual.

Internally, he was far from calm. He had been furious about Dean, and confident it was a one-time mistake that the tribe would soon rectify. No one had managed to even draw blood on them before, and they had been doing this for years. Men, women, it didn't matter, not a single time had it even been close. He even started to think the loss of Dean would strengthen the pack, remind them that they had to stay hungry. Now, in the space of forty-eight hours, a lone man was chewing them to ribbons. Three dead on their side, and as far as he could tell, not a scratch on him. The shit with Robbie made it seem like he might even be having fun. What was this guy made of? Chief had known a few Marines from his years in law enforcement. They tended to be tough and capable cops, but nothing that far out of the ordinary. Four years of brain washing, some extra bluster about being Jarheads, and maybe a little above average physically. He had never met a former sniper before, but he couldn't imagine them being that much different. Something was nagging at him, and the investigator inside him wanted to dig at it.

He was caught in a dilemma though. He had a tag number, a full name, and a vehicle registration complete with address, more than enough information to find out anything he wanted to know. With modern police resources, he could know where he went to fucking elementary school if he wanted to. But any searches he did in the official system would be logged, and that could potentially create a trail. Chief wasn't stupid, but he knew computers weren't his strongest suit. He wasn't positive he could cover his tracks all the way, and that might matter if Mike found an FBI office willing to listen. He could log in using a deputy's credentials, but that would still bring the trail back to the Lehmi County office. Worse, if Mike's file was already flagged by someone else, it could bring questions to his doorstep right now.

It wasn't adding up. Sniper gets his rifle back, has opportunity, and doesn't shoot anyone? For that matter, he had a rifle when he killed Robbie, but didn't use it. Why didn't he just steal a car and flee? He could have been all the way to Bozeman before they figured out he was gone.

In the end, he decided to call in a favor. He knew the Sheriff from Twin Falls pretty well, met him at a state forensics conference a few years back. Liam was an ex-Marine too, liked to talk about the Gulf War when he had been drinking. Maybe that would provide some further insight. Switching on his Sheriff Bob persona, he concocted a story about a woman he was involved with over in Boise, ex-boyfriend going a little stalker, not wanting to use his own computer in case it turned into a civil. Pretty standard cop to cop favor, they looked after their own. Liam said he understood, he would run the plate and get back to him.

Next morning, Chief went to see old man Johnson. Johnson greeted him carrying an old double barrel, thankfully pointed at the ground. He must've been really tweaked out, normally he had the sense to put that away before he approached Bob. He needed Johnson to do him a favor, which kept him from teaching him an object lesson just now. But he logged it for later. Can't ever let the local riff raff think you are getting soft on them. That is how problems get started. If Johnson survived this, he was going to need a beating later on principle. He must've needed the money desperately. He agreed to run his dogs for the $2,000 Bob had managed to scrape up. Half up front, half when the job was done, and not a word to nobody. Bob had a thought that he might just let Johnson's business partners know where he was, and that no patrols would be around here some Friday night in the near future. Tweakers talk too much, and they will do anything to weasel out of trouble. While Johnson got his dogs ready to go, Chief decided to be seen at the office before he left for the day. With a bit of luck, this would all be over and right with the world by sundown. Then he would set about cleaning up the mess that had been made.

While he was having coffee and reading last night's reports, his phone rang. Liam skipped the formalities.

"What did this woman tell you about her ex-boyfriend exactly?"

Fuck. Liam was in business mode. Time for some ass covering. Dealing with criminals his entire life had at least made Chief good at that. "Not much, he was some kind of military before, roughed her up a few times, kind of a violent streak when he was drinking. Like most shitbags we see."

As Liam replied, Chief was certain he was choosing his words carefully. There was a kind of gravity to what he said, no banter or cut ups like he normally used. " Well if you have to get into it with him, bring a fucking SWAT team. This isn't one you want to try and strong arm."

Chief went pale, but tried to keep his voice even. " What do you mean?"

"I mean this guy's career reads like a demon's resume. Scout Sniper, Amphibious Reconnaissance School, multiple deployments to war zones. Those Recon guys are some hard boys."

Chief tried to inject a humor he didn't feel, see if Liam would give him something else. " Oh, all you Marines are big tough guys, I know. We did have one fail the academy over in Nampa though, that I remember. And I seem to think I also saw a State Policeman beat the ass off of one a few years back, on video at a use of force lecture."

Liam leaned forward on his desk, trying to convey a message to this friend." There are Marines, and then there are other Marines. I drove a tank, Bobby. Other guys are in motor T, or office clerks."

"Or they make omelets." Chief interrupted. Trying to keep his tone light, slightly annoyed at being called Bobby. Like he was a fucking kid again.

"Yes, some of them make omelets. But let me tell you something about Recon Marines. They make those guys out of something else. Back in the Gulf, there was a setback most American's don't know about. It was on TV and all, but it's turned into a forgotten event. Days before we invaded Kuwait, that is, days before we were ready, Saddam's army sucker punched us. Two of his armored divisions invaded Saudi Arabia, a little place called Kafji. About the only force there was a six-man Marine Recon team. They not only held out for forty-eight hours until we could scramble enough tanks to help them, they inflicted damage. Real damage. This was the old Iraqi army too. Actual professional soldiers, trained and using the best Russian weapons available. Six men rocked them back on their heels, evaded every attempt at capture, and walked out without a scratch among them."

Chief sat down. This was not what he wanted to hear.

"It gets worse. Your boy has two DD-214's on file. That was the first one, from his USMC days. Starting the day after that discharge, he enlists in the Army. Special Forces, Green Beret. That is where he eventually retired from, about three years ago. Got some medals, and they don't hand those out easy over there. Whole lot of training and schools, some combat, and some gaps. Do you know what gaps means on paperwork like this?"

"No idea Liam. I'm just an old country boy when it comes to this military shit."

"It means he was doing some spooky shit. They don't slap that on your discharge paperwork, but it's the government. They have to do something. So they leave gaps, knowing most people can't read between the lines. He ends up retiring out of the 3rd Special Forces Group support battalion. But none of his listed specialties have anything to do with support. "

"In English please? What exactly is spooky shit?"

"There are all kinds of clever ways the military phrases these things. Ever heard of MACV-SOG? Most people think SOG stood for Special Operations Group. It didn't. The whole thing stood for Military Assistance Command Vietnam- Studies and Observations Group. It sounds like a bunch of nerds reading reports right? Easy for Congress to rubber stamp a budget, and never ask what for. Thirty years later, we find out the SOG boys were highly selected warriors from across the DOD, doing all the dirty shit in Cambodia and Laos. Phoenix Project, that was your assassination program. Near as I can tell, your boy was in the modern day equivalent to a Hatchet Force. And that euphemism isn't meant to be cute."

Liam was quiet a moment, letting his message sink in. Then he continued." Tell your girlfriend to move. And if this fucker shows up looking for trouble, you shoot his ass, and quick. At trial, scared for your life is totally justifiable."

Chief hung up, and weighed his options. Jesus Christ, it's like Tim handpicked the Devil himself, and then pissed in his cheerios for good measure. Still, he had the dogs, and he had six men with assault rifles. If he left this alone, everything he had done was for naught. He knew what he was facing now. With surprise on their side, they might just be able to still get this done. Kill this one guy, and all the problems were over.

Chief went to the FEMA trailer to borrow some radios, he wanted good command and control this time. Every stop was being pulled. For good measure, he borrowed an unmarked car from the pool, and left the registration at his house while he changed. It was a different game now. He hadn't been around the camp much, it was still possible Mike didn't know the County Sheriff was involved. He had addresses and names for everyone else but Tim, and he knew how to find Tim. If this went pear shaped, being an unknown was a big plus in the positive column. He left his vest on, and switched from his uniform into hunting camouflage. Time to hope for the best. He retrieved Johnson, who followed him out to the camp.

Chief parked behind one of the damaged trucks, in the hopes of protecting the engine in case shooting was on the menu again today. Driving in, he was secretly proud of his tribe. There they were, all alert in the morning light, laid out in a circle pulling security. Maybe the night in the woods free of shelter had hardened their resolve. He felt a surge of hope that they were going to pull this off.

He wasn't even out of his door yet before Zeke and Wade were on him.

"We gotta get the fuck out of here Bob." It wasn't lost on Bob that they used his name, not Chief. He doubted it was for the benefit of Johnson, who was out of ear shot getting his dog team together. Wade was near panicked.

"He's not kidding. This whole situation is fucked. We gotta go."

Rapidly it was explained that the stranger had slipped into camp, roasted Bo like a marshmallow in his bag, and vanished again like an apparition. Garrett had burned the hell out of his hands trying to help Bo, and he needed medical attention. Bo had finally died screaming, after they put him out and tried to peel the charred nylon shell off his body. He went hard. His face was a mask of twisted flesh and blackened skin. Everyone had been wide awake ever since, scared stiff to even think about sleep.

Chief grabbed his first aid kit from the trunk and went to find Garrett. For the first time, he noticed the smell. The bodies of the women they feasted on smelled nothing like this, but then they were properly butchered first. The aroma of burned hair, evacuated bowels brought to a boil, and melted plastic was almost overwhelming. His men looked absolutely horrified. Wide eyed, they looked at him for an answer, gaze darting back and forth between Bob and the trees. They were spooked, and he had to get control. Fear was contagious, and he felt himself catching it. No one had made Sheriff Robert "Bob" Harvey afraid in a very long time, and he didn't like it. He wrestled the terror into anger. The last bastion of bad leaders the world over. But he only needed it to work for a short time. Once the dogs were on the trail, the troops would feel the dynamic shifting. Following the baying pack would give them strength once again, he just had to get them on the path.

He called them over to his car, both to get them away from Bo's stinking carcass, and to hand out radios. The magic of technology, holding the power to convince men they have the upper hand. He needed all the help he could get at the moment.

He held back what he had learned from Liam. That knowledge was sure to unnerve them further, and might even lead them to stampede out of here on foot. They looked like husks of men, ready to bolt at a moment's notice.

"Men, I need one more hard day out of you. I brought the dogs, just like promised, and that changes the equation. I am also leading this charge personally. I know it's been a bad couple of days, but I'm here now. Together, as one, the tribe is complete again. And together we have never failed." He neglected to mention he had left Tim home on purpose, and that four of them were dead. Chief was never one to let facts get in the way of a good motivational speech." We have been through a test, and it has hurt us. But it has also made us stronger of character. Today, we are pitting the life we want against a force of civilization that wants to take it from us. All that is wild and free demands that we answer that challenge. If we prevail, we prove ourselves truly worthy of the Return of Kings. And if we fail, we die. But at least we all die together. As it should be. One tribe, one shot at redemption left. TO THE RETURN OF KINGS!"

The answer he received was a muted "Return of Kings."

Not what he was looking for. "TO THE RETURN OF KINGS!"

The volume went up, along with spirits. Chief could motivate other men to do his bidding, it was one of his best tools. One more time.

"TO THE RETURN OF KINGS!"

A thunderous "RETURN OF KINGS!" echoed back to him. He could see life breathing into his ragged force. He hoped it was enough.

CHAPTER TWENTY-THREE

Mike awoke at the first rays of dawn, fully rested for the first time since his ordeal began. He munched a granola bar, folded the wrapper neatly into his pocket, and headed out to see what his quarry would do today. Finding a vantage point on a rock outcropping well above the camp, he lay down to watch. Automatic rifles changed the dynamic, and it made a random hit a lot more likely. Out of caution, he positioned himself much further away today than in the recent past. No point in letting some dickhead get lucky by accident.

He was enthused to see the tribesmen all awake and facing out in a makeshift perimeter. It looked like they got the message after all. There was a charred body in the remains of a burned out sleeping bag, so he could chalk that up to a success. Wounded would have been better in many ways, it would have tied up more resources. But he would settle for dead. Dead was good too.

Watching, he wondered what would happen next. Maybe they would come after him again, and maybe they were broken. If they made a move to walk out of here, he would have to go cut them off. No one gets to leave the party until it's over. If they stayed in their little perimeter, they would eventually run out of water, which offered its own opportunities. Where the fuck was the Sheriff? His minions couldn't keep absorbing losses with him not present, it would look bad on his leadership. And Mike really wanted to kill him out here in the wilderness. Preferably with one of his own men's guns. Let the FBI run forensics on that, see how the story shakes out.

"Ah, here he comes" Mike mused, watching a dirt cloud form up the road. As long as he wasn't in a van, everything was fine. It wouldn't do to have the capability to take everyone out at once. A brown sedan congealed into view, which was curious to say the least. Personal car perhaps? Didn't want to risk a 300 Norma taking out the Crown Vic? That would make things easier, thank you.

As Mike was formulating a new strategy, a second vehicle appeared on the horizon. Mike focused his binoculars, and his happiness evaporated. A truck, but more importantly a truck with kennels on the back. The Sheriff had brought in the dogs. Fuck!

Mike hated dogs. At least he did if they were on his trail. Once a year or so, a training event would be against dogs. It did double duty, teaching the dog guys how to pursue, and the Team guys how to evade. From day one at SERE school though, one lesson remained. You cannot beat a dog. No one can. No neat running water trick, no doubling back, and on a long enough timeline, not enough speed or head start. You can't hide your trail, and you can't outrun them forever. The only thing you can do with any hope of success, is beat the handler. Mike was not amused by the idea of being chased by dogs today.

Only one thing to do. He needed a count of how many dogs, and what kind, since that information was available. Watching the dogs unload, he was further dismayed. Bloodhounds are excellent trackers, but they aren't vicious enough to attack a man. That influences strategy. The three dogs circling the new skinny man obviously in charge of them were the furthest thing from. They were massive, probably over 100 pounds each, and looked like wolves. Leave it to fucking Idaho to have some kind of half wild vicious mongrels to track convicts. The handler being a skinny fellow also meant he could probably move. No time to go dig up his rifle, Mike was working with what he had in hand now.

The best way to handle this problem was going to be to separate the dogs from the handler, and then the handler from the group. The second part was probably going to be easy. He was fresh, while no one else was. Also, he probably wasn't part of the tribe, or else he would have been brought in earlier. That meant they held less sway over him, and cared less about his fate. Creating distance between him and his dogs was going to be the problem. The dogs were sniffing around the truck he had used as cover last night, that meant they were minutes at best off the trail. Time to get a move on. He took his jacket off and rolled it into a long tube, tying it across his body. Plenty of heat would be coming from the chase ahead.

Mike took off at a jog, tracks and noise meaning a lot less than scent. Scent, there was nothing he could do about anyway. He stayed to the ridgeline as much as he could. Vertical distance helped separate the men from the dogs, but dogs could climb faster than him too. Ridgelines were the path of least resistance. He had a spot in mind for dealing with the furry missiles at his back, but it was going to take some creativity to reach it. Knowing he had a lead in distance, and for once there was no risk of stumbling across other enemy forces, Mike moved toward a wide-open area he had spotted the day before. Easily a half a mile wide and steep of slope, it must've been burned out in a forest fire, and then collapsed in a mudslide later. The other side followed a crescent shape ridge, effectively creating distance while turning his field of view back to the grassy open field he crossed before. The distance was around 600 meters across, plenty to keep him safe in the trees from casual observation, but close enough he wouldn't miss the pack of hounds on his trail. He needed to know the time lag behind him, and this was a good way to find out. Once he was parallel with the open spot, he slowed to a fast walk. Conserve energy for what could be a long day, and to make sure he didn't miss his pursuers. Snarling cries of beasts on the hunt preceded them, echoing across the canyon between them. Mike shivered involuntarily. Canine howls tugged at his primate brain, back to the race memory of a time when wolves had been a constant threat. That his ancestors had fought hordes of them with not much more than a sharpened stick was humbling. A bravery and ferocity that allowed his bloodline to survive down to him inspired renewed awe. He would make them proud this day.

Not long after, the animals appeared in a triangle shaped formation, following the pack leader. Noses to the ground, they moved like a force of nature. No chance of tiring these beasts out, they were ravenous for a kill. Mike checked his watch. Ninety second later, the skinny man followed right behind. Mike guessed he was following the barks and yips mostly, no way he was keeping them in sight. Good enough for his needs. Mike resumed running, and saw the first of the tribesmen break into the clearing just as the dog handler exited the other end. They were sucking wind for sure, the last few days taking its toll.

Mike needed an accordion effect, now that he understood the timing. A chance for the dogs to have to wait for the handler, and an open sprint after. That would give him the space he needed for a magic trick. Running towards the flowing river, Mike read the terrain looking for a sharp incline. That would denote a section of very hard rock, not easily eroded, likely to still be standing over the riverbed. He found what he wanted as he felt a slight drop in the ambient temperature, telling him he was close to water. Bursting out of the timber, he found himself ten meters above the stream. Perfect. The only thing men can do, terrain wise, that dogs can't is climb sheer rock face. The height was enough they were unlikely to jump, something he would have done himself if he was sure of the depth. Mike lowered himself over the edge, thinking of the dark sorcery that is the opposable thumb. It had brought man to the top of the food chain with all the things it could do. Hold a club, fire an arrow, cord a rope, and certainly provide purchase in granite. When his feet touched the water, he let go with his hands, and fell less than foot to the hard stone bottom. Bounding through the flowing water, he turned upstream for fifty feet, and then exited the opposite side. He was sure to leave plenty of visual sign, he didn't want the handler wasting time. On the other side, he headed upwards in a zig zag pattern, the switchback style of an experienced mountain climber. Just like back in Kosovo. The end game neared.

Finally, he arrived at the place he had been searching for. High above the river, a flat outcropping of stone, sheer cliffs on three sides. The peninsula of rock offered an ideal setting for his trap. Looking down, he saw the beasts dumbfounded. Back and forth they ambled, unwilling to give up the trail, but too smart to jump. The biggest sniffed down the rock ledge, and suddenly turned to snap at one of the others that had gotten too close to him. Frustration was visible even at this range. Mike breathed deeply, forcing oxygen into his burning muscles. Pulling out his binoculars, he set in to watch the show.

Minutes passed, and finally the skinny man found his animals. They turned to him as if expecting an answer. The man puzzled a few minutes, looking at the scuffmarks traveling down. His gaze turned to the far riverbank, taking it in with slow precision. His face grew animated as he spotted disturbed earth on the other side, and he led his dogs back into the woods from the embankment. A short time later, they reemerged at ground level with the water, across from his tracks. Money. Mike had gambled that his ruse was common around here. Most people assume running water is a way to evade dogs, but only to a point. You have to exit the water sometime, if it's even deep and fast enough to mask you in the first place. A tracker just has to follow both sides of the river until he picks your trail up again. Mike had gone upstream, as most will do, in the mistaken belief that the water will carry your scent away downstream, leaving you free and clear. The handler probably assumed Mike slowed down after this, as most will do once they think the chase has ended. Leading the hounds across the water, he put them back onto Mike's trail, and turned them loose. Confident they would have their prey in short order, he sent them charging into the woods.

Sitting on his stony perch, Mike continued to watch the man. He waited for the others behind him, finally growing impatient and drawing a large arrow in the sand with a stick, pointing the direction he was headed. Mike set his binoculars down, and reached into the pouch behind his holster, retrieving his 10mm suppressor. Men were one thing, attack dogs quite another. Taking on three with primitive weapons was suicide. Besides, the dogs were in this against their will. They had no capacity for judgement in action, and had been bred for this one task. They couldn't understand right and wrong, only instinct and whatever training had been beaten into them. They deserved an easier death than the men that wielded them. Weapon assembled, he waited, back to the cliff. The terrain he had chosen would channelize them together, ensuring he didn't get flanked. Torn apart by sharp teeth was not a way he would choose to go.

He heard the howls of blood lust closing in on him, and the hair on his neck stood up. The wolves smelled victory close at hand, prey drive pushing them faster to the kill. Poor dumb bastards. Not that they would have listened, but this wasn't a lone hairless ape clutching a flint spear in terror. It was a man holding the cumulative power of 100,000 years of evolution in weapon form in his hand. He lowered to a knee, giving him a better optimum angle for shooting targets low to the ground. The wolves broke the cover of trees and sprinted straight at him, Alpha in the lead.

Mike didn't want to cut it to close, but he also wanted them well outside of a range they could retreat once it started. Suppressors sound like pin drops on TV, but in real life they barely make guns hearing safe. He hoped he could kill these animals without the men hearing the shots, hence the can. But inside of pistol range, it would still sound like thunder claps.

The distance closed. Mike wanted Alvin York targeting for this, taking the targets in the back first. If the others did turn and flee, that gave him the most chance of cutting them down before escape. It was harder to calculate, but necessary to ensure he wiped them out. Animal behavior is unpredictable. The leader was bearing down on him fast, so close now Mike could see the froth on its teeth, its hunger to sink fangs into flesh. Its ferocious eyes shown its one minded task, warm blood and torn meat. Mike willed himself steady. Decades of combat time or no, he felt the primal fear. Adrenaline charged his system, and he tamped down the desire to turn an flee. Somehow fur and fang was scarier than bullets and bombs, deeper felt. Pack predators have been enemy to man longer, and the sight of three in a full charge tugged all the way back to stone age instincts. Mike raised his pistol, setting the red dot electronic sight on the left most target first.

The load was a custom build, 200 grains of XTP hollow point moving at 1,250 feet per second. That was right at the chamber pressure max, and only a fool would shoot it often. But as a defensive round, it was second to none. The recoil was so hard, only years of heavy handgun shooting and inhuman forearm strength combined made it possible to shoot quickly. As the trigger broke, Mike was already pushing the gun hard to the right, acquiring the next target. The dot was true and the trigger press clean, no need to see if it hit. He knew it did. The heavy 10mm slug hit the first wolf in the top of its left shoulder, mushrooming with the impact of bone, and driving a ruined wad of meat through the rib cage and out the far side. It was dead before it hit the ground. Firing solution acquired on the far right, the Dan Wesson barked again. 200 grains of expanding lead and copper smacked the target square in the chest, turning sternum into jagged, sharp projectiles of bone, and dragging them along as it exited the rear hindquarter, thirty-four inches of penetration. A muffled yelp escaped its throat as it crumpled face down against the stony ground. Slide still moving to the rear in cycling the gun, Mike slammed it left again to the last target, slack coming out of the trigger. He felt the wrongness of it the millisecond the recoil impulse ended. Years upon years of experience told him without looking his gun had failed to fully eject the spent cartridge, and had slammed a new one home behind it. Double feed. The longest malfunction to correct, and the most involved. On auto pilot, he automatically turned the gun sideways, locked the slide back with his left hand, and ejected the magazine. Looking over the top of the gun, his conscious thought processed impending death. There wasn't enough time. Double feeds can be cleared by very quick hands in 2.5 seconds, and Mike's were superhumanly quick. But in less than a single second, his face was going to be torn off by the pack leader. If those gleaming white fangs sank into him, he was a dead man. No time for another weapon, and not enough space to bring the pistol down like a club. Out of options, Mike sank his butt to the granite, and tucked his support leg underneath him, and grabbed the pistol with one hand on the warm suppressor, the other on the grip. Hands lowered slightly, his neck and face presented an irresistible target, burned into canine DNA since the dawn of time as the optimal choice. The wolf leapt for his jugular, and as he did so Mike snapped the steel and titanium boat anchor sideways into its mouth, at the same time kicking his forward foot up under the animals rear leg, and rolling backwards with all this strength. Sutemi Waza, the sacrifice throw. Mike hadn't done that throw in years, but it flowed through his muscles as natural as rain falls from the sky. A gift from the Gods, or his subconscious, or luck, or maybe just programming down deeper than we like to admit is possible. 120 pounds is heavy for a dog, but very light for a man. The wolf sailed over his head, jaw clenched around the pistol, eyes wide open in disbelief, hanging on for all it was worth. Rolling all the way up onto his shoulders, Mike snapped his arms to the ground with all the strength he had left in them, accelerated by the combined momentum of both bodies. The animal impacted on its back with a bone crunching snap, half its body over the ledge, but still it held on. Mike could smells it's breath, ivory colored daggers less than a foot from his own face. Quickly, he rolled to the right, twisting the dog's head in a savage jolt. Dragging his knees closer to the edge of the cliff to deny his opponent footing, he stood. Raw hate and terror reflected back at him, front paws holding tight to the ground, rear paws scrambling for purchase. Hanging tight with his two handed grip, Mike brought a knee up in a savage blow to the wolf's lower jaw, finally breaking its bite. As it released, Mike whipped the pistol into the air one handed, crashing it down on the beast's head, sending it tumbling to the rocks below. Gulping air, he forced his shaking hands to reload the pistol with his only spare magazine, racked the slide, and recovered the one he had dropped earlier. Every survival instinct in his body screamed run. Almost being eaten had jarred his nerves something fierce, but he had a task to finish. He mentally double-checked the timeline, figuring it had taken all of about five extra seconds to deal with the last creature. It had seemed like a lifetime, but it was over in the space of a few heartbeats. "Good luck not dreaming about that." He said out loud to himself. He had at least two minutes of prep time, more than enough. Finding his other two victims fifteen meters away, he selected the lightest looking of the two. The other he pitched off the cliff to join his friend. Scooping the carcass up onto his shoulders, with the chest wound facing down, Mike created a blood trail off the ledge and back into the trees. Finding what he wanted, he faced the body into a bush, concealing its wounds with foliage. Time to handle the sick fuck that had created these monsters and turned them against him.

Mike correctly assumed the skinny man would get here first, and most importantly alone. The others seemed to have learned that particular lesson, but this guy was new. No matter how craven a man like this might be, he would still be concerned about the welfare of his weapons. Whether because he felt the sacred bond of dog and man, or he wanted to know the status of his investment was immaterial. If it looked like they might be hurt, the first instinct was to find them and be sure. In a low crouch, he came to the scene of the battle clutching a shotgun. Out in the open, Mike thought he looked ridiculous, but no doubt thought he was moving tactically. Given an enemy with projectile weapons at his disposal, Mike would have watched that open area for hours first before he dared step foot in it. If ever. The handler found the blood trail right on cue, and began following it, head down. That would be acceptable behavior with a posse at your back, someone to cover your six. He had defaulted to prior habit, and now it would cost him. Mike pulled his borrowed hatchet from his belt, a gift from one of his kidnappers. He had carried this useless extra two pounds of steel all day, time to get rid of it. He thought about ditching in many times during his movement, but somehow kept forgetting. Mike peeked from behind a thick pine, less than six feet from the furry bait. The skinny man saw his treasured pet, and lost all sense of situational awareness. He dropped next to the dog, stroking its fur and calling its name. As he pulled its head up and noticed its injury, Mike stepped to the side of him opposite his barrel. "Lizzy Borden calling mother fucker!" He said smiling, as he cleaved the hatchet down, striking him square in the forehead with all his might. His victim had a flash of recognition before his eyes rolled back in his head and he collapsed in the dirt.

Dog and handler threat eliminated, Mike circled back to a patch of high ground overlooking the killing field he had created earlier. He was very curious to see how the Sheriff handled adversity when it was right up close and personal, as well as how the troops would handle this added insult. He might even get to see a mutiny, with the rest of his enemies cleaning each other up for him. Extreme trauma can show the cracks in the cohesion of even hardened, battle tested units. He wondered what it would do to psychotic, untrained, amateurs. Mike and all his kind had been psychologically evaluated to ensure they had a good chance of surviving things like this unfazed. He had no idea what his would do to a gaggle of random mortals, especially the kind that were used to consistently winning.

Not long after, he got his answer. The rest of the party showed up, and began sorting out the carnage. Following the blood trail first, they found the handler and dragged his body out into the open. Milling about a bit, they found the pool of blood where the other wolf fell, and followed its obvious drag marks to the cliff. Looking over, one man went white in the face, and had to step away to vomit. The horror of it had become too much for him, or maybe he was just abnormally afraid of heights. That gave Mike a brilliant idea. He pulled the pistol out, and screwed the suppressor back on. For the first time, he noticed the dents left behind by teeth. He shuddered at the thought. A bite like that could easily snap a forearm, and he never would have broken a hold like that in time with a knife. He had gotten extremely lucky. Looking at the pistol as a whole, it didn't appear the barrel was bent, a real possibility with that much weight hanging off it. He would have to send Dan Wesson and Sig a thank you card. He also took a moment to vow no more fancy guns. Tight, 1911 style fitted pieces are more accurate, but they are not more reliable. Adding the suppressor on back then had also been stupid, it cuts the reliability of any pistol. It was all combat Tupperware from here on out, provided he wasn't killed or jailed before then. Checks complete, he looked back to his prey. An argument seemed to have broken out, heated for certain. Mike wanted to fuel that fire with some added horror. Always a winning combination. The bearded man was pacing back and forth, looking down occasionally at the shattered corpses below. Maybe he was thinking about jumping, ending his agony. Best to help him along then.

Two hundred-fifty yards was a far shot with a pistol, even in expert hands. But it wasn't impossible. And this opportunity was so good, Mike was certain the God of War would begrudge him one bullet. The combination of eliminating one more enemy while striking unholy fear in the rest was too much. He had to try. The one with the beard stood at the precipice, hands raised, bellowing at the Sheriff. The other four stood to one side, not having chosen a side yet. Mike had laid the pistol in the V of a tree branch near the trunk. Every added bit of stability mattered at this range. Red dot turned low for minimum distortion, he raised it two feet over beard guy's head. Steady, he slowly eased pressure on the trigger. The gun barked, and Mike waited for impact. Time of flight would be a full second.

Just as he started to think he had missed, he saw Beard crumple. The bullet hit him low in the hip, and his collapsing weight dragged him backwards. In slow motion, he fell over the edge, disappearing from sight. He screamed the entire way down.

CHAPTER TWENTY-FOUR

As the chase wore on, Chief was more and more certain the dogs would run him down. He felt his old confidence returning as the tribe found the river crossing. Chief had chased a few convicts in his time with Johnson, and this looked exactly like what they would do. Desperate but futile hope of flowing water, and they were always surprised when the dogs found them anyway. Following the arrow Johnson had drawn, he kept after the footprints and broken limbs like his own yellow brick road. He just wished he could be there to see the beasts extract a terrible vengeance for him. Johnson's dogs were half breed grey wolves, and meaner than the Devil himself. They would tear Mike's guts out, and smile the whole way home over it. They had been little slow in catching up a few years back, and the carnage they found was sickening to look at. City Council had raised stink with him about who exactly he was contracting, but the voters seemed alright with it. The escapee had been a kiddy diddler, and that didn't garner much sympathy in these parts.

He was thinking they must be close when he heard muffled gunshots, two of them. Maybe Johnson had fired into the air to get his dogs off. That would be keen of him. Chief would much appreciate a seat at the show. He pressed his men onward, which was getting harder to do by the minute. These boys were dead tired, they would need a long rest after this. "Come on you curs, it can't be much further" He yelled, leading from the front. Rising up the side of the mountain, he finally stepped out into a clearing. Curiously, he didn't hear anything or see anyone. Finding the first pool of blood, his heart fell through his stomach. Creatures like Johnson's don't let a victim loose once they latch on, and a man is too big of a meal for even three of them to drag far. Fear rising, he set the boys out in a search pattern. It didn't take long to figure out the story. Liam had been right. A demon had been unleashed, and it was cutting them down like a threshing machine. The loss of the dogs was utterly incomprehensible. Two had been shot, but how the fuck did the third one get tossed off a cliff? There was no blood, only scuffmarks up to the edge. Sheriff Bob felt something new forming in him. He had been slightly scared before, but now he was terrified. He had to keep that under control. Had to think of something quick too, or else the men were going to bolt and run.

He had lovingly built this tribe, a collection of men he had molded into his shape. Others, to share his vision of the world, and his hobbies. It was nice being able to talk about these things, after being forced to keep them bottled up inside for all those years. His police job gave him insight into the commonalities among serial killers, and he knew this was one area where he was outside the bell curve. Most of them are loners, and anyone acting in a size beyond two-person team is always caught very quickly. Even pairs are exceedingly rare. But Bob was a social creature. He liked the sport of others participating, and he liked the power he wielded by the taboo things he coerced them to do. He had invented the rituals and mythology whole cloth, but that was part of the fun for him. He truly enjoyed watching the tribe grow in audacity and skill, each of these men felt like a son to him. But it was time to put the icing on this cake. If they continued this path, everyone would die. The fate of the wolves and Johnson put a guarantee on that.

Gathering the survivors close, he told them the only way out. "Men, we are in deep shit here, no question about that.

I've never seen anything like this, or even heard about it for that matter. But our man did fuck up. He left us a murder, with a murder weapon, that I guarantee has his fingerprints on it. I don't see any other way but to shift strategies. What we need to do is think through a plausible story, iron out any holes in it, and bring down the power of the office I hold. I am talking full blown National Guard helicopters, State Police, FB fucking I, the works. Good chance this guy is so nuts, and I'll help enhance that story line, he doesn't get taken alive."

Jessup was the one to dissent. Apparently he had found his balls again, must've had a pint stashed somewhere Chief thought as he started to argue. "You out of your fucking mind Chief? You know how much dirt is up here on all of us? Tracks we couldn't cover in a month of work. We just need to get the fuck out of here, lay low for a while, and this mother fucker will go away."

Chief folded his arms and looked stern. This wasn't the time to muscle his authority, the rest might crack. "Jessup, you saw the registration in Robbie's mouth. He probably kept the rest, he knows where we live. And what about this son of a bitch makes you think he's the quitting type?"

Jessup was pacing, stopping suddenly and throwing his hands in the air. He was yelling now, a tone he would never even have considered with Chief a week ago. "Fuck you Bob. You haven't been out here. You've been back at your fucking desk, while we are out here getting chewed the fuck up. We stay out here, we all die. We call in the goddamn Police, we are going to jail. Me, Zeke, and Wade have all done time, it isn't fucking pretty. I'm not going to live in a fucking cage again. They would put us away for life if they found the bone pile. Bury us under the goddamn jail. We are leaving. Your happy ass is going to drive us down this mountain, and we are gonna hide out for a while. End of story."

Chief started to respond, when Jessup folded at the hip. The four tribesmen not in the argument looked defensively at Chief, sure he had just shot him, Zeke raising his rifle. Chiefs gun was still in the holster. A second later, the sound of a gunshot reached them. The bullet had already gone subsonic, eliminating the crack of a bullet flying past. Jessup tilted his head up in a look of betrayal as his legs gave out, his mouth opening to scream as his crippled body pulled him over. His voice grew distant, followed by an unearthly wet splat, like a bag of meat hitting a countertop magnified by thousands. Dumbfounded, Zeke looked over the cliff to be sure. The other three stood frozen. As Zeke turned around, he caught a glimpse of Chief disappearing into the timber, back the way they had come. Panic struck, Zeke took off after him, the others following in his wake.

Bob hauled ass back toward the camp. He knew his only salvation was to get to his car before Mike disabled that too. Even before Jessup was shot, Bob knew the game was over. The only way out was to sacrifice the rest of his men, and hope Mike had never been close enough to identify him. He hated it, but he could build again. He had a nest egg saved; he could buy some land in neighboring Montana. This site was done, that was certain. And he couldn't call in any outside law enforcement, Liam would spot the holes in that right quick. Whoever he brought in, word would get around. Statewide manhunts are rare in Idaho, and cops gossip like old women. He couldn't even do that if he knew they would burn Mike down. The body would be identified by dental records or fingerprints or DNA, and there was no good answer for how the "stalker" had ended up on this side of the state, in Bob's own turf. He also knew that if any other bodies got found, Mike had an alibi of not even being in the country for some of them, no doubt. His boys were not going to survive this. Bob could get away though, and that was what mattered. Run back to town like nothing happened, let Mike clean up the mess and possibly Tim on his way out, Sheriff Bob has no leads. Forgotten by next Christmas, life goes on. After the amount of felonies he had committed himself, no fucking way Mike was going to the Feds. "Hey Agent Johnnie All American, I had a chance to escape, but instead I ran around the woods carving people up like Thanksgiving turkeys, but let me tell ya something." No chance of that.

His guys might have figured this out after his hasty escape, they might even be pursing him now. But he had much fresher legs than they did, and he had slept in the last seventy-two hours. He hoped it was enough, because all five of them were running for their lives right now. A fox only has to beat the slowest rabbit, but the rabbit has to beat the fastest fox. Bob pushed himself faster, chest heaving, trying to keep oxygen in his system. The terrain started looking more familiar, he was getting close! Hope sprung in him like a governors reprieve. He was going to make it! Into the clearing he ran, past the charred remains of the tent lodge and Bo, never looking back. Like Lot's wife and the pillar of salt, he knew that to do so would be his end. Single minded purpose, he kept his eye on the prize. Grabbing his car door, he almost ripped the handle off trying to get it open. He didn't remember locking his door this morning, and he frantically felt his pocket for the keys. Oh fuck, he lost them in the pursuit. He pulled his pockets inside out, staring at them in disbelief. Jacket pockets! Of course! Oh sweet mother Mary, there they are! His hands felt like he was wearing oven mitts as he separated the car key from the rest. The door unlocked, and he scrambled inside, firing the ignition before he even pulled it closed. Ripping into reverse, he J-turned in a cloud of dust, braking hard. Slamming the shifter into drive, he floored it. Faintly he heard the crack of a bullet as the engine roared to max RPM's. Disappearing around the first corner, he slapped the dashboard. He made it! He fucking made it! Sorry men, but it was you or me. And I always pick me.

CHAPTER TWENTY-FIVE

Zeke ran as fast as his legs would carry him, Wade, Garrett, and Tony not far behind. At first he thought Chief was just getting out of the line of fire, smart tactical decision. As the miles wore on though, a different line of reasoning started to meld in his mind. Why hadn't Chief stopped to regroup with them? Was he running in a panic? That seemed like a good way to get ambushed. But staying back here with a killer on their tail didn't seem like a good idea either.

It felt like Zeke had been running forever. Like he might keel over and die at any second, and that would actually be a welcome relief. He was exhausted, wiped out, so far gone he was starting to see things. He thought he caught a glimpse of Chief up ahead of him, and stutter stepped to pull his rifle up in case it was the stranger. He tripped over a root and lost sight of whoever. Picking himself up, he resumed his flight. Finally, the terrain looked familiar again. Breaking into the clearing that had been home for so many years, he finally knew what Chief was actually doing. As the brake lights went off and Chiefs car lurched forward, Zeke unleashed a torrent of rifle shots. Wade bounced into him from behind, the other two piling into them both.

"That's Chief dumbass, he's going to get help." Wade yelled, knocking Zeke's rifle barrel high. He looked at Zeke like he had just committed sacrilege.

"No, he isn't. Chief isn't coming back. He left us. Left us out here to die." He turned to face the remaining survivors.

The looks he received in response told him they knew it was true.

"FUCKING FUCK!" Wade screamed." No good, coward mother fucker!" The abandonment by Chief was the last straw. His entire belief structure crumbled in front of him. It was like getting to the Pearly Gates and having Saint Peter ask you if you had been a good Shinto. The walls came tumbling down, and there was no answer.

"Johnson's truck, maybe we can hot wire it. Or he has a redneck key!" Garrett chimed in. Holy shit! Wade had forgotten that in all the excitement! The foursome found the strength to run to the old diesel truck. What greeted them added insult to injury. Keys were in the ignition, but Zeke's bullets had found a back stop. It would turn over, but something under the hood was hopelessly damaged. Absolute crushing defeat settled over them, made all the worse from a glimmer of hope. For a long while, they sat next to the truck, men at the gallows resigned to fate. Zeke finally spoke.

"I have one last idea, and it's not a great one. But I just don't figure any other way, and I'm not about to sit here waiting to get shot, or burned up in goddamn sleeping bag tonight, or some other terrible fucking way to die we haven't heard of yet."

The other three perked up. At this point, anything beat nothing. Zeke continued, "We are gonna surrender. This guy was a Marine, they don't shoot prisoners. They let fucking 'Old So Damn Insane' surrender, and he did way worse stuff than us." That had actually been the Army's 'cough' 4th Infantry Division 'cough,' but no one was around to give a history lesson. Zeke let the idea sink in, waiting for someone to object.

"Are you fucking crazy? Surrender to this guy? What if he just decides to kill us anyway? And if he doesn't the State is sure as hell gonna after they sort all this out." Wade was having none of it.

"If he wants to kill us, he could've done so with a rifle already. Anytime since after he killed Robbie up to now. We can't get him in the woods, and we don't have a tracker or dogs to try again anyway. The only other option is to try and walk out, but I don't think he's gonna let us do that. Surrender is the only way. Them Marines are full of honor and shit, I don't think he'll just kill us if we aren't a threat anymore. And as for the State, we get a plea deal for turning Chief in. Fuck him. He left us out here to die. We use the State of Idaho to bury his ass instead. We play our cards right, we might only do a dime or so. Long as we don't confess to any of the weird shit."

His story was gaining traction, the survivors were in like rats from a sinking ship. He had their rapt attention. Bring his head down in a huddle, he spelled out the last piece in a whispered tone.

"That last part was in case he can hear us. Unless he saw Chief leave, or has his eyes on us right now, he don't know how many of us is left. We get out to an obvious spot, clearing West of here smaller than this one, build a big ole fire, call out we give up. Tony is laying in the woods, all covered in branches, I give a signal. Tony shoots this mother fucker, we call it a day. Deal with Chief's ass later."

Now we were talking! Renewed vigor, the four left for a small meadow Zeke knew nearby. On the way, they worked out the details of a plan. The stranger tended to prefer to strike at night, at least it seemed that way. Sundown was only a couple hours away. They could bury Tony in brush, keep him pretty close though, since he would be shooting in the dark most likely. A big fire would help that, and Zeke's signal would be a Copenhagen tin. Filled with gunpowder they could get from a few bullets, and with holes drilled in the back, it would make a good flash bomb. The added light should help Tony make his shot, and distract the stranger long enough to die. Natural enough that if they sat around throwing pinecones in the fire, the motion would be missed at go time. Hastily, they set about making preparations.

CHAPTER TWENTY-SIX

Mike was delighted with his shot on the bearded guy, that was too perfect. A hit anywhere would have been good, but to get a hip shot? Dropping him off the gorge, still screaming? That was textbook. He hoped he could tell his boys from Bragg about it one day. That was a shot worth bragging about. And it seemed to have done the trick for inducing panic. The Sheriff took off like a scalded cat, his minions not far behind. Mike considered following them, but he would have to run to keep up. And that was a damn good way to get counter ambushed and killed. Not exactly what he had in mind, but if they all managed to escape in Chief's car, he could always find them later. The more pressing issue at the moment was a tactical blunder he had committed. He had spent so much time on a battlefield, ideas like evidence trails didn't always factor into his planning. His bare fingers had buried a hatchet in a man's head, and he had three shell casings along with an unfired round to account for. The last check back in sniper school at the end of the day was always the same. Lay out your boxes of ammo, and every piece of brass had better be accounted for. Burpee's and pushups in a healthy volume ensured it was a mistake you only made once. In school, you paid in pain. On a battlefield, you might pay with your life. It was a lot easier with bolt guns than auto's for sure. This was a lesson so ingrained, Mike had actually asked after his first firefight, riding a machine gun no less, if they had to pick up the brass. Fucking new guys, they ask the dumbest things. Out here, though, things were different. He was starting to see a limited advantage in carrying revolvers, no need to go looking for evidence.

Off he went to clean up his trash. The last one took some time, but he eventually accounted for them all. Pulling the hatchet out of Johnson's face took some doing, it had gone in deep. Probably never felt a thing, which was a shame. Just in case forensics became an issue, he went ahead and dropped the handler over the ledge to join his dogs. With a bit of luck, the birds and mice would clean up anything that the fall didn't. The hatchet he would drop in a deep section of the river very shortly.

Work completed, Mike took a circuitous route back to the old camp. He had no doubt that is where the survivors were going. Habit made him move slowly enough to avoid an ambush, he arrived as twilight was setting in. The Sheriffs new car was gone, but the truck for the dogs was still here. Curious. He hadn't thought to check the old fellows pockets for the keys. Observing with his binoculars, he couldn't see the obvious trace of any people, which was mildly uncomfortable. In all the time he had been out here, he had known exactly the location and disposition of his enemies every moment since the hot springs saved him. It was possible they had all escaped, but he needed to be sure before he made his next move. Skirting the tree line, he moved toward the higher ground to the North of the desolated camp. From an elevated perch, he saw a dim sign of firelight to his West.

Carefully moving through the night, quiet as the grave, Mike followed the increasing signal of the flames. Every five steps, he would stop and listen. When he was able to barely make out shapes by the fire, he crouched down to make sense of what was happening. Had these clowns learned nothing? Laid up in the dark, they would have survived another night. He didn't have night vision goggles, no way he would have found them without them. But here was a blazing fire, beacon to come find them. He settled in for a bit of surveillance.

He could hear snippets of conversation, but nothing helpful. Then, out of nowhere, one of the men stood up, cupped his hands, and yelled, "We surrender. We're done. You win. Our weapons are stacked back at the old camp." Then he sat back down. Conversation continued as normal, with the others alternately stoking the fire to keep it burning high.

This was curious. Not a turn of events he had anticipated. Most of the really bad dudes Mike had ever been after knew the drill. No quarter asked, and none given. A short time later, a man stood up and repeated the call. Mike checked his watch. Thirty minutes later, it was repeated again. These guys looked serious about the surrendering bit. He could go back and check for an arms pile at the old camp, but that wouldn't tell him much. He had no idea how much hardware they had started with, nor what should be left. And why was the fire in a different spot? They knew he knew of the old camp. Why not just build it there? He doubted the fates of Bo and Robbie had enough impact to scare them out. And they could have turned all the vehicle lights on, that would have been sure to get his attention. Very interesting. Mike decided to cloverleaf around the area, see what else he could find out.

For two hours, Mike skirted the perimeter, learning what he could. Three of them were left, and from what he could see, they were in fact unarmed. They kept the half hour pace, probably wanting to ensure he didn't have enough time to kill one of them without the message getting out. He could wait until the morning light, when he could see everything, but he didn't like the idea of resting without finishing this. Holding his pistol in his right hand down by his leg, he walked into the firelight.

Zeke almost shit himself as a ghost appeared before his eyes. He barely kept his voice from saying "Tony!", but this wasn't Tony. It was going to work. After all this, his plan, his brilliant idea, was going to save their skins. Forcing down a smile, he sat, holding his hands up. In a serious tone, he started talking, if for no other reason to get the strangers attention.

"We give up. You bested us. We are unarmed, and we surrender."

Mike wasn't sure how to handle this exactly. It was new territory. "What makes you think I'll let you? You guys had a bad fate in mind for me, and it hasn't exactly been kittens and flowers since we met."

Zeke continued to talk, while Garrett and Wade continued to toss twigs and pinecones in the fire. Just a couple of dejected souls, resigned to fate, occupying their hands. Just like the plan. Why the fuck hadn't Tony taken the shot? The friendlies were sitting down, all he had to do was aim high. " We know you were a Marine. Chief told us. So I don't think you will shoot unarmed men that are giving up. And we are prepared to confess to our crimes. Turn States evidence against Bob. Bob is the local Sheriff, in case you didn't see him. He wasn't here much, except today." Zeke slowly reached into his pocket for the tin of Copenhagen, showing the lid to Mike as he pulled it free. He didn't want to get shot over moving too fast.

Mike noted the new object in play, his mind absorbing new facts. That meant Chief had run his plates, which made getting rid of him a little more difficult. But he must not have run them very well, or he would know the rest. Maybe he just decided to keep that to himself. Might also explain why he left his boys out here to their fates.

Zeke held the can of tobacco close to his mouth, pretending to take a pinch. This had better fucking work. Half a second after this flash bomb went off, the stranger was likely to plug all three of them on principle. The stranger was looking off into the woods, actually in the direction of Tony. Creepy. Did he have a sixth sense about danger?

Now or never. Zeke gently tossed the can towards the open flames, closing his eyes at the same time. Mike reached out absentmindedly, left handed, and caught it.

"That sounded too full when you packed it to be throwing away, unless you dip a whole can at once." Turning to face Zeke, he tossed it back. "Besides, I killed your sniper an hour ago."

CHAPTER TWENTY-SEVEN

An hour ago, when Mike was walking the cloverleaf of his recce, a thought occurred to him. He didn't know exactly how many were left, but it was a pretty good chance the Sheriff ducked out alone. He ran first, odds were he left by himself. That left four, not three. And he could only see three. Slim chance that the car was a ruse, and the Sheriff had doubled back on foot as well, but not likely. Most men can't navigate very well in the dark, that is an acquired skill. And nothing from the last seventy-two hours made him think anyone here had the touch. That still left one missing though. Chances were exactly zero that he got lost in the woods and didn't make the rendezvous. So what would Mike do in this situation, how would he set up?

With iron sights, shooting in the dark at any kind of distance is difficult. Shooting downhill is harder, you lose your target against the ground shadow, if you can even see them at all. The easiest way is to shoot uphill; your target stands a much better chance of sky lining themselves, with either natural light or fire light. On top of that, people tend to follow the path of least resistance. If you were going to walk into a circle of people that might be hostile, would you plan your escape to move uphill, or downhill? Downhill let you accelerate from danger quicker. Both of those things pointed to a triggerman, if there was one, being on the downhill slope. Mike decided to check that side first. Carefully moving at just beyond what he would have considered shooting range given the light, he was rewarded with an unmistakable sound. Snoring. The trigger had been very well camouflaged, mostly buried under branches, a bed of pine needles on top. He looked just like a lumpy piece of ground. Mike might have missed it completely without the sawing of logs. His designated killer had gotten cozy in his nest of straw, no doubt comfy and warm, and had nodded off to sleep. Mike gently removed the rifle from his hands and cut his throat. The razor sharp Randall had killed him before he knew what happened.

Continuing his conversation with Zeke, Mike picked up where he left off. "Next time you pick an assassin, pick one that doesn't snore."

Zeke's face went white with shock. Garrett and Wade stared at Mike like he had just grown a unicorn horn. Wade pushed off the log he was using as a chair and bolted. One handed, Mike shot him twice in the back. Turning his attention to the others, Mike spoke again.

"Let me tell you two the universal law of beheaders, torture cell members, and IED makers. You don't get a chance to go quietly. There are some crimes so heinous, there is no possibility of redemption. You fucking clowns, with your ritual sacrifices, are well past that line. Did any of your victims get the chance to give up? You assholes show any mercy when you had the option? I didn't think so. Besides, you angered the God of War. You pretended to be warrior caste, when you're weaklings. Slimy, soft, pathetic little men, trying to pray to a God you couldn't fathom. It's why he sent me to test you. And I judge you to be, unworthy."

With that, Mike shot each of them in the head. Pushing the bodies out of the way, he sat down on the log they had previously occupied, warming himself by the fire. It was a luxury he hadn't enjoyed for quite some time, and felt all the better for being earned.

CHAPTER TWENTY-EIGHT

Rising the next morning from a well needed sleep, Mike recovered his shell casings again. He also went ahead and rifled the wallets of the departed, spoils of war. You never know what you will need next, and cash is always handy to have for contingencies. Next, he recovered his rifle, stripping it down and applying oil recovered from one of the dead engines. Not what the SAKO manual recommends, but it would do in a pinch. He was happy to see that his scope had not leaked any moisture. He decided to wait one full day, to see if any other shenanigans were in store, before he walked out. He set up at the high edge of the clearing, just inside the cover of the forest.

Around noon, a shiny F-350 he hadn't seen before rolled up the road. The driver parked and exited, wonder in his eyes. Who was this, but his old friend Tim. The sneaky little fucker that had dragged him into this whole mess. Behind his rifle, Mike waited for a clean shot. The second Tim cleared the front of the truck, Mike dropped the hammer on his custom tuned long action. The 230 grain Berger bullet took Tim's left leg off at the knee, dropping him like a screaming pile of mush. Mike hurried down before he bled out.

Stanching the flow with a makeshift tourniquet, Mike introduced himself and asked the questions he still needed answers to. Where was his Bronco? Who else was involved? Why him? How often had this happened?

Satisfied with the answers, Mike unceremoniously tossed Tim in the back seat like a trussed pig. He found his Bronco in a large barn outside of town, owned by one of the men he killed earlier in the week, keys still in the ignition. The engine hummed to life without missing a beat, and Mike noted he had three quarters of a tank. Plenty to get him away from here, but he topped it off with cans in the barn to be sure. No telling where these men had friends, best to get as far away as possible while the getting was good. He pulled Tim out of the backseat by his neck, letting him drop to the ground, eliciting a scream of agony as his new stump hit the dirt, muted by his gag.

Mike had a decision to make, which he war-gamed as he wiped down the interior of the truck he had touched. Killing Tim put one more witness out of the picture, effectively making Sheriff Bob the only one that had seen him around here. He had only kept him alive this long in case his first set of answers were lies. And he deserved a killing, same as the others had. But there was some power in keeping him breathing. For one, Bob might have a soft spot when push came to shove about his friends. He had left them to die the day before, but that could be argued as self-preservation. In the end, it was an Officer-thing to do, in the military sense. Sometimes people have to be sacrificed. Mike had done it leading indigenous allies, and it left a smudge on your soul. Necessary, but not the easiest thing to live with. It was one thing for the Sheriff to abandon his men to their fate, it was quite another to let one bleed out when he could prevent it. If that was the case, leaving Tim hurt but alive would cost the Sheriff time. He would have to concoct a story and get him help before he could focus on Mike.

Secondly, Mike knew he couldn't kill the Sheriff. To risky. He loathed the thought of leaving him still breathing, it was like fire in his veins. He needed to die more than anyone, but it just wasn't possible at the moment. He had felt the same way with some of the Warlords his team had to use in his other life. Monsters, all of them. In desperate need of a dirt nap. But it just wasn't feasible, they were needed to fight bigger monsters. The taste it left in his mouth was like licking an ashtray, but sometimes you just have to soldier on. Sheriff Bob was the same way. But maybe him seeing Tim walking around on a prosthetic leg would serve as a reminder, he got off easy. And best not to go looking for the man that did it. It was funny, the way things worked. The dead can be forgotten, but the mangled? Walking wounded among you doesn't fade the same way. Let him chew on that before he decided to play cowboys and cannibals again.

Third, if Sheriff Bob did let Tim live, and this went to a legal showdown, some kind of frame up, Tim was another liability. One man can keep a story straight, but two rarely works out under close scrutiny. Mike seriously doubted anyone wanted to drag this week's events into a courtroom, but it was a contingency to mitigate. That settled it. It was counter to his nature, and a long way from what he wanted to do, but it was the best move. At the moment he would rather eat broken glass than let either of his last two targets live. Pragmatism won out over emotion though. That is how you stay alive. He was out of options, at least if we wanted any chance of walking out of this unscathed.

Slapping Tim to get his attention, he held up Tim's mobile phone. "Call the Sheriff. Personal line. Right now."

Tim had regained some defiance it seemed. At least enough to shake his head no. Mike sighed, went to a nearby workbench, and returned with a set of tin snips.

" Look Timmy, I'm done fucking around. We can do this the easy way or the bloody way, and I think a look at your legs tells you which I prefer. Call him, or I am going to start snipping off fingers. I'm feeling a bit impatient today, best not to fucking test me."

Tim decided he felt cooperative after all. He dialed a number from memory, and Mike snatched the phone out of his hands while it was still ringing.

"Tim, I'm fucking busy. I'll be by to see you later." Bob answered his phone by way of greeting. He was at home, ironing his uniform for tomorrow. Business as usual, nothing to see here.

"Sooner would probably be better. I have your man." Mike retorted in a detached tone. The momentary silence was deafening.

"Who is this?" Bob demanded.

"You know who it is. The question is why are we talking? So do you want that answer?"

Bob sat, suddenly afraid his knees might give out. The hot iron burned away at his uniform, forgotten in the change of priorities. "Why are we talking?"

"You are a harder man to get than the others. Your position dictates that. At least if I want to keep the heat off me. I want you to understand that. Your badge is the only thing keeping you from joining your pals. And I did say more difficult. Not impossible. Are we quite clear?"

Checking the load in his revolver, Bob answered like the weasel he was. In case this was being recorded. Bob might not be rocket science material, but he wasn't stupid. "I don't know what you are talking about. What friends?"

Mike read between the lines, pacing as he talked. "Good enough. I saw you yesterday, so you know your little housedog with me didn't sell you out. We could be meeting face to face, but I don't think either of us wants that. Feelings tend to run high at times like this, and I've had enough excitement for one week. I also understand your reluctance to speak on an open line. So I will do the talking. I am willing to call a cease-fire if you are. This can be over. But if you try anything, anything at all, from this point forward, even if you get me, it won't be enough. I already phoned a friend, one that owes me his life. If I'm not home in forty-eight hours, you're the one he's going to come asking questions. Do you understand? Our bonds run deeper than a cockroach like you can fathom. So either we are done, or you can spend the rest of a short life looking over your shoulder. Are we done?"

Bob absorbed this new information. All of it was true. Killing a law enforcement officer brought out the heavy guns. No one in the state would rest until they solved it, and there was enough to pin it to Mike. At least enough to make him worry. Bob was safe behind his tin shield, as long as he let this go. The friend part might be a bluff, but the last thing Bob wanted was investigators combing the hills. "I understand. I accept those terms."

"Your buddy from the bar is with my Bronco. He needs some attention, but I am sure you can think up a plausible scenario. I am leaving, right now. I will be out of your town in ten minutes. If I see you, I am going to assume our deal is off. I believe firmly in judged by twelve instead of carried by six. Are we clear on that as well?"

"Yes, I think we understand each other." Bob's heart rate was starting to subside. He had been found out, but he was going to survive. The badge had saved him, not the first time it had done so. He took a moment to admire the brilliance of his career choice, counter balanced with his hobbies.

"Good. And your little circus in the woods is over. I might just come back and check on you myself. I get an inkling you have started again, and I'll end it." It was a weak threat, but Mike felt he had to issue it. People like Bob and Tim were beyond help, beyond redemption. But fear was a powerful weapon. If it just kept them out of the game for a while, it was better than nothing. Tim was going to be spending some time learning how to walk again anyway, so there was that. Feeling the burn of a failed mission, Mike finished his thoughts. Leaving two pieces of shit like this alive was going to hurt for a good long while. "I hope you understand that Bob. I'm not the kind of person to issue threats idly. You ran my records, you ought to know that. Goodbye."

Hanging up, Mike wiped Tim's phone down, and tossed it across the barn. Didn't need this pussy panicking and calling 911 or something. As a parting gift, he stepped back and kicked Tim in the face. It didn't put him out, but it did crack some teeth. Small victories.

Back in the Bronco, Mike headed North out of town. It wasn't the shortest way to Montana, but it was the least likely to have an ambush set on it. Crazy people are unpredictable, and Bob might just have the stones to try one more go if he thought he could win.

CHAPTER TWENTY-NINE

Fayetteville, North Carolina, 15 months later……..

Mike was tying off the last ratchet strap holding a late model Jeep Cherokee to the flat bed, late afternoon. A gentle breeze was in the air, keeping the temperature from becoming uncomfortable with constant humidity. A perfect weather day, the rarest of times in the South. In just a few days, the summer would take hold in earnest, making a task like this oppressive. The trailer was attached to a late model Diesel crew cab, taking up a plot of real estate at the end of the cul-de-sac, typical of the Fayetteville suburb. Some planner had clearly decided no one wanted kids playing on a through street, and now every new edition was a maze of dead ends, branching off a single main artery. Three identical sedans pulled onto the street, parking a vague distance from him.

He half expected this, but was just starting to think he might have shrugged off further scrutiny. He knew they were there for him, but he still hoped the occupants went to a different door as he busied himself checking trailer lights and lug nuts. Fayetteville was a weird place. They could actually be here for anyone on the street. Not likely, but a man could dream. He didn't turn and look, but he could feel a presence at his back, getting closer.

Footsteps stopped right behind him, from the vibe Mike guessed the owner would be just outside his reach when he turned. Not looking for conflict, so not directly in his personal space. That would make for an easy assault charge to haul him in, but even easier to beat the rap with instinctive lash out.

"Michael William Bryant?" a voice asked.

Mike stood up and slowly turned about. No point in making these guys twitchy. From the number of cars, they had done enough homework to consider him dangerous already. Getting shot wasn't on his agenda for the day. Facing the voice, Mike noted nine agents, spread out in a non-confrontational posture, that conveniently cut off any avenues of escape. Professional. Nine was a lot. That showed some serious commitment to whatever happened next. Mike looked at the likely source of the voice, front and center, but remained silent. A man about his age, maybe a few years younger. Dark grey suit, conservative monochrome tie, clean shaven. Blond hair combed to the side, posture that of authority, but not violence. Might as well be wearing a blinking neon light that said FBI. Mike made eye contact, but remained silent.

"Sergeant First Class Michael William Bryant, more commonly known as Mike?" The agent implored again. His voice was steady, showing just a bit of irritation creeping in.

That was an act, and Mike knew it. Agents senior enough to command a team of nine don't get flustered. This was a play, and everyone had their part. The agent would start with standard street hood posturing, because that was the default setting. And usually it worked, even against people it shouldn't. Hell, dirty cops broke in the interrogation room all the time, and they were used to playing the game from the other side. But Mike had performed exceptionally well at SERE, absorbing all its lessons. And in several investigations since, a by-product of the uniquely American way of war, for war crimes, murder, and once stateside for assault. Each of the seven times he was dragged before a JAG officer and read his rights, a line from the classic *Apocalypse Now* would echo in his head. "Charging a man with murder in this place was like handing out speeding tickets in the Indy 500." It was all trumped up bullshit, and it flowed off him like water off a ducks back. Good luck playing CSI in a war zone if you want to make this stick. The neighborhoods Mike and his crew usually worked in, you would need an armored regiment to hold the block while you dusted for fingerprints. Especially after they had already kicked over the hornet's nest with a lightening raid. Usually some fucking idiot new officer that didn't understand how war was fought. Still sticking to his West Point ideals, or the fantasyland belief that the bad guys dressed in uniforms and always carried weapons. He had even been told once, by an attached JAG major, that sniping was premeditated murder since the target had no way of displaying hostile intent to a hidden gunman. That was kind of the fucking point, jerk off! Fair fights are for suckers and rubes. The way of the jungle is to kill with as little danger to yourself as possible.

The best move Mike could make, in terms of his present situation, was to invoke the Fifth Amendment and not say a word after. Whatever slip up had brought them to his door, talking wasn't going to make that evidence go away. They could also be here on a hunch, but that was reaching. The safest thing was to say nothing. If for no other reason, it is remarkably difficult to stop talking once you start. And career cops tend to have a mind like a steel trap. One slip in your story, one minute change, and they have a thread to pull. But invoking the Fifth right off the bat also lets them know you were absolutely guilty as hell. Assessing the danger, Mike decided to handle it like he would secondary at a foreign airport. Confirm nothing, pause long and hard before you answer, and try to talk your way out. While hopefully finding out what they know in the process. Besides, his identity wasn't worth bracelets, not right this minute. They could run his plates, look at his wallet, and had undoubtedly seen pictures of him. Casually, Mike responded with a simple "Credentials?"

The agent reached into his jacket and produced a folding leather wallet the size of a passport. His guess was correct, Special Agent Justin Moore, FBI. All in order, and as far as he could tell, authentic. Satisfied with the look, he turned back to the face.

"What can I help you with Agent Moore?" Mike put on his best innocent face, golly gee, just a guy standing in his driveway.

The agent stared at him, silent, hoping the uncomfortable situation would cause Mike to ask something else. This was another great tactic; silence will draw out all sorts of details while revealing none of your own cards. Most humans can't handle an uncomfortable quiet, and will start talking just to break it. No such luck, Mike had played this game before.

Mike turned to leave, taking one step toward his truck before he felt a hand gently press him back. Touch barrier was a big no no, and Mike resisted the urge to snap the wrist like a twig. Holding down the violence in his soul, he faced Agent Moore once again. "Am I being detained? Because if I'm not being detained, I'm leaving."

Mike stared hard now into his eyes. This was the play. They could arrest him, but it was obvious he was up on his constitutional rights. And if they had done a real background check, they knew he was going to lawyer up immediately. The next move would tell Mike a lot. If they put him in cuffs, odds were good they had some real evidence. The FBI is not in the habit of locking people up that are going to walk six hours later. And if they didn't, it meant they had jack shit, and needed either a verbal clue from him or evidence in his possession. His fingerprints and DNA were on file in the Federal system, same as every other DOD member in the last thirty years. They wouldn't book him just for prints or blood.

"Right now we are just two guys talking Michael. Whether it stays that way depends a lot on you." Moore retorted. This was a sticky spot. They hadn't gone for the cuffs, which made Mike breath a sigh of relief. Whatever they had, it must be thin. But he was now engaged in an interview, which is a form of detention.

"Seems to be your party. What are we talking about exactly?" Mike casually replied. He was good at keeping a poker face, but inside he felt the pressure. No matter how many times you have done this, it's never simple.

Moore smiled. "We can start with this warrant, authorizing a search of your home. Signed this morning in Federal Court in Raleigh." A carbon copy was torn off and handed to him, Mike noted the case number and address. "Then, you can tell me your whereabouts on the fifteenth of March."

Bad form, Agent Moore, bad form. Mike couldn't suppress a grin in his response. "Good luck with your warrant, this house closed two hours ago. It has new owners. But it's unlocked, so not my problem."

Agent Moore flashed a hint of surprise, and rapidly locked it back down. Guess they didn't see that one coming. He murmured to one of the other agents, who walked to the house and back.

"Empty. Not a speck of dust, clean top to bottom." The agent said upon his return.

"That doesn't change much. You know I can search your vehicles without a warrant just by them being on this street." Moore quipped.

"Do what you need to then Agent. If we are playing that game, I'll need to go make a phone call." Mike answered just as quick back. He left that the phone call would be to his lawyer as an implied.

"Where were you the night of the fifteenth?" Moore shifted suddenly, hoping to catch him off guard.

Mike leaned back on his trailer, folding his hands into a steeple in front of him. He could have thought through an alibi, but that would have required someone else to confirm it. And when the chips are down, the only person you can truly count on is yourself. There was no truer words ever spoken than Ben Franklin with "Three can keep a secret, if two of them are dead." He wasn't touching an answer to that one with a ten-foot pole. He looked at the Agent, his expression his response. Not happening.

Goddamn it, Moore thought, not the way I wanted this to go. His case was paper thin, even the judge had looked at him a little skeptical before he signed the warrant. If it wasn't for Moore's reputation for closing cases, they wouldn't even have that. Moore knew he was right. This was his guy, without question. But knowing and proving are two different things. The stick hadn't worked, maybe some carrot would. A little time to build rapport, maybe something would slip. If pressure didn't work on guys like this, arrogance often did. Plenty of criminals thought they were so much smarter and craftier than the cops, they would play right into a trap. Get a little too friendly.

"Alright, I see how it is. But I didn't come all this way not to check. That's my job. So we can either search your remaining property right here, or we can take it to our warehouse and not scatter your business all over the street. Choice is yours."

Mike considered. Right here was likely to be more uncomfortable for the agents, and they would have to keep traffic off the road. It was also going to take longer. There was nothing for them to find anyway. "Acceptable terms, your place is fine. Let's be clear I am not consenting to search, you are exercising your warrant. But the second I get anywhere near an interview room, I am demanding representation."

They didn't let him drive his own truck, no surprise in that. One of the other agents was given the task, and Mike herded into the back seat of a brown Impala. FBI cars were funny. No cage, and leather seats to boot. Just some friends out for a cruise. No one said a word on the way to the field office near downtown. And that is how he came to find himself in a waiting area, coffee and water in urns with Styrofoam cups, ten chairs but all alone. Presently, Agent Moore arrived with a grey haired, spectacled agent in tow. The man could have been his ghost of Christmas future. Moore introduced him as Agent Allen, local HMFIC. Curious, that confirmed Moore wasn't from around here. Moore started into him with a passable good cop persona, shifting from "your in big trouble mister" to "we can help you, little buddy, but you have to help us first." Mike hoped he could learn some more details from this change in tactics. An intelligence operative doesn't miss anything, and cognitive leaps can spring from the tiniest fact.

"Look, Mike, I know you prefer to be called Mike. In fact, I know an awfully lot about you. Military career, past relationships, I've even talked with some of your friends recently." Mike new that part was bullshit. Any of his friends had a run in with the Feds, his phone would be ringing the second they drove off.

"I know you came off a contract job three months ago in South Africa, and what you made for a year long stint. The IRS documents I saw made it clear you took a lower paying job than Iraq or Afghanistan would have offered as a contractor. South Africa is a curious choice. We technically have an extradition treaty with them, but it is common knowledge it's paper only. South Africa doesn't like us nosing around, and they have been quite blunt about that. Much more difficult to nab a man from there, than a place we own like the Middle East. Curious, don't you think?"

Mike remained silent. It didn't exactly take Sherlock Holmes to figure that part out, and he'd paid his taxes.

"And then we have a curious set of circumstances way out in Goose Neck, Idaho, three weeks after you step foot back in the States. Ever been out to Idaho? Beautiful country, world class fly fishing." Moore was studying him for any hint of recognition. Mike remained passive.

"A female bartender remembers a guy about your description, North Carolina plates on a black Ford Bronco, about this time last year. Must've made quite an impression to stay in her memory this long. Her boss goes missing for a while, then shows back up missing a leg. Hunting accident he says, got hit by a 12-gauge slug. Rehab in Boise, takes a long time to get back to functional. The fifteenth of March, he winds up dead. Real gruesome. Kind of a funny set of coincidences right?"

Fuck. Mike hadn't calculated the bartender remembering shit. Or even still working there. Small town America he guessed. Not like she had a lot of other prospects. Movie star contracts didn't fall out of the sky places like that, or winning lottery tickets. As Moore continued to talk, Mike walked back over the operation in his memory, searching for a detail he had overlooked.

CHAPTER THIRTY

Driving across the country as fast as he could manage, Mike plotted his next move. His paranoia was so high at the moment, he wouldn't even check into a hotel. Too many possible questions, to many logged plate numbers, to many walls. He slept in rest areas when he had to, or on back roads when available. He calculated the ways the Sheriff could plot against him, how evidence could be fabricated to implicate him for the entire mess. They might not, but then again they might. Arriving home, he stashed some of his hardware in a place it couldn't be found, and dove into his network of contacts. Time to find an overseas job, a good place to be out of reach of any US law enforcement. Iraq and Afghanistan were out, the FBI maintained a presence in both as part of its counter terrorism mission. He would be trapped if they came for him. It wasn't like he could slip the walls and disappear into the local population. That would be trading a trial in US court for an immediate sell out to a beheading cell, the highest offer standing for captured American contractors or soldiers. Eventually a British friend turned him to a contact in South Africa, looking for his skill set to use against poachers. The work was hard and the pay comparatively low, but the Boers weren't keen on selling out a friend to anyone. If the long arm of the law reached out, he was likely to hear about it. And with the money he was making, he could live semi-civilized in Africa for a very long time.

Two weeks later he was in Johannesburg, and threw himself into the task of being useful to his new employers. A long year of waiting for one of his trip wires to go off produced nothing. In the meantime, he made it his business to rediscover the gym, and take training seriously for the first time in many years. He helped develop a sniper capability for his hosts, and learned a great deal more than he already knew about bush craft and man tracking from an ex-Rhodesian SAS trooper on the team. In between stories of slotting floppies of course. When his time was up, it was hard not to renew for a second. But there was something he needed to finish. The men he had left standing back home were in his thoughts every day. Sons of bitches walking around free and breathing his air. Like an itch that couldn't be scratched. He had looked evil in the eyes, and he knew he could never rest until it was extinguished.

Flying back into Raleigh, he was pleasantly surprised he wasn't detained at customs. A reasonable assurance no one had come looking for him. He had his Bronco tuned up by a mechanic in Greensboro, this wasn't the time for a timing belt to go bad. Long hours spent in planning back in Pretoria were set into motion. A few bank withdrawals of $5,000 each might be abnormal most places, but Fayette-nam was an exception. With the number of deployed troops returning and contractors to boot, cashiers didn't bat an eye. Many a fresh-faced paratrooper had burned an entire enlistment bonus at strip clubs in a weekend, a story as old as soldiers. Fifteen thousand dollars in cash was enough to handle any contingency Mike could think of. He would prefer to buy his way out of problems on this one, but shooting was always an option too.

Next, Mike went to visit a friend in an industrial area in Sanford. One of North Carolina's best-kept secrets, the manufacturing base kept the town alive. From chicken processing to brick yards, warehouses as far as the eye could see. Mr. Joshua owed Mike some deep favors, so burying a pallet of hardware at the back of his distribution center no questions asked was a cinch. If someone did come looking, they had 40,000 square feet to comb to find it. From a large PVC tube, Mike retrieved what he needed. It took most of two hours to scrub the Cosmoline off and return it to proper working order.

Shopping was next on the list. Ten spare fuel cans ensure he wouldn't have to refill much, and wouldn't look that out of place where he was headed. A handheld GPS, purchased in cash, from a Cabela's, not one of the local tactical shops. In the off chance it was found, better to have a huge serial number list to sort through. This stop also afforded him the chance to pick up camouflaged clothing. He wanted to look like a hunter if he was spotted, not a soldier, which made most of his personal kit a no go. He opted for A-Tacs pattern, a nice blend of concealment and fitting a role. He bought out multiple Walmarts of Mountain House freeze dried meals, along with a new Jetboil stove.

Heading Northwest out of state, he stopped at the Low Moor sight in range in Covington, Virginia. He had resources back home, but didn't want to risk anyone he knew sighting in the rifle. The Low Moor was a free range, provided by the Forest Service, and thankfully mostly empty as he arrived. His weapon was a little large for deer, and the report could garner unwanted attention. All shooters love the big bores. Happy with his preps, he continued to the North.

In Thief River Falls, Minnesota, Mike stopped to top off all of his fuel. Ten miles outside of town, he stopped for one last arrangement. His SAKO TRG M10 was originally designed as a switch barrel model, capable of changing calibers by the user. Considering its overall length, this was also very helpful in concealment. Pulling the barrel loose, he fit the pieces in the hollowed out rear seat. A special compartment he had built himself using expanding foam and a razor knife fit it snugly. It wouldn't stand up to a full search, but it would pass cursory inspection. He had originally thought of using the top of the gas tank, but the concern of breaking a crucial piece on the long road ahead forced him to reconsider. His SIG P320 Compact he kept in an appendix carry rig. After his last road trip, he wasn't straying far from a gun anymore, regardless of the situation. From Minnesota he crossed a logging road into Canada, the world's largest unprotected border. Post 9/11 it had become a little bit harder to do, but far from impossible. Most of the checkpoints were on major highways. There was just too much empty space to bother securing all of it. There were so many crossing points in North Dakota and Montana, he wondered why they bothered at all. Just like door locks, mostly keeping honest people honest. Driving through Canada with his cargo was risky, but not terribly so. US plates were as common there as Canuck ones at home, no one was likely to suspect anything. Maybe a bit less so in the winter, but still plausible. The advantage was immense. The roads of the United States had become a veritable hornets nest of cameras and electronic tracking. You were still likely to slip through the cracks, but it was too easy to get unlucky. Canada was further behind, and also didn't share things like that with US law enforcement routinely. Maybe in a nationwide manhunt, but he didn't plan on letting things go that far.

A nervous drive across Canada took him to Medicine Hat on the first leg, and down toward a place called Creston the second. He had a moment of white-knuckle poker with a Mountie at Fort MacLeod, the officer manning a checkpoint to ensure he had chains. It took Mike a few minutes to realize the Canadians are just too friendly, he wasn't being grilled for answers. In the weeks leading up to this, he had rehearsed a cover story to the smallest detail, just in case. Cover for action is a way of life. A confession of an unmanly fear of flying combined with a too good to be true oil patch job in Alaska did the trick. The admission of a phobia was designed to mask any nervousness he displayed, and the story to cover his cargo. He even had a card from the foreman in Prudho Bay, name taken from LinkedIn, and printed at a Raleigh Office Max. Details matter. The Mountie wished him the best without asking to see his passport.

From the Canada side, using the standalone GPS unit, Mike reentered the US into Idaho, moving in from the North. Just two miles away from his destination, he pulled off the highway. From Google Maps, he had selected a narrow ravine, unlikely to be used by hunters considering it proximity to the road. Not caring one bit for the paint job, he shoved the Bronco deep into a grove of pine saplings. The green sprouts popped back up in his wake, bending like grass. A camouflage net completed the illusion, and would cover him from the air if needed. Packing a ruck with his needed equipment, Mike prepared for three hard days. From a scrap of paper in the glove box, stowed in the middle of the owner's manual, he plugged in the coordinates to his first target.

Tim was first, he was less likely to be missed. Mike found his trailer by the glowing porch light within a few hours. Keeping the front door in sight, he located a vantage point far enough away to avoid detection. Tim lived at the end of a dirt road, nearest neighbor a good half mile away. Perfect for what was in store. Pleased with his vantage point, Mike moved East away from it, following his feet downhill. Not long after, he found a thick nest of elderberry bushes with a downed Douglas fir. Caching his pack and heavier gear, beside the trunk, he removed his food stores. Those he hung in a bag from a tree fifty yards away. It wouldn't do to have a bear ransack his stash at a time like this.

This set Mike with three locations. An observation point, a place for eating, and a harbor site. They were segregated to keep animal traffic to a minimum. Any food consumed was going to leave crumbs, even if too small for a human eye to notice. But mice, wolves, and birds wouldn't miss the smell. Best to keep time spent there to the least possible. The harbor site was for sleeping, and only for sleeping. Under normal conditions he would never use one for more than twenty-four hours, but he reasoned he stood a better chance of being seen looking for a different one in these conditions. Besides, running recon on two targets by yourself is not exactly by the book. To help him in that regard, he had packed two high end trail camera's. Carefully reading the owner's manual to ensure he had any flashes disabled, Mike had preset the programs at home. He had also looked for them with the naked eye and NVGs, to make sure they didn't emit a visible light at any point. The NVGs picked up the infrared lighting they used for night shots, but that was hardly a threat. Down to just his jacket, pistol, and a full topped off water bottle, Mike moved back to his observation point. Watching Tim's house, he saw the television go off around 2 a.m., and the remaining light shortly after. Thirty minutes later, he crept down to emplace the camera. Adding natural vegetation with a small bungie cord, he set it to cover Tim's front door.

The Sheriff was a more difficult target. Two miles from Tim, he lived in a suburb, homes set right next to one another. This was going to require most of the actual eyeball work. A short ridge overlooked the area, three streets between wilderness and front door. This had the effect of making the distance seem longer than it was, as well as making him near impossible to detect. The second trail camera went in on his own position. He wanted to know if it was frequented by any locals.

For the next three days, Mike spent most of his time observing Bob, taking breaks to check up on the electronic leash on Tim, and keep the batteries fresh in the camera. He took his sleep breaks when both were always out of the house, noon to seven. Three days wasn't the best pattern of life indicator, but most humans are creatures of habit. Given his operational constraints, he was willing to gamble it. The pictures from Tim's and the long hours at Bob's gave Mike a window to complete both tasks in one night. Time to finish this.

Tim seemed to be low on visitors, no one else besides the mailman ever came near his house. He would leave for work around two in the afternoon and returned right after midnight. Mike waited until darkness fell, and moved to the rear of the trailer. A design that seems to never go out of style, single wide trailer houses are predictable. Front door on the right side, back door on the left side. Donning disposable gloves, Mike stopped at the back door. He listened for a while, making sure he hadn't missed anyone inside. A dog would have also been bound to smell him and raise a racket, forcing him to make a plan B. Satisfied, Mike used his pick gun to defeat the doors deadbolt. Trailers don't have the best of hardware; entry took him seconds. And considering the age and use of the doorknob, there was no way anyone would notice turning tool marks. Careful not to disturb anything, Mike checked the premises for stragglers anyway. It wouldn't be a fun surprise to have Granny come out of the back room with a shotgun while he was saying hello to Tim.

The house was a disaster, beer cans and titty mags all over the living room floor. Mike was glad he didn't have to sit in the lazy boy. On the end table next to it was a .44 magnum. Over the oven he found a hi point pistol, and a sawed-off shotgun in the bathroom. Timmy, it seemed, was still scared. Well, he should be. Mike stood watch at the front of the trailer, waiting on Tim's return. Through a gap in the living room curtains, he could observe the driveway. If Tim was alone, game on. If he had miraculously found company, it was an easy slip out the backdoor before they got to the front. Not trusting a stun gun, Mike held a blackjack in his right hand. Sometimes, the old ways are the best. Just after midnight, headlights lit up the interior. A Honda Civic parked, and Tim exited alone, still uncertain on his fake leg. Serious downgrade from an F350 Mike thought, medical bills must've been pricey. He took some satisfaction in even that small victory. An audible thump echoed every time Tim's prosthetic landed. Mike used the noise to get to the backside of the door. Tim paused at the top of the steps, keys in his left hand, .38-snub nose in his right.

Just like in the pictures the game camera had snapped, Tim pushed the door open and looked left, then right before he came in, covering the room with a wide sweep of the revolver. But like most people, he didn't look far enough to the edge of the wall. Lesson one of CQB training, look deep before you commit. A man with a day of urban combat experience would have hugged one side of the door, flat to the aluminum siding, and then the other before making entry. Like the TSA in airports, Tim was mostly making himself feel better with a half assed solution. Satisfied, he stepped inside and reached for the light switch. As he did, Mike rained a crashing blow of the black jack onto his gun hand, forcing him to drop it. Radial nerve strikes work in theory, but crushing blunt force trauma to the thumb works in practice. Before he had time to process the damage, a follow up to the side of his head put him under. When Tim came to, he was zip tied to his recliner.

Mike needed him to know. Tim deserved it, after all the pain he had caused in the world. So he turned on a lamp, waited on Tim to wake up, and waited again for the recognition. "Time to pay for your sins," Mike said, before he plunged a knife into his chest, opening him up like a Christmas turkey. He pulled his still beating heart from his chest, and held it up to his eyes before he expired. Tim dead, Mike set about carving the lat long of the old camp into his chest with an Xacto-blade. So much for subtlety. That would be pretty hard for whoever found him to ignore.

Under cover of night, he moved next to Sheriff Bob's house. His observation point was 700 meters away, excellent line of sight, and covered egress routes. SAKO reassembled, he settled in to wait for the morning light.

Mike didn't want tracking him to be easy. Seven hundred meters is a lot of ground to cover looking for sign, or trying to get a dog on a trail. Right at 7:30, Bob walked out of his house, coffee cup in hand. The ever-faithful Sheriff, off to another day of protecting the townsfolk. Even after all this time, the hypocrisy of it made Mike nauseous. His range finder and ballistic computer had worked out his elevation hold with the first ray of dawn. Left to right wind, five mph, Mike made corrections in his head. Not that five mph was going to mean much to a 300 Norma Mag at this range. He corrected two tenths of a mil left as Bob presented a side quarter shot as he unlocked his car door. The rifle bucked, and Bob folded like he was hit by the fist of an angry God. His hip bone was shards, caught longways across its axis. The odds of him surviving that were near zero, but Mike didn't come all this way to half ass it. The man needed to know he was dying, hence the hip shot. Mike hoped he had the presence of mind to know who did it. He decided to give him two minutes, to be sure. Bob clawed his service weapon free, propping himself up on one elbow. Tough old bastard, Mike thought. At least we have one fighter to the end. So he gave him another one in the chest to be sure. Gunfire wasn't uncommon in the woods around here, but two shots supersonic through a neighborhood was still hard to miss. As a neighbor ran to the Sheriff's side, Mike picked up his equipment. Warm brass in his pocket, he took off through the woods like all the forces of hell pursued him. Two hours, he figured, to get the word out and the road blocks up.

An hour and a half put him into Montana, eating up road into the Kootenai National Forest. Moving into the back country as far as a Bronco could go, he did the last thing a manhunt would ever assume in the winter. Having packed accordingly, he went to ground for two solid weeks. Camping out gave him lots of time to consider "what ifs", but it was ultimately the safest bet. Even if it came to helicopters and high-level assets, ten square meters in a sea of wilderness is damn hard to spot. His Bronco stayed cold and under branch cover, making it virtually invisible to thermal imaging or aeriel spotting.

More than enough time spent for any pursuit to die out, Mike followed the same trail home. Even if someone did check cameras for his plates, Minnesota was a long way off to start. One local Sheriff wasn't worth the effort of checking every CCTV tape in the nation, and two weeks after the fact was a long time to stay the course. A President or Supreme Court Justice maybe, but not some two-bit local.

CHAPTER THIRTY-ONE

Mike came back to the conversation as Agent Moore was wrapping up the Sheriff's part.

"Bullet did so much damage, it looked like a car crash happened inside his chest. We initially thought 338 Lapua, but the forensics specified it as a 300 Norma Magnum. Pretty rare round, and that pointed us to military snipers. NC plate, Bragg and Lejuene both in the state, still a pretty big pool. We ran that list through the DMV for Black Ford Bronco's, which returned a list of four. Two out of the country at the time, one a 19 year old from the 82nd Airborne that was on staff duty, and you."

Mike still knew he had nothing to worry about. It hurt his poor boy heart, but the SAKO took a swim. An amphibious background gave him knowledge of the ocean, and he knew enough to go the eight miles out to get over the continental shelf in North Carolina. A long trip in a borrowed zodiac, but necessary. The ocean was deep out there, well past what a scuba diver could do, and besides the Atlantic here was dark. Those tools would be dust before the technology existed to find them. It had cost him all his reloading dies and brass too, but never too safe. The Dan Wesson 10mm had been melted to slag with a torch the year before. There were four bodies on that gun, not a souvenir worth hiding.

"So now I find you, and you seem to own, recently acquired, the two most inconspicuous vehicles on the road. Where exactly is your Bronco at Mr. Bryant?"

Good luck with that one too. It paid to have the kind of friends that didn't ask questions. The Bronco had been drained of fluids on his return, and was currently buried in a pond over in Chatham County. Private property, it had been in a buddy's family for 100 years. Grain of sand on a beach, figuratively speaking.

A junior agent called Moore out of the room, and from the look on his face it wasn't good news. Nothing incriminating could be in Mike's current possessions, because nothing from the op existed anymore. All told it had cost him about $25,000 to do, but that beat prison any day.

Moore was less than enthusiastic, his face said he knew he was beat. "It seems you own six rifles and ten handguns, not a one of them in 300 Norma or 10mm. How very convenient."

Mike looked at him deadpan. Cards were on the table. "So, are we done here?"

Moore was exasperated, but completely out of options. "You're a real asshole Mr. Bryant. I know you were in the area last year, a department 100 miles south ran your tags. We log that you know, out of state and all. But we both know that isn't enough. Not for an indictment. And we aren't stupid. As we started finding bodies, it was obvious the local boys planned on adding you to the tally. But a year later, and the goddamn Sheriff? That is some cold work. Premeditated as the day is long. This isn't the Wild West, we don't do frontier justice. No matter how dark things get. You can still clear your conscience. Cleanse your soul. We could probably get that charge down to third degree. With your history of service, we could call that crime of passion. Just tell me why you went back, why you didn't call it in as soon as you could."

Mike looked at the Agent like he had just escaped the asylum. Was he out of his fucking mind? Mike knew he was on a slippery slope. The best thing to do right now was walk out the door. They had all but admitted they didn't have enough to charge him. But he couldn't resist an object lesson. After all the blood and pain he had shouldered for this nation, he was owed somebody listening. For once. Maybe he could actually get through to this simple mother fucker.

"You by chance search the Sheriff's property?"

Moore made a face like Mike had just pulled a quarter from behind his ear. After a moments pause, he answered. "Matter of fact I did. On a hunch, I took the cadaver dog over. We had to bring one in for the mess up on the mountain."

"And?" Mike gently prodded.

Letting out a long breath, Moore decided to give him this one. "Two more bodies, underneath the garden shed. Female, probably been there 10 years."

Mike's eyes blazed fire. "Well let's have a little hypothetical then, just between us. You're not my priest, so I'm not confessing anything. I hope you find your guy. And when you do, you give him a pat on the back, a medal, and some extra bullets. We need law and order in this country, which is your job. It keeps everyone honest, and playing by the rules. But once in a while, something truly evil rears its head. And the only thing you can do with pure evil is shoot it in the fucking head. No negotiation, no reforming, no debt to society to pay. No technicality to get off on, no million dollar legal team. Kill that motherfucker graveyard dead. As they say back in Texas, kill him and tell God he died. It's the only course of action."

Mike stared at him as he let that sink in.

"Now Agent Moore, you can charge me, or its time for me to go. I have places to be."

Begrudgingly, the agents put Mike's truck back together, and turned him loose.

CHAPTER THIRTY-TWO

Driving across the badlands of South Dakota, windows rolled down, Mike thought of how much things had changed. He had been adrift, a ship without sails, a man with no purpose. And now he had found redemption. He knew why he was still walking the Earth, why he had survived when so many of his teammates and friends hadn't. Because he still had work to do. He had a seat in Valhalla, but they would hold it for him.

A phone rang from the glove box, which was weird since Mike's was on the dash. And there had been no service for over an hour. Realization dawning on him, he popped the latch and pulled it out. It would be asking too much to think it belonged to the former owner.

A single text message, from a number he didn't know. Virginia area code. Very subtle guys, very subtle. It read "Abandoned gas station in three miles, pull over." Not the kind of message it pays to ignore. Mike saw the exit coming, and eased the truck down the ramp. Pulling up to the long defunct pumps, he stepped out into the sunny afternoon. A few minutes later, a black Volvo station wagon pulled up on the other side. A tall, light skinned black man stepped out of the driver's side, dark ray bans masking his eyes.

"How have you been Mike?" He asked, pulling up his shirt and turning in a circle.

"I was actually having a wonderful day up until about five minutes ago. You'll forgive me if I don't do the same.

I'm carrying, and it seems pointless to put it away. If you wanted to kill me, I suspect we wouldn't be talking right now."

"Curiosity gets the best of me. How would you do that in our shoes Mike?"

Mike looked around casually, taking in his surroundings. "Long gun, right over there on the high spot in the rocks." He was greeted with sunlight glinting off glass, an obvious tell. And a gift. Any sniper on this payroll would have a shade over the scope. "Or I'd just run me off the bridge over the next gorge, probably with a semi to make sure it worked."

Ten seconds later, an unmarked big rig flew down the interstate, well above the speed limit. Now they were just showing off.

"Very fucking funny Colonel Nuvy. Or are you Mr. Smith today?"

The black man smiled. "Mr. Nuvy actually, thought it would be rude to play otherwise."

"Well, you came a long way to see me. What is this about?"

"Like you don't know. Be serious Mike. The FBI can't access Canadian traffic cameras, but we can. Now I want you to know we aren't upset about the cousin fuckers. They had that coming. But the Sheriff, really? You couldn't be a little more discreet? Like maybe a shotgun at close range? That would have done the job too you know. How the fuck am I supposed to blame a 700 yard shot on pissed off white supremacists?"

Mike hadn't really thought that part through actually. When you have a hammer, everything starts to look like a nail. It had been childish, but he really wanted to use that gun. "Yeah, I guess you have a point there. So am I in trouble?"

Nuvy looked at him like a disappointed father. No, you can't use the car tonight. "We are willing to let one go. But just one. We don't really care what happens out here, not our business. But we do care if it looks like one of Uncle Sugar's killing machines is about to go totally off the reservation. We can't have that. Makes the rest of us look bad, and people start asking questions. So try to keep it a little more refined. Next time, it won't be me you see."

Mike shuddered. He doubted it would be anyone he saw. Probably a pressure plate at the end of his driveway, or some poison soup. He wondered if they had traded the Russians for any Polonium 210 recently.

"Fair enough. Things got a little sporty for a while back there. My bad."

Nuvy shook his head. Some things never change. "Alright then. Make sure you keep it off the radar if it happens again. Looks like you are headed out West. You'll want to take this." He said, handing Mike a Post-it note." A member of the Association, personal friend, he can help you start over. He knows the ground out there. Best of luck."

Mike took the Post-it. Nuvy turned and walked back to his car, driving away without another word.

Notes about the Characters

This is a work of fiction. But like all stories, the characters are based on real people. The main character Mike Bryant is based on two good friends of mine, and I hope this page will cause you to take a minute and remember the real heroes in the world. And all the ones from the GWOT that never got to come home.

CW2 Mike Duskin was a giant of a man, standing six foot, eight inches and weighing in a 280 pounds of twisted steel. His hobbies included shooting three guns with his son, and "picking heavy things up and moving them over there." Despite his intimidating size, Mike was a fantastic mentor and teacher, and he always left his ego at the door. I lost the fast rope gloves he loaned me at SFAURTEC when I was a student and he was an instructor, and he gave me zero new guy shit about it. Later we became fast friends. My favorite story about Mike involved him beating one crackhead with another crackhead in the foyer of a Fayetteville Waffle House when they started some shit. If I had made him the actual central character of this novel, it would have ended many chapters earlier. On realizing he was captured, Mike would have busted the handcuffs and beat everyone to death on principle. It was a terrible blow to the Regiment the day we lost Mike Duskin, and you are missed. Killed in Action, 23 October 2012, Wardak Province, Afghanistan.

Sergeant First Class William Brian Woods Jr., was a very good friend I met during the Special Forces Qualification

Course. Like myself, Brian was a former USMC Scout Sniper, having done his hitch with 7th Marine Regiment. Brian was the best Weapons Sergeant in Special Forces, which is pretty incredible since his actual MOS was Medical Sergeant. Brian became Bryant in the novel, because Woods would be a strange last name in a book set in the forest. Brian taught us more during the Q about weapons than I knew was possible, his hobby while cramming four years of medical school into a year of hell known as the 18 Delta course. Brian always had a hold out piece, which would also have ended the novel much sooner. Even if it was a keister stash. You are missed old friend.

CHAPTER ONE

Preface

I remember where I was when the War started. Not the little brushfire war we had with Iraq and Afghanistan, though I remember where I was when that one started too. No, I mean the big one. What some people would eventually call World War III, though it made the previous two looks like a dust up in the school yard. The one that took us to the brink of extinction. How we got there didn't seem to matter at the time, it never does in a crisis. All that mattered back then was staying alive. Age and what I hope is wisdom has changed my perspective a bit, but it is tempered with a healthy dose of cynicism. I've always had that, and what I saw over the years didn't do much to dissuade it. I don't think even foreknowledge of what would happen really would have changed anything. All the warning signs were there, but the population chose to ignore them, a recurring theme in history. People were busy going to the mall and watching reality TV, nothing bad could ever happen to them. The political class was busy getting rich off the backs of everyone else, maintaining the status quo, business as usual. Much too busy to think there could actually be a crisis big enough to upset the trough of easy money. The cable news liked to talk about dirty bombs and EMP attacks once in a while to boost ratings, but none of the so called experts saw what was really coming. All the conventional wisdom of the day liked to tell us that terrorist were outliers, Islam was actually a religion of peace, the mad mullah's were just barking. We rattled sabers and talked a good game about keeping Iran and North Korea from acquiring nukes, but that was mostly just to keep them away from the big boy table. Pakistan acquired its doomsday weapons well before that, and was subsequently invited to be taken seriously. Nukes had so many safeguards in place, red phones and direct lines and serious looking diplomats, that they had basically become status symbols for statesmen. If you had the goods, you could run with the grown-ups. If you didn't, you could expect to have your nose rubbed in the dirt at will. No more no less. No one really expected the missiles to fly, not when there were so many luxuries for leaders of nuclear nations to indulge in. They might occasionally puff up at the ancient enemies, but that was theater for the peasants. The elite class was never going to end life as we know it, not with so many pleasures to keep them entertained.

I suppose no one ever sees a paradigm shift coming. But one was on the wind. And it would answer a question the soldiers from the pointy end of the stick already understood, but that no Washington Beltway or Downing Street desk jockey could fathom. What would happen if one of these savage eyed Bedouin lunatics preaching about a new caliphate ever actually acquired a doomsday weapon? Simple. He would use it.

My name is Derek Martell, and this is my story. The story of how mankind was almost pushed into the abyss. How we fought back, how we bled and died by the thousands to claw our way out from the darkness. The terrible price we paid, and how I survived. At least for now.

CHAPTER TWO

The day the world almost ended, I was manning a mostly irrelevant outpost on the Iranian border. It was a long fall for a man like me, but the pay was decent, and the odds of getting shot were higher in Chicago. So I had that going for me. Officially, the name of the place was Combat Outpost Cramer, named after some poor bastard that bought it back in 05. The plaque near the front gate said he was a paratrooper from the 82nd, so he deserved better than what COP Cramer had become, which was a glorified gas station. We called it 7/11, and unfortunately home. I was not that long retired from 3rd Special Forces Group, a victim of Obama's purge of the warfighters in the years leading up to the end of his second term. Why was I at a refueling depot in a god-forsaken corner of the sandbox, not running Commando Steve missions of derring-do and glory? Good question. I asked myself that plenty of times, too.

Most of it had to do with the great purge, which had driven down the price of labor across the board for all of us former ninja's. 2021 was a rough time to only possess the skill set of killing bad guys, with the decline of American power abroad. Our first Orange President had lasted only long enough to wipe ISIS off the map before the opposition party managed to have him and his VP impeached, mostly on some made up charges and some highly sketchy testimonies. The Soy Boy Speaker of the House became President, and picked a recently pardoned Hillary as his second, hoping to appease the populace since she "won the popular vote.

A few days later he resigned, and the circle was complete. Wrath of the Clinton beast soon followed. There were some predictable protest, and some III% groups even tried to start an armed rebellion. Kill-ary responded with a jack booted lesson that would have made Janet Reno blush. The deep state, so bent on the destruction of Trump, had closed ranks to protect their Queen. Military men quit in droves, most of them heading out West. The ones that didn't hang it up in disgust at the banana republic politics left not long after, when the full-fledged tranny circus invaded all the services. The once great US Military, praetorian guard of the world's only superpower, crumbled from within. Twelve years of combined social experiments and humiliation did what no foreign power ever could. It reduced our forces to ashes. The new military was a giant welfare leach at best, often proving incapable of tying its own proverbial shoes. I guess that is a skill you learn after you decide what genitals you want to wear.

Anyway, the flood of surplus labor wreaked havoc on the contracting market. Even a year before, I wouldn't get out of bed for less than $750 a day plus per diem. And we better have all the new Arc'teryx Gucci kit to boot. Now, when you couldn't swing a dead cat without hitting ten pipe hitting Special Operations Tier eleventy bad asses, the game had changed. Contracts that once had prerequisites like "must be breathing, two years military service (waivable), and reasonably capable of hitting the floor with a dropped pistol" now said things like "if we could print the name of your Unit, please do not apply" and filled up overnight. I was caught with my pants down. I had made some bad choices after I got bounced out of the service, spent time like an idiot figuring out what I wanted to be when I grew up. Hiking the Appalachian Trail, enjoying nature, exploring the country I had defended but rarely seen all those years. Stupid, but I did it. The few coins I had made from contracts I had mostly blown on fast cars and faster women, which didn't seem like a mistake at the time, but certainly did when they were over. Not to mention, I felt something like patriotism rising in my throat every time I saw that traitorous bitch on TV. I had a lot of years of experience on a sniper rifle and a bad whiskey habit, I needed to get out of the country for a while. Before I did something me and the Secret Service both regretted in the morning. I just needed a little nest egg to buy some land in Wyoming before the revolution started. You have to have somewhere to make popcorn for the fireworks show. With a national divorce on the horizon, Wyoming's low population density made it unlikely to be strategic ground for either side. So I took the first job I could land, which took me back to Iraq at half my usual pay. And what a miserable job it was going to be.

COP Cramer was located North East of Al Kut, which is to say in the middle of nowhere. It existed only as a midway refueling point between Firebase Apache in the North and Firebase Clark in the South, on the rare occasions supplies or troops needed to move between those two points. Most people thought Madam President would appease her base by pulling all the forces out of Iraq, especially since ISIS was gone. She must've owned stock in KBR though, there was still a large troop presence conducting train and advise missions. These days that mostly meant salsa night and an excuse to ask for a discount at Home Depot back home for the rest of your life, though there were still some Green Berets and others trying to do the right thing. The tide was against them, but God bless them, they were trying.

The COP was part Old West fort, and part prison. At least it felt like a prison to those of us stuck there for a year. We had an exterior wall of Hesco barriers, 400 meters to a side in a square. The Hesco itself was a wonderful invention, basically a wire mesh basket lined with a thick canvas material. Fill it up with dirt from a back hoe, and you have a six foot by six foot Lego block you can stack and build with. It has a side benefit of being able to stop anything short of a direct hit by an artillery round, and it better be a big artillery round. Inside the walls we had a living quarters, a gym, a 50 meter range for test firing weapons, a chow hall, and not much else. In the back left corner was the fuel farm, further protected by 20 foot concrete Jersey barriers. The fuel farm was segregated into smaller sections, also with concrete walls, to lower the chances of a direct hit from indirect fire. In theory, the same walls would contain most of the blast if one of the massive fuel blivets did happen to go up. At least that was what we told ourselves.

At least I wasn't alone, though there were days my guard post felt like a life sentence in solitary. I had a good crew with me, and we were making the best of a bad situation. Scott Dodge was a fellow 3rd Grouper, though our paths hadn't crossed much before. His left arm was mangled from an RPK round in Afghanistan years before, same night his team earned all the Silver Stars in the inventory. I think they had to melt down J. Edgar Hoovers earring collection to make the last one, but they deserved them. Scott was an 18 Charlie (Special Forces Engineer Sergeant) in his past life, which meant he was good at demo, which was pretty much useless at the moment. Fortunately the other Charlie job is team supply monkey, which was useful. Frank Gold was a former 18 Delta from 10th Group, which means he must've been more hard up than I was, or he had some bad black marks on his resume. 18D denotes Special Forces Medic, and they are the best in the world at trauma management. If I was all shot up in the street, I would rather have an 18D working on me than a Vascular Surgeon. A surgeon can fix things a Delta can't spell, but a Delta cannot be beat at keeping you alive long enough to ride a chopper to the hospital. Those boys are looked at like they are made of gold in a combat zone, and I was very lucky to have one on hand. Even if he was a veritable midget, at five foot six wearing boots. Maybe he liked the not getting shot at much part of our new job. Rounding out my American contingent, Willie

Pirelli, an old hand from Force Recon, then MARSOC (Marine Corps Forces Special Operations Command), then Force Recon some more. I liked making up new acronyms for his unit when I introduced him to strangers. I really wish the USMC would figure its system out, it gets confusing for us Army types. Willie was from New York, which also gave me reason to abuse him over his accent. Poor bastard. Stuck on a COP as the only Jarhead with three SF guys, and a Yankee to boot.

Our host nation force was 30 Kurds, which was a godsend. Kurds were by far my favorite partner forces to have, and it also meant we were unlikely to get killed in our sleep by our own guys. I also insured that they stayed happy by supplementing their paychecks with gasoline every month, thanks again to Scott's creative ledgering procedures. It may sound strange that fuel would be such a precious commodity in an oil rich nation, but it always was. Iraq had almost zero refining capability, so it's finished fuel products were mostly imported. Gasoline was scarce, and was often hocked on the black market at upwards of fifteen dollars per gallon. Not like I really cared what happened to KBR's fuel anyway, especially not if it bought some added loyalty out in Indian country. Once a month a real bulk fuels specialist from the Army would drop by to check our stocks. We figured out early that a case of Jack Daniels, brought back from Kurdistan, covered any discrepancy we might have. Circle of life. Cue the "Lion King" music.

In keeping with Iraqi Army tradition, a third of our force was on leave at any one time. Of the remaining twenty, ten were on guard duty, and the other ten were on training or patrols. We didn't patrol as aggressively as we would have if we were on offense, but it did pay to know what was going on outside your wire. In place of Humvees, we had a gaggle of armored F350s, the contractor standard by this stage of the war. I don't want to know what they cost, but they got the job done. Two Americans on patrol and two at the COP stretched us pretty thin, but it was manageable for keeping watch on the area directly affecting us.

Our weapons and communications equipment left a lot to be desired, another reflection of our low importance. We were technically State Department (DOS) employees on a sub-contract, which meant we weren't authorized to have big boy toys. The Diplo-wieners at Foggy Bottom were very specific about the armaments we rated, the biggest of which were 240G medium machine guns for the guard towers and trucks. 7.62x51 belt fed weapons might not sound small to civilians, but for old Iraq hands, they felt like pop guns compared to 50 cals and recoilless rifles. We had been on the job for months and I still felt naked. We had a few 5.56 SAW machine guns as well, along with M-4 rifles, pistols for decoration, and AK's for our Jundies. I suppose that was an extra insulting term for our Kurds, since they hated Arabs, but habits die hard. Early on, I had my friends over at Barnes Precision Machine mail us new upper receivers for our M-4's, a small comfort. Technically illegal, the BPM upper with its Nickel Boron bolt carrier offered enhanced reliability and much improved accuracy, otherwise it changed nothing with the weapon. We kept our DOS uppers handy in case our management team decided to drop by. Two pins had us back to inspection ready, and being way out in the boonies made sneaking up on us hard. Scott and I also opted to run personally bought Bushnell 1x6.5 scopes on our rifles, a game changer in the open country of Eastern Iraq. Willie and Frank stayed the course of being extra cheap, sticking with the issued red dot aim points. For pistols we had the new M-18 Springfield Armory XDM, standard DOD issue by that point. Worrying about your pistol in a firefight was akin to worrying about what color your socks were, but I did like them. And at least we had enough 9mm laying around to keep ourselves entertained on our range. We had a beer shoot every Friday, with Willie and I usually jostling back and forth for the title belt. In spite of my many protests, we didn't have a suppressor or heavy weapon among us.

The communications equipment was worse by far. Being 50 miles from the nearest friendlies, I was positively aghast at the issued gear. We had VHF (Very High Frequency) radios for the trucks, and some old Harris personal size ones for us and each tower. VHF, as configured, had a range of about 8 miles, which meant our patrols where blind as soon as they drove past the curve of the Earth. After much complaining, we finally received one ancient SATCOM model for reaching our bosses in Baghdad, or anyone else in country on the nationwide "guard" frequency. Since we were not authorized military crypto for the SATCOM, that was all we could reach. Our real contingency was locally purchased cell phones, with a handful of SIMM chips to cover the 3 main networks. Like every backwards nation thrust headlong into the technology age by force, Iraqi's loved them some cell phones. So at least we had the potential to die looking totally baller, desperately trying to text in some air support on a limited edition Nokia.

We did have one other avenue to communicate, one that would pay many dividends in the coming days. Not long after we were in country, we had our first visit from the local spooks. They were hard wired the same way we were when it came to spreading an intelligence gathering net far and wide. The CIA loves having sources, from bought cabinet ministers down to the lowliest gas station attendants, which included us at the moment. Who should step out of that tinted window armored Suburban, but my old friend Paul Tiberius. At least this way he didn't have to give me a bullshit fake name. I went to the Special Forces course with Paul, which can make introductions awkward given our new employers. I waited on him to say his name first, then it was all bro hugs and "what in the hell are you doing here?" Paul is what we call in the business vaguely ethnic, some flavor of Asian. But with his newly shoulder length black hair, he could pass for almost anything. His guys had named him Comanche, which was fitting from what I knew of Paul. We spent time in the same group, but never on the same team. Still, his reputation preceded him. He was a little guy like Frank, but vicious as the day is long. All sinew and CrossFit, he was the kind of guy that made you self-conscious about your cardio just by showing up.

Paul gave us the run down, which was basically a formality given the collective history of my guys. I was a fully badged 18F, or Special Forces Intelligence Sergeant, Frank had spent most of his career on "long hair" intel teams, and Scott and Willie were far from wet behind the ears. Would we kindly report anything out of the ordinary, use fake plate and vehicle descriptions should we need to refuel Paul's trucks, and let him meet his sources outside our back gate if the need arises? No problem buddy. Would you kindly give us some government sanctioned air power if we start getting over run, and let us know if we are standing in the path of a turf war? Can do easy. Our radios were incompatible, and it was well outside Paul's mandate to supply us with crypto. Instead, he gave us a new agency toy that was a wonder. Named Venona Tempest, or VT for short, the toy was an app for either phones or computers. VT could use either cell networks or HF radio to transmit secure messages using public and private key encryption. The public key was like an address, so messages were routed to the correct receiver. The private key did the decryption, ensuring only the intended user could unlock the message. The messages were limited to roughly twitter sized 160 character messages, but that was good enough. Pictures smaller than two megapixel could also be sent, though it took a while in HF mode. The real benefit here was the HF radio part. Unlike our regular spectrum radios, an HF radio could reach anywhere on Earth with the right antenna. HF was used by Ham Radio nerds to do just that on a daily basis. HF was ancient technology, but it did tend to work when all the fancy stuff failed. I was fortunately old school enough to have cut my teeth on HF as a radioman. One off the shelf Ham Radio later, courtesy of my new Agency pals, I was practicing my antenna theory again in my down time. It beat knitting.

To the West of us, our closest other Americans, was a small firebase manned by an ODA (Operational Detachment Alpha) from 5th Group. They had been tasked with rebuilding a battalion of Iraqi troops, the same clowns that had melted in the face of the ISIS onslaught not that many years before. To say they were jaded was an understatement, but they were doing the best job they could. Scott and I did the secret SF handshake after crossing paths on a patrol one day, after which they became regular visitors at the 7/11. They were beyond the range of our normal patrols, so it was generally them coming to us. We had enough bunks to be able to tie on a powerful drunk and not force our guests to sleep in their trucks, and the respite from normal duties was good for both of us. They were a mix of old and new hands, with the old guys trying like hell to make twenty. A few of them had been with the Iraqi Counter Terrorism Forces in the glory days, actually doing hand offs with Scott and later me, though none of them were recognizable. The change overs had been fast and furious back then. We talked for hours about the old times, running and gunning across all of Iraq with the Iraqi Counter Terrorist Forces (ICTF). The Battle of Baghdad in 07, how the ICTF had stopped ISIS cold at Ramadi, though abandoned by all the regular forces. And how difficult the ODA's present task was, turning a battalion of bricks into something resembling a military fighting force. Somehow Scott even managed to trade for a 300 Winchester Magnum Mk13, which we had to return before the ODA left country. Like many of us had in the past, they were casually ignoring the mandate to create a battalion sniper platoon. It just didn't seem prudent, given the present political climate.

As contractors often elect their own leaders, I became de facto boss of COP Cramer. It certainly wasn't my innate leadership ability, and Scott or Willie could rightly claim more experience. Mostly it was temperament. I do a lot of things wrong, but I do have a tendency to remain cool at all times. It takes a lot to get me really angry, well beyond the usual guy that does violence for a living. Between that and my propensity for fairness, it just kind of happened. Along with my new call sign, which per the custom of SF, was also an insult. "Mother Hen", shortened to "Mother", had the helm at the 7/11, and everything was going to be alright. Or so we thought.

CHAPTER THREE

The days turned into weeks, which turned into months, which turned into a cliché. We pumped gas twice a week, we patrolled often enough to keep a howitzer battery from setting up on us, and tried to maintain our sanity. Using our locally purchased internet connection, we maintained something like contact with the outside world. As soldiers, we often talked about guns and equipment. Now we watched our stocks and talked about money. Politics went from bad to worse, so much so that I didn't even bother to check the news anymore. I just needed the dollar to stay strong enough for the next six months to buy my mountain top, then I didn't give a damn what happened.

The armored trucks gave me a bad case of claustrophobia, it felt entirely too much like cramming myself into a sardine can. My last combat tour had been at the trail edge of the armored Humvee development, and even then, most of us still rode in the open back. In theory the armor would protect you from small arms, but in reality it also had a bad habit of mangling in roadside bombs. This had the negative side effect of leaving you to burn alive in a hopelessly twisted ball of steel, futilely kicking the door until your boots melted to your skin or smoke inhalation finally overcame you. Such thoughts were never far from my mind when I was looking through my two inches of bulletproof glass, waiting on the trash heap or false section of curb that would be my end. They did have the added bonus of air conditioning, so I could imagine my fiery death in relative comfort.

Fortunately, IED's had largely gone out of vogue, at least in our sector. Or maybe they were saving them for better targets. Mostly what we dealt with was the occasional mortar round, and those were usually badly lobbed. I developed a theory that the local militia's let the new guys practice on us, warming them up for the fight against the Sunnis over in the West. We would respond with what we knew to be ineffective machine gun fire, and an aggressive immediate rolling response to a plausible firing point. It was a high stakes game of cat and mouse. They might have sucked with the indirect fire, but they only had to get lucky once on a fuel depot. We had almost no chance of ever picking the correct firing point, but if we did, we would easily be able to massacre the gun crew. A stalemate ensued, with no one really wanting to up the ante.

The day humankind almost ceased to exist was like any other. Willie and I had just come off a six hour patrol, covering enough ground to really be looking forward to a shower. No armor seals tight enough to keep out the moon dust of Eastern Iraq, and we were absolutely covered head to toe from being in the middle of a three truck convoy. We liked our Kurds, but if anyone was going to eat a buried anti-tank mine, well, we didn't get paid enough for that. In sha Allah, the guys that live their whole lives believing in fate can go first. Back inside the safety of the wire, I was stripping my armor off, my helmet already sitting on the hood. My phone chirped, a text from Paul.

Voice comms up?

Double checking that I had my Iraqna chip in the phone, best for voice in this area, I dialed him.

"Your medic at the base today?" he said without an introduction. That wasn't a fun way to start a call, it usually meant someone was shot up.

"He's here, but we don't have a lot in the way of med supplies. What's the crisis? How many hit?" I was already moving toward Frank's hooch. The more he could glean from my side of the call, the faster he could start prepping for triage.

"No one's hit, no trauma. But my Ranger is sick, running a bad fever, and I don't think I can get him all the way to Nasiriya before the weather closes in." Baghdad was actually closer in direct distance, but traversing the traffic of a major city would indeed make it take longer. This also told me Paul wasn't concerned enough to call in a medevac chopper, something he could still do with his official government status.

"Yeah, my guy can probably handle it then. And what weather? You know something I should know Comanche?" I defaulted to call signs on the phone. Even if the Iraqi Government couldn't fully intercept cell traffic, which was doubtful, Iran and the Russians certainly could. In fact, I had it on pretty good authority the Russians owned the internet hubs in Iraq too. I always made sure to keep my email traffic vague.

"Jesus, you didn't hear? The whole eastern half of the country is under a haboob warning. Suppose to be a bad one. You should really try working for people that care about you more."

"Yeah, I'll get on that. Right after I hit the Powerball, and the Hawaiian Tropic girls drop by here on a USO stop."

"That's what I like best about you Mother. Always an optimist. I'm 45 out, see you shortly."

"Thank you come again" I hit him with my best Simpson's Apu voice, and hung up. Haboob, peachy.

To those that have not experienced a Middle Eastern dust storm, it is hard to describe just how much they suck. The winds are often only about 60 mph, but it feels much worse. Since the environment is mostly super fine "moon dust", standing outside in one is like being in a sandblaster. Given enough time, they actually will rip your skin off. You have to turn off your air-conditioners and tape the vents, or else the units will self-destruct. Any crack or opening in a building will be found, and after a while it hurts to breathe, even indoors. Aircraft won't fly in them, no matter the need. If you have any sense, you spend a haboob inside your hooch, with all the doors and windows duct taped shut. The only positive was that the chances of getting attacked in the middle of one was zero. Nobody on Earth could navigate in one, at anything beyond dead reckoning an azimuth. I had seen them so bad you literally couldn't see your hand in front of your face.

Waiting for Paul to arrive, I called a rapid meeting of my Americans, and the Kurdish leadership. Willie hit Baghdad on the SATCOM, which did indeed confirm we could expect the storm to hit anytime in the next two hours. They were very sorry for neglecting to ensure we got that information, which is a nice way of saying they simply forgot us. That was at least something I was accustomed to after my military career.

Frank was already busy in the med shack, doing whatever it is medics do. I suspect inventorying Tetris shapes on his phone, given his experience with trauma and my description of our inbound patient. But you are allowed to act like a Diva when you are a Diva, so I didn't bug him as we started sand storm prep work.

"It's been a while since I saw a haboob, and the weather dorks say this has the potential to be an epic one. Obviously I am not concerned about an attack in the middle of one, but we won't know exactly when it lifts. I recommend we put four men to a tower, with food and water. Sleeping kit too, and tape for the seams. Power will necessarily be out, we can't run the generators either. Can you organize that Bazan? I direct the last part at Bazan, the closest I had to a ranking Kurd. The contact specified manager, but Major felt closer to correct.

"No problem boss. I get the man in the tower, bing bang boom" He returned in passable English, clapping his hands on the last part and smiling widely. With sixteen of his twenty guys in towers, and two others likely on another detail, he knew he would be riding the storm out with me, and therefore my Jameson stash. Oh, the burden of command. The sacrifices really bring a tear to your eye sometimes.

"Awesome. Scott, can you shut down the generators, and do you need any help?" Scott was the closest thing I had to a mechanic, since one of his hobbies was modifying his jeep back in the real world. I think it spent more time on the rack than the trail, but he did know what he was doing.

"Can do easy. Spare set of hands would be nice, it will go a lot faster if I don't have to depend on ole lefty here." Scott was already grabbing duct tape and plastic bags out of the supply locker.

"Nemo, always jockeying to a supervisors position. Are you sure you were never a Warrant Officer?" I had to get a jab in when I could, Scott was quick with the wit most days. Always best to do so when he was distracted with a real task. Nemo was his call sign, after the Disney cartoon, an obvious barb about his mangled left hand. "Take Bazan's left overs, but be quick about it. Bazan, best English guys for Scott." Scott shot me the bird as he shoved his supplies in a backpack.

"Willie, that's you and me then to string a rope between the med shed, the chow hall, and our TOC." The TOC was our Tactical Operations Center, at least in theory. Old habits die hard, the word TOC would indicate we were doing anything tactical. Mostly it was a glorified radio room, with some maps on the wall, and some sofas. We tried to stay by the radio as often as we could, but it wasn't like being in the real Army. It wasn't a requirement that we man it 24 hours a day. Still, being close to it let us keep an ear to the ground, and by default, it became our usual hang out spot. The ropes were the only way of ensuring we could travel between the three in the sand storm. A hand on the rope, or better yet a carabiner on your belt snapped into it, would keep you from getting lost. A bad enough storm, it was entirely possible to wander around your own tiny compound until you died. "Did I miss anything?"

Willie chimed in, "Worst haboob I have ever seen lasted four days, best we prepare for slightly longer. Let's drag some bunks into the chow hall, we can sleep there. Hooches will turn into easy bake ovens without the power anyway."

That was a valid point. Our living quarters were CHU rooms, or containerized housing units. Often called the tactical trailer park, the CHU was ubiquitous across Iraq. It looked exactly like a tin shoebox, usually five feet wide by twelve feet long. The door and window were on the short side, and they were bolted together to make blocks of any length you liked. It was said they could also be double stacked tall, though I had never seen that. Leave it to the DOD to send American's to war in micro sized camping trailers. The CHU was great for quick housing solutions, and offered a level of privacy unseen in any other war at any time. But the sheet metal walls wouldn't stop a Red Ryder BB gun, and they became stifling sweat boxes the second the air conditioning went out. The TOC or ops cen was a plywood building with a 10 foot roof, it would be a lot more comfortable.

Just then, Frank burst in the door, dragging a large plastic box, backpacks on his front and back.

"Jesus, Frank, not really the time for a garage sale" I said to him with a smirk.

"I'm not spending a potentially multi-day haboob holding hands with a dying man in a roaster pan. My med shed is too small to circulate air with the door sealed. Besides, if he is contagious, Paul and his crew already have it too. Unless you plan to quarantine them, we might as well all be in here. Maybe one of you knuckle dragging idiots can play nursemaid too, learn something for your trouble." Medics are notorious for telling you how they deserve more pay than everyone else, usually about the time they are patching up your stupidity. And when you have pieces of you on the outside of your skin that should never see daylight, you tend to agree with them. There is a time to tell your medics how the cow ate the cabbage, but this didn't look like one of them.

"Alright, Princess, you can have a sleep over. Anything else from your shed?" Even when they are making sense, a smart leader takes shots at his medics on principle. Just to keep them on their toes.

"Yep. My table and IV stands. Best not to do this on the floor like savages if we don't have to."

I walked into that one. The patient table was heavy, I had already helped Frank re-arrange his shop once. Me and my stupid mouth. "That's not what your mom said," I quipped as I ducked out the door, barely dodging a roll of gauze.

Not long after Willie and I finished Frank's move, in rolled a tinted windowed Suburban. On my orders, men on the gate didn't even stop them. Paul and his associate Jim popped out of the front, moving to the driver's side rear to help the last of the team out of the truck. Paul's Ranger was a giant named Alan, easily six foot five and two eighty. We just called him Ranger as a matter of course, since he was the only one around. His relative youth implied that he also had limited service time, no way the kid was over twenty-five when most of us were past forty. How he ended up with Paul's crew, I had no idea. Rangers are not known as the smartest guys around, in fact mostly they are known for hitting things with a hammer exceedingly well. Ranger smash! Compounded with this one's immense size, I had no idea what he was doing out here in the employee of the agency. Maybe they used him to squish the skulls of the guys that wouldn't talk. Whatever he was for, today Ranger Alan was a mess. Paul and Jim looked like kids trying to support him as they pulled him out of the Suburban, and I was thankful they were able to get his legs under him. This wouldn't have been a fun stretcher carry, even the 30 feet into the TOC.

At Frank's direction, the four of us got him maneuvered onto the table. It was also made for a normal sized man, so his legs hung off the end. Frank went to work with his tools, checking his temperature and heart rate while quizzing Paul. Ranger Alan was pale and sweating buckets, way too delirious to answer any questions of his own. Paul was clearly not accustomed to being asked about his whereabouts anymore, and had to focus to keep from being evasive. Willie and I went outside, hoping to make Paul a little more comfortable about the OPSEC. A few minutes later, he joined us.

"Thanks for giving us some shelter from the storm. I owe you one. You guys need any help?" he asked.

Willie and I were taping the door seals on our trucks. Save us some detailing work later." The rest of the 240s still need to come off of these turrets, so you can start with that. Then I recommend you guys grab some lickies and chewies from the chow hall for tonight. We have mostly dark booze, so grab your mixers accordingly."

Without a word, Paul set to pulling the machine guns free of their mounts. I always liked working with other team guys. They asked what needed to be done, and then did it.

Less than an hour later, all of our collective jobs were finished. I had just finished checking the last of the guard towers, and met the rest of the guys in front of the TOC. Everyone was enjoying some last moments of being outside, in spite of the heat. Like a switch had been flipped, suddenly the light got dimmer. On the horizon, like a tidal wave of dust, the lead edge of the haboob came into view. Two thousand feet high, a solid wall of flying sand. Above that, lighting flashed in dark clouds. You could actually watch the storm eat up the distance between you and it, one of the strangest parts of a haboob. As it relentlessly crashed towards us, the air picked up speed. First a gentle breeze, then a blowing inferno of superheated air. I always thought a haboob coming on looked like the beginning of the apocalypse. Unfortunately, this time I was right.

http://wbp.bz/sotca

ENEMY OF THE PEOPLE by PETER EICHSTAEDT

http://wbp.bz/eotpa

Read A Sample Next

Chapter 1

Tariq stared at the camera. *I will do this.*

Hot wind swept across the desert, pushing against him, rippling his black cotton shirt and blousy pants. A black scarf encircled his head, exposing only his dark eyes.

Two nine-millimeter automatic pistols hung loosely at his sides, each in a brown leather holster dangling from shoulder straps. A knife in his left hand, he felt invincible.

I was born to jihad. I have known that since I was very young.

Tariq put his right hand on the shaved head of the American journalist who knelt at his feet, a knee against the bound man's back. The journalist wore orange prison garb, mimicking the men in Guantanamo who Tariq considered his brothers in global *jihad*.

They stopped me from going to Somalia to join al-Shabaab. They stopped me from marrying the woman of my dreams. They wanted me to betray my Muslim brothers. They will suffer and pay for their arrogance.

Tariq glanced pitifully down at the journalist's pale skin and scruffy beard, the hands bound behind his back.

The prisoners call us the Beatles because we are British. But, we are not British. We were born on sacred Arab soil, then raised among the infidels. It was not of our choosing. The others say we are not true jihadis. But they lie. I will show them what a true jihadi does. They will tremble in awe.

Tariq lifted his eyes to the camera, drew a breath, and began to talk, his voice deep and resolute, muffled by the scarf. "I'm back, President Harris, and I'm back because of your arrogant foreign policy towards the Islamic state."

Tariq pointed the blade at the camera.

"You continue to bomb our people despite our serious warnings. You, President Harris, have nothing to gain from your actions but the death of another American. Just as your missiles continue to strike our people, our knives will continue to strike the necks of your people. You, President Harris, with your actions, have killed another American citizen."

Tariq waved his knife.

"This is also a warning to those governments that enter an evil alliance with America against the Islamic State to back off and leave our people alone."

Bracing his knee against the journalist's back, he grabbed the man's chin with his right hand and pulled up, exposing and stretching the throat. Tariq's stomach knotted. His heart pounded.

Do it! Do it!

With a furious burst, Tariq drew the thick blade across the American's neck, the blade biting , unleashing a torrent of blood spilling over the man's chest.

Moments later, Tariq's hands shook, his body pulsating with the pounding of his heart.

Calm yourself. This is for the glory of Allah.

The eyes of the American were empty, lifeless. He bent over the body to finish the job. He rolled the American's body onto its back and placed the severed head on the chest. He stood back to inspect his work. He exhaled, the task complete, his hands still shaking.

"How does it look?" Tariq asked the *jihadi* behind the video camera.

"Excellent," the *jihadi* said. "God is great."

"That will show the American infidels that we are serious," Tariq said. "God willing, they will all die if they try to defeat us."

Another *jihadi* handed Tariq a bucket of water and a rag. "Tariq, you are destined to be the face and the voice of all *jihad.*"

"*In'shallah,*" Tariq said. He dipped the knife and his hands into the water and washed, turning the water a deep pink.

http://wbp.bz/eotpa

- Chapter 1 -

Jake Silver inched his way across the dimly lit bedroom of his Manhattan apartment.

Stopping by the bed, his eyes were drawn to the woman's prone form, and beyond to the far nightstand where a pair of champagne flutes—one on its side, the other upright, its silhouette clear through the tiny garment flung over its mouth–recalled visions of an evening well spent.

And, though the night had been special, it had not yet occurred to Jake that it was the first during which his sleep, however brief, had not suffered the nightmare and its aftermath. That this gutsy woman had chosen to remain by his side, would serve as adequate good fortune for the moment. Though they'd known one another a mere 36 hours, Jake felt an uncommon affinity for Sandy McRea.

The bedroom was comfortably warm against the crisp autumn dawn, so *Cassandra*—as the decidedly unaffected Ms. McRea would soon become known—had let the bedclothes slip below her waist. Jake made no move to raise them, but instead allowed his eyes to wash slowly over his new lover's sculpted upper back, indulge the ivory sweep of torso, the narrow waist, the sensual, summoning breadth of hips laid bare by the retreating folds of linen.

He wanted to wake her, lift her to him. But he knew she'd need her rest if only to survive the upcoming day of job interviews at what seemed every ad agency in town. So Jake ever-so-gently moved an amber curl away from her face and bent to softly kiss her cheek.

Opening one eye, Sandy smiled sleepily. "Is it morning already?"

"Not for you. Not yet." He adjusted her blankets.

Reaching up to touch his face, she said, "You slept well, peacefully."

"I was tired. Can't imagine why," he teased.

"Well, you think about it," she countered, suppressing a mischievous grin, hoping he'd find himself able to think of little else.

Both eyes open now, she girded her courage and asked, "Will I see you again?"

"We both know that answer," he whispered, pleased as much by her candor as her interest. "I'm flying back tomorrow night. We'll put on our big-boy pants and celebrate your success."

"Success?" she laughed. "I haven't landed anything yet."

"You will," Jake said. "You're beautiful, brilliant, *and* talented."

"Right," she yawned, a hint of cynicism aimed less at the choice than the order of his words. "Maybe the last two qualities will carry the day for once."

Their faces nearly touching, Jake understood the distraction such a face as Sandy's might impose upon a hapless interviewer of either gender, especially those unable to see the aspiring artist as anything other than an "aging" ingénue. He smiled. "I've seen your renderings, kiddo. Those drawings are gonna knock 'em dead."

With that bit of encouragement, they shared one long and lingering last kiss before Jake playfully pushed Sandy's distracting face into the overstuffed pillow, teasing, "Now, stop pointing that thing at me, or I'll never get out of here. I'll see you tomorrow night... and remember, big boy pants."

They exchanged a smile, she closed her eyes, and Jake turned to leave.

Suddenly, in wrenching contrast to the moment, he recalled the horror and the visions that had overwhelmed him two nights past. As he stood in the doorway, his back to the bedroom, vivid images of the recurring dream shattered his idyllic morning.

Once again the specter emerged and walked toward him. Once again he saw its wet garments, its shredded hand beckoning, looming, horribly cold as it drew near. But this time, like no other time, the hand had touched his face. With no little embarrassment, Jake recalled how he'd awakened then to pitch his sweaty, shaking, combat-veteran's fit, all of it playing out before the wide-eyed and terrified Sandy.

Now, a full day and night later, Jake tried to shake the memory as he turned back to have one last, bittersweet look at the extraordinary person still sharing his bed, and despite himself, despite the nightmares and learned caution, despite Sandy's earlier terror, despite all of it, he allowed himself to feel the rush of new romance.

Stepping back into the bedroom, Jake picked up a pen from the nightstand, and scribbled a few words of endearment, along with an admonition—his second—that Sandy use the apartment for her remaining few days in New York. He closed with a promise to call when he got to LA.

Tucking the note under his alarm clock, he also left a key.

It meant taking things another step, leaving that key. But, he clearly cared for this woman, eight years his junior. He wanted her to feel at home at his place, safe, comfortable, naked, but most of all *here* when he returned.

Setting the key atop the note, he checked the night table drawer. His pistol was there. Sandy, who liked to call herself a country girl, should have found that New York made her nervous. Since it didn't, that made Jake nervous. So, and since this Iowan knew how to handle a weapon, he'd decided to leave the gun out of its locker for her quick access.

With slight apprehension, he slid the drawer closed, and left the apartment.

It was slightly past 6:00 a.m. when Jake stepped from the building's lobby and into a fast-building rain shower.

A few cabs drifted by. None were available.

Then, just as he turned back for the shelter of the lobby and was about to ping Uber, a medallion taxi pulled up to the curb, discharging a man.

His hat pulled down against the weather, the guy left the cab's door ajar while gesturing for Jake to do the same with the apartment building's door. On impulse, Jake obliged, but regretted his rote courtesy the moment the stranger disappeared into the building. Uttering a muffled, "Dammit," Jake ran for the cab.

"Airport this morning?" the cabbie asked, recognizing Jake's uniform.

"Yeah, JFK," Jake responded, absent mindedly while looking back and making a mental note to find a new place, one with a doorman.

As the cab wove its way east through an awakening Central Park, Jake peered from the window, impressed by the number of people out jogging so early on so dismal a morning.

He recalled having once shown similar discipline as a light heavyweight boxer in New York's Golden Gloves.

Always disdainful of bullies and bullying, young Jake had found amateur boxing a sensible outlet for his adolescent-male aggressiveness. What began as an outlet grew to an avocation he'd later carry into intercollegiate competition. But despite his emerging pugilistic promise, everything changed when, in the final second of the final round of an otherwise unexceptional bout, a blow to the head caused Jake's vision to flood white.

And though he'd neither gone down, nor lost consciousness his clearest recollection was of a doctor shining a light into his eyes as he sat on his stool in a corner of the ring while the referee raised his opponent's hand in triumph.

Given that the study of head trauma to athletes was in its infancy, Jake was simply declared fit, sent on his way and no medical record established. Only later did he learn that following the blow, he'd continued throwing punches despite that the bell had rung and his opponent had returned to his own corner as the crowd roared with laughter. The revelation so disturbed and embarrassed Jake that he'd never climbed into a ring again.

So, these days, Jake Silver liked to boast that he kept his fitness regimen limited to the rigor of chewing an occasional airline steak.

To the annoyance of some male colleagues, Jake's cynicism was not entirely without motive. A darkly handsome six-footer, he was among those fortunate few who need put forth little more than a shave (and what his airline considered a too-infrequent haircut) to maintain his masculine good looks. In fact, the only thing at which Jake seemed to toil was the public projection of himself as the carefree New York bachelor: a less-than-accurate image, yet one he did little to assuage.

Because, to Jake's mind, despite his entreaties that Sandy stay on at the apartment, and despite her clear desire to do so, once the woman now asleep in his bed stirred to wakefulness, he suspected she would come to her senses and take flight as had so many before her, wisely choosing to disappear before anything akin to real feelings for Jake could develop. Yes, Jake Silver had long ago convinced himself that as long as his nightmares and nocturnal ravings continued, each new liaison, however promising it might first appear, was likely to end with a frightened woman beating a hasty, often pre-dawn exit, leaving Jake's ostensibly precious bachelorhood securely, if not preferably, intact.

So, on this fateful morning, he would do that which he'd done on so many mornings; he would steel himself against what he'd come to consider inevitable. He'd endeavor to deny his feelings for the alluring, but ultimately sensible woman of the moment, and prepare to face the day, his singular expectation being that Sandy McRea remember to leave his key as she left his apartment, his life, and in time, his thoughts.

The latter, he'd learn, was not to be.

As the taxi pulled up to his airline's curbside entrance, Jake over-tipped the driver and made a dash for the crew room.

The brightly lit room was empty but for the lanky form of Ed James, a first officer with whom Jake had trained a few years back.

A compulsive talker, Ed was the kind of roommate Jake knew awaited him in hell.

Without looking up from his newspaper, and before Jake could bolt, the rangy Southerner drawled a hearty, "Jake-boy!"

"Mornin' Ed. What brings you to the frozen north? I thought you were living out your golden years on the Miami milk run."

"I'm deadheading to La La Land with you and Cap'n Willie today." Ed spoke the words with a wink and a smirk. "I got some important bidness out there, if you catch my drift."

"Would that *bidness* be of the blonde or brunette variety?"

"Oh, my Yankee friend," Ed admonished, "a Southern gentleman does not kiss and tell."

In contrast to his own romantic reticence, Jake suspected that Ed did a great deal more telling than he did kissing.

"So you won't be regaling us with details of your little peccadillo?" Jake said.

"My little *what*?"

Leaving the answer to Ed's question dangling, Jake decided to forego his coffee, and as he turned back for the door, he fibbed. "It'll be nice to have some company up front this trip."

Jake was pleased to see Captain Bill Gance already seated in the cockpit when he arrived. Gance was talking to Operations on the company channel. Jake, who had a special affinity for his boss, had given up a regional captain's spot so that he might spend a year or so flying the big iron beside this universally revered chief pilot. To the younger man's mind, knowledge gained at the knee of Captain Gance would prove more meaningful than a seniority-based promotion. A pilot to the core, Jake placed profession before career.

"Mornin', Number One," Gance said warmly, welcoming his copilot as Jake took the right hand seat. "She's holding thirty-four tons," meaning fuel, "and three-hundred souls." Turning then to their hitchhiking colleague, who'd entered behind Jake, Gance added jovially, "Top-o-the mornin' to you, Edwin."

As Ed wiggled into the small jump seat, Jake's brow furrowed at the clutter of planes on the JFK ramp. Though the rain had subsided to a mist, he was eager to climb into the sunlit upper air.

"Get me the current ATIS, please," Gance directed Jake, ATIS being the airport's automated terminal information system for flight crews.

While Jake and his captain worked as one, the radio crackled with the ground controller's instructions: "NorthAm Two-four heavy, Kennedy Ground, taxi runway Three-One Left at the Kilo-Echo intersection, via left on Bravo, hold short of Lima. Holding short of taxiway Lima, monitor tower, one, two, three point niner. They'll have your sequence. Good day."

As the big jet pushed back, Ed said, "Looks like we'll get out on time this mornin'."

"Clear on the left." Gance announced.

"Clear right," Jake responded in the opening movement of a cybernetic ballet that would ensure safe carriage of this crew and its charges across a continent.

Again, the radio crackled to life. "North Am Two-four heavy, Kennedy Tower. Wait for and follow the second heavy Boeing 767 from your left at Lima. They'll be your sequence. You'll be number eleven for departure."

Groans from the two younger men.

As the plane slowly moved up in line, Jake felt a tap on his shoulder and turned to see Ed holding up a rumpled copy of the New York tabloid he'd been reading in the lounge. "Seen this yet, Jake-o?"

Looking over his shoulder, Jake read the headline whose font size would overstate Armageddon: IRAQ WAR HERO KILLED IN DRUG CRASH.

"Yeah, right," Jake said, his voice dripping with cynicism as he turned to Gance, whom the younger pilot knew would disapprove of Ed's cockpit discipline breach. "Everybody's a hero now. Some drunk drives into a tree and it's news because he's a vet."

"Not a car crash, y'all," Ed corrected, shaking the paper, demanding attention. "This boy flew an old Charlie-four-six, Commando into the ocean. Thing was full of drugs. So was the guy, I reckon."

Annoyed by both the breach and Ed's penchant for military nomenclature, Jake grabbed the newspaper from Ed's outstretched hand, aware, as was Gance, that acquiescing to their dead header's compulsion would be less distracting than ignoring or upbraiding him.

Reading the article, Jake became visibly upset, frantically leafing through the paper, looking for the continuation of the story, tearing pages in his frenzied search.

"Knock it off," Captain Gance barked, tired of the whole affair.

Rather than comply, Jake crumpled a page in his fist and said, to his colleagues' surprise, "We gotta go back to the gate."

Incredulous at his normally disciplined first officer's behavior, Gance looked askance at Jake over the half-lenses of his wire-rimmed reading glasses. They'd already advanced, and were now fourth in line. "Go back to the gate?" Gance asked. "Is this your hobby now?"

Not responding, his breathing coarse, his expression somber, Jake stared straight ahead.

Gance realized his copilot was serious. "This's a helluva time..." The captain paused, took a breath. "What is it, Jake? You sick? Got a pain?"

Jake could see his captain's patience dissipating. "It's personal," he said.

"Nothing's personal on my flight deck. Spill it."

Two airplanes were released in rapid succession.

Gance picked up the microphone as if to abort, but Jake raised a hand to stop him.

"Talk to me, Number One," Gance commanded, inching toward the runway. "We're runnin' out'a yellow lines, here. What's this about, son?"

"I'm sorry, sir," Jake said, embarrassed, forcing calm against the gravity of his outburst. "It's...it's this story. It's about Swede Bergstrom."

"Bergstrom?" Gance replied. "Oh, sure. Bergstrom," the captain recalled, keeping his gaze straight ahead. "Your flight leader in the sandbox." Sandbox being GI slang for the Middle East. "He got hit on your first sortie. Right?"

"Right," Jake said, reigning in his emotions, "after saving *my* sorry ass."

Unlike Ed James shifting uncomfortably in the jump seat behind him, Bill Gance had not seen the newspaper article. "What's it say?"

"Says Bergstrom was killed yesterday flying dope out of South America. Claims he got lost and went down off Cuba, a hundred miles west of his flight planned route."

"Really?" Gance asked, surprised. "He was flying an old Curtiss Commando?"

"This's bullshit, Skip," Jake affirmed, "Pilots like Bergstrom don't get lost, and c'mon, what drug runner would be dumb enough to file a goddam flight plan? I gotta find out what's behind this."

"North American Two-Four-Heavy, I say again, this is Kennedy tower," said the irritated voice of the overworked controller, indicating the crew had ignored his initial call.

"North Am Two-four," Gance responded. "Go ahead, tower."

"I repeat. North Am Two-four is cleared for immediate takeoff, Three-One-Left, Kilo-Echo. No delay on the runway. Take off or get off, sir."

"Roger," Jake responded to the tower in a reactive protocol breach that preempted his captain. Turning to Gance, he then said, "I'm good to go, Skipper."

Knowing his first officer as well as a mentor could, and ever conscious of both the CVR and sterile cockpit rule, Gance found himself committed to act.

His eyes burning into those of his errant copilot, he pressed his transmit button. "Two-four is rolling," he growled at the mic.

"Are you...?" Jake began.

"Harness," the captain barked, cutting off the younger man, and asserting his authority.

"Harness secure," Jake responded, relief evident in his voice.

"Flaps."

"Fifteen and fifteen. Two green..." and so on the pair went through the takeoff checklist.

When Gance eased forward on the thrust levers he felt Jake's hand come down gently atop his own. "No sweat, Cap," the younger man said, his voice calm yet well aware that he'd not only abused his authority but compromised his captain and would be called to the carpet—or worse—for his actions.

Equally aware that the CVR was recording the crew's every word, Jake said nothing more.

Gance nodded and both men applied power exactly as they had hundreds of times before and the big jet accelerated.

"Vee-one," Jake called.

"Rotate," Gance replied, and they were flying.

As the airplane rolled into a climbing departure turn, Manhattan's sun-draped spires glistened vermillion through the mist. And, though disappointed by his copilot's brief but serious transgression, Captain Gance took confidence in Jake's recovery and in doing so allowed himself to be awed by the beauty so unique to their vantage. Knowing, too, that he needed to ease the residual tension on his flight deck, the captain waxed poetic, saying, "Red sky at morning..."

No one heard Ed James respond, "...sailor take warning."

http://wbp.bz/thestraita

Made in the USA
Columbia, SC
07 October 2023

24116208R00130